The Hwanung Solution

Euan

Hope you enjoy it!

And [illegible].

[illegible] 2017

The Hwanung Solution

David Middleton

Matador
9 Priory Business Park,
Wistow Road, Kibworth Beauchamp,
Leicestershire. LE8 0RX
Tel: 0116 279 2299
Email: books@troubador.co.uk
Web: www.troubador.co.uk/matador
Twitter: @matadorbooks

ISBN 978 1788039 307

British Library Cataloguing in Publication Data.
A catalogue record for this book is available from the British Library.

Printed and bound in the UK by TJ International, Padstow, Cornwall
Typeset in 11pt Aldine401 BT by Troubador Publishing Ltd, Leicester, UK

Matador is an imprint of Troubador Publishing Ltd

FSC www.fsc.org
MIX
Paper from responsible sources
FSC® C013056

This book is dedicated to my Mom who elected to adopt me when medical advice was telling her not to. She gave me a chance in life that is an unpayable debt.

I remain indebted to numerous people but especially my long suffering wife Jennie, grown up and discerning offspring Caroline and Anthony, Peter Gibbs who is back in my life after 30 years away and advising now on publishing and promotion, mentor and red pen ace Debbie Dorman, hawk-eyed error spotter Mike Dodman and long-time friends Kevin Walsh and Wayne Livick. They all gave me great encouragement and guidance.

The Hwanung Solution is my third novel and completes the trilogy. It follows *The Final Shah Mat* (2014) and *The Acionna Projects* (2016). Many of the same main characters are re-established in another adventure that provides a cocktail of fact and fiction (see Fact & Fiction Appendix). The focus this time is on climate change, said by some to be the most important and perilous challenge facing our modern world.

Our main character and reluctant hero (who has a contentious surname and a confusing first name) becomes embroiled in a story that includes the north coast of Scotland; the exotic Flying Bird Tea Shop in Seoul; a deserted nuclear town in Siberia; various locations in Alaska; 40 miles of waterway separating America and Russia; Brussels; and finally Wales but probably not as you know it!

The Final Shah Mat: self published via Amazon-2014

The Acionna Projects: published by Austin Macauley-2016

This book is a weave of fact and fiction – see Fact and Fiction Appendix. Most characters and the events are pure fiction and drawn from my imagination though the majority of places in the story do exist.

About Me

Always a keen writer, I was given a chance at the age of 20 to become a news reporter on the weekly local newspaper, the Walsall Observer. I spent a few years in local newspapers and radio before becoming a motor sport photo journalist. Via time in commercial PR, I moved into the world of exhibitions and conferences which took me across Europe, Japan and the USA. In 1988 I had my "green epiphany" standing on a bridge in Pittsburgh. In 1991 I helped launch the MEBC, a business group dedicated to the subject of sustainable development. I became its CEO. I was Secretary General of TURF – The Urban Renewal Foundation. I later also added the role of CEO of the UK branch of the World Business Council for Sustainable Development to my activities. I retired from these responsibilities in 2013. Since then I have become involved in various projects. In August 2017 I was appointed as a Fellow of the Royal Society for the encouragement of Arts, Manufactures and Commerce.

See www.davidmiddletoncommunications.uk

I have now taken to writing fast moving adventure stories with the central themes based on various elements of sustainable development in the hope this may be an effective vehicle by which to carry important messages to as wide an audience as possible.

See www.davidmiddleton-author.com

Chapter 1

Crawling slowly across the debris and dust littered floor, bits of wood and metal occasionally digging painfully into hands and knees, dragging his aching, exhausted body towards the glassless window with its shattered, twisted, rusty frame left him drained and panting for breath. Breathing was difficult and he desperately gulped for air. But what he inhaled burned his lungs. It was so cold. The fierce, icy air penetrated not just his physical being but cut like a knife deeply into his mind and soul. Clearly he could not last much longer. But he needed reassurance his hiding place was still secure and uncompromised, that a line of hunters was not at this very moment closing in on him. It would drain his already depleted reserves of energy to take a brief look but he felt it worthwhile.

Reaching the wall he stretched out and upwards to grab the edge of the windowsill. Bugs of various sizes and descriptions, unused to such an intrusion, scurried in all directions. Agonisingly he hauled himself up into a kneeling position so he could see outside. There was no military line. No police. Nobody. No animals. Nothing. The abandoned town looked soulless and decayed with its rotting buildings, decomposing advertising hoardings promoting products to a long departed community, and cracked and broken roads. Only the weeds moved in the wind. It was eerie.

The nausea wracked him and the pains in his stomach were excruciating. He heaved frequently, doubling up in pain as he did so. But there was nothing left to vomit. He shivered constantly and felt burned up from within but freezing from without. He pulled the oil stained sackcloth further round him and stared at the view before him. Despite everything, this decaying world had its own beauty. It was extraordinary. It was also unnerving.

Anadyr-1 nowadays offers nothing to anyone except its place in history but it was providing him with a temporary hideaway – or a place to die.

Before him stood the long deserted Siberian town, once the centre of a Soviet military establishment with a population at one time reaching 5,000. With the collapse of the USSR the cluster of RSD-10 Pioneer nuclear missiles programmed to launch towards Alaska and onwards to strategic US targets, together with their store of warheads and support equipment, were all dismantled some decade and a half ago. Now, as he could see, Anadyr-1 is a ghost town, utterly dead, sadly derelict and almost forgotten. Immediately in front of him stood a railway trolley, as rusty as the rails it stood upon. Grey, crumbling apartment blocks, houses, supermarkets, offices, disintegrating roads and surprising amounts of slowly rotting equipment, remnants of its former importance, spread before him with distant, ice and bare rock patchwork covered hills providing a backdrop to this largely monochrome scene.

The reassurance of his solitary position was reward for the exertion made in moving, but he paid a cost for the effort and fell back to the floor panting for breath.

His first response to the accident had been to escape and find nearby cover. Now the formidable challenge was to somehow get from here to Ugolny and the one airstrip that served the area. Here, hope beyond hope, he might somehow board an aircraft bound for Alaska, or perhaps find help through one of the increasing number of tourist expeditions here to explore the Chukotka tundra, or from the traffic related to the growing minerals extraction boom.

If he had been fit and well the challenge would be mind blowingly daunting and probably unachievable. In his current state he gave himself no odds on success. He had no idea how far away the airfield was or even in which direction. Yet Anadyr-1 was no place in which anyone should die.

The seeming lack of attempts to find him confirmed his growing suspicion. What had happened was not official – not a police, political or military matter. If it were, surely there would have been more activity around the deserted town. Officialdom would be hunting him down. There was no sign of such activity. Maybe the crashed bus had not yet been discovered. But if it was not the police or military that had dragged him and Mabel from the hospital, who was it? Now Mabel was perhaps dead and the mystery remained as to what happened yesterday in Anadyr hospital.

For four days the two of them had endured confinement in the modern hospital, a development owing its existence to the internationally renowned ex-Governor of the town of Anadyr, Roman Abramovich, who had shaken it from its past and dragged it closer to the 21st century. This included not only modernising the hospital and other key municipal elements but enlivening the drab arctic city by painting many buildings pink, yellow and blue to create a startling contrast to the grey surrounding tundra. How ironic, he thought, Mabel was a Chelsea football club supporter. Or perhaps had been.

Their visit to this extreme eastern prong of Siberia had been strange from the outset. Both he and Mabel, highly regarded environmental geophysicists, were called in by Imperial Mining Inc. This London based former shelf company was acquired by a group of entrepreneurial speculators who wanted a corporate platform from which to explore new gold extraction opportunities in Siberia. Their forward programme had been interrupted and potentially prejudiced by the appearance in some parts of Siberia of a series of mysterious large holes. The first was found by reindeer herders in the Yamal Peninsula, sometimes known as 'The End Of The World'. It sparked widespread speculation as to what it was and what had caused it. Interest in the hole was made keener because it appeared less than 20 miles from Russia's biggest and strategically important gas field at Bovanenkovo. Opinions varied widely as to how the holes had been created and ranged from incoming meteors to subterranean explosions.

Whilst the Yamal Peninsula was some distance from the more Eastern area of Siberia in which Imperial Mining hoped to operate, consternation grew when more holes were discovered including one in the Chukotka tundra in the Chukotka Autonomous Okrug of Russia which covers an area some five and a half times the size of England. In this vast and desolate frozen wilderness is the remarkable Kupol Gold Mine, a town in which the buildings are so inter-connected nobody needs to venture outside into the deep freeze. Here live some 1200 workers who extract gold and silver. The nearest civilisation is the port town of Magadan to which it is linked by a 220 mile long ice road which exists between January and April. Otherwise the mine is connected to the outside world only by air services.

The site of the mine acquired by Imperial Mining Inc. is further east than Kupol and closer to the town of Anadyr than anywhere else. Whatever was causing these holes their sudden appearance was enough to potentially unnerve investors and Imperial Mining wanted a clear, concise and independent assessment of what was happening.

Jack Bailey and William Patterson were despatched to the cold bleakness of Siberia, travelling via Alaska and then onwards to Anadyr, a port town that can only be accessed by air or sea and the latter only in the summer before the seas freeze.

Jack Bailey came from Yorkshire. He was a dry humoured, no nonsense man who delighted in quoting sayings from "God's own county." Ask him how he was and the inevitable response would be, "I'm as fit as a flea on a butcher's dog." He was known laughingly to some of his close friends and colleagues as Mabel because he ended his answerphone message saying "… I'll get back to you as soon as I'm able." To his initial disquiet, a distortion of the last two words created his nickname.

William Patterson, better known as Bill, originated from Glasgow. He and Bailey had worked together for a while in the London office of an international engineering consultancy. It was whilst there he had conjured Bailey's nickname. Jack Bailey said he would never forgive him.

The journey to the newest Siberian hole, a day's trek north of Anadyr, was fraught with problems but there was nothing unusual about that and nothing for these seasoned travellers to become concerned about . A small scientific observation camp had been established a kilometre away from the hole which was about 16 metres wide and, as far as best evidence could so far suggest, 90 or more metres deep.

The origins of the holes had by now become the subject of wild rumours and speculation. Media attention was global. In the US it was said one hole was 70 miles deep. According to one report, a microphone had been dropped down it and the sounds it picked up were like the roar of a furnace but with human screams and howling in the background. Played on American radio it created panic. These holes, it was being said, reached to hell itself. The screams were from the lost souls of Hades! Increasing numbers of people were saying the recording proved it – until an audio expert dissected it and found it to be the re-mixed sound track from an ancient sci-fi film. A con though that was, it encouraged and stimulated media interest in the Siberian holes which were real enough. Media curiosity in any form was definitely unwanted attention as far as Imperial Mining was concerned.

Patterson and Bailey shared a portable hut as a home for four days while they conducted their own soundings. They also continued to monitor the worldwide scientific debate about the mysterious holes. Various theories were being promoted. Some scientists thought they were sinkholes caused by water from melting permafrost or ice creating some sort of explosion deep underground caused when ice cold water hit underground hot rocks. Extreme cold meeting extreme heat was a recipe for explosions.

Alternatively, much focus had turned to the high concentrations of methane inside the first crater, known as B1. Even whilst the two of them were on location more and more holes were being found, some 20 to 30 in total. This gave rise to the theory that the explosions were caused by the release of methane because global warming is melting the permafrost. This was being countered by yet another school of thought that attributed the holes to mounds of earth covered ice in the Arctic and subarctic known as pingos. These are plugs of ice formed near the surface over time which have a small mound or hill on top. The theory proposed that as an ice plug melts rapidly – as many have done thanks to unseasonably warm temperatures in Siberia in recent times, it causes part of the ground to collapse, forming a crater.

The geophysicists were also well aware that from Alaska to Siberia, right across the planet's frozen north, climate change was causing the permafrost to melt. It was producing an array of new problems. Buildings which had their foundations locked into the permafrost were beginning to lean and even collapse and, right across the north, trees were falling as the ground around them melted. Huge amounts of forest area were being impacted. And now more and more of the mysterious holes were appearing.

The hole they were exploring was located in an area of flat tundra. It had all the appearances of not being a natural phenomenon at all. Conspicuously, nothing similar was anywhere nearby making the hole with its symmetric dimensions and smooth sides look like a vertical, manmade tube that had somehow been drilled into the land. In the same way a volcano throws materials into the surrounding area, so a circle of black rocks up to ten feet high surrounded the hole. This helped exaggerate the strange appearance in the otherwise flat, green and grey surroundings with its occasional patches of ice. Inside, at the top of the hole, rugged, vertical scars had been cut into the otherwise smooth surface of the hole, presumably made by the materials that now surround its brim. This scarred area at the top of the hole looked just like solidified lava with the vertical cuts close to each other. Below, some 20 feet from the top, the sides of the hole were smooth, giving the appearance of a vertical steel tube. But even here, the sides were marked with a pattern of vertical lines, more like scratches than cuts. All the visible evidence suggested some subterranean explosion had occurred, throwing material upwards to form the hole and its rim of black rock.

On day four out on the tundra both scientists started to feel ill. It developed fast and they did a rapid retreat back to Anadyr where they reported to the local hospital. The attention they received was thorough but somehow impersonal. There was not a lot of humour in Anadyr hospital. Patterson concluded this perception was probably more to do with the language barrier than anything else. Only a handful of people spoke basic English and between the two of them they had little Russian. Initial medical tests indicated the two scientists had some sort of virus. Samples were despatched for analysis. It would take two weeks to get the results.

On day five in the hospital Bill Patterson was roused from a half sleep by raised voices echoing in corridors within the medical centre. Somehow, instinctively, he knew they related to himself and Mabel. Minutes later a group of four men, rugged, stubble faced and wearing jeans and black flying jackets with a yellow flash badge or symbol on the front, marched into the side room where the two had been kept in semi isolation. They were accompanied by two nurses and a doctor all arguing furiously and loudly with the intruders.

The leader of the group snapped orders to the other three men and to the medical staff, ignoring what Patterson took to be their protests. It was a chaotic group that had descended on them with voices raised and energetic amounts of gesticulation. Two of the men, including the leader, headed straight to Bill Patterson, the other two going to Jack Bailey where they grabbed him to shake him from his deep sleep. The action generated more protests from the medical people.

"You come with us," the man growled at Patterson. "Now!"

Patterson and a sleepy Jack Bailey joined the chorus of protests from the medical team.

"Who are you?" Patterson asked the leader. "What authority do you have? Where are you taking us?" The questions were totally ignored. The intruders were focussed on what they wanted and nothing would stop them, not even when the two geophysicists complained they had no clothes. Amidst the unruly disorder, bedlam and general confusion, their clothes miraculously appeared and nursing staff, reluctant to be party to what was going on, were ordered into helping the two get dressed.

As soon as they were fully clothed they were taken from the hospital. Virtually carried out, two men to each of them with burly hands under their armpits lifting them off their feet, Patterson and Bailey, and an entourage of medical people still maintaining their noisy protests, were rushed along crowded corridors. Onlookers, startled by what they were seeing, were rudely swept aside. At the front door there were more protests, this time from what Patterson took to be senior hospital officials. It had absolutely no impact and they were whisked out through the front door and into a wall of freezing cold air.

A dirty green, battered, well used KAvZ bus with smoke darkened windows had been reversed up to the hospital door and they were unceremoniously bundled in and onto benches either side of the bus. Their kidnappers, which is what Patterson took them to be, sat with them, Bailey opposite Patterson and two men on each side of the geophysicists. The Yorkshireman looked extremely ill and had difficulty raising his head to try and speak to Patterson. As soon as he tried to talk his face was slapped.

"Not talk," barked the man who had slapped him.

Mabel looked forlornly and in dismay at Patterson before his head slumped down onto his chest.

The moment the door crashed shut they were off, the engine of the old bus revving to almost valve bounce degrees, wheels spinning. Sitting secure on the bench was no easy task. The bus lurched crazily on its high speed journey and in their weakened state the two geophysicists had difficulty in remaining seated. But every time they came near to falling, burly hands pulled them back.

Bailey was in a bad condition, his head rolling around uncontrollably, his eyes now shut. Patterson was not sure if his colleague was even conscious. He too felt himself slipping from being awake and he forced himself not to drift into sleep – or worse. The bus was being driven fast. From the noise of the tyres on the icy road surface they were often sliding. Sometimes an exceptionally sideways slide was followed by a crash as the bus regained all four wheels. It was manic progress. Lurch after lurch sapped his strength. Even their guards became uneasy about the ridiculous way the bus was being driven. At one stage the leader shouted at the driver, presumably urging him to slow a little. It had no effect. A bent, flattened self-rolled cigarette hung from his lips. Patterson wondered what was in it and thought he could smell the sweet aroma of cannabis.

Through fleeting glimpses forwards and to either

side of the driver, Patterson caught brief images of the world through which this crazy journey was taking them and for a while he realised they were on the road leading to the ice road across the frozen sea. Even in his poor state his mind pondered the question as to how long the ice road would remain open and how soon climate change would mean the roadway would be replaced by the ferry that operated during the summer months. Through the haze of semi-consciousness, Patterson fathomed there could only be one reason for them speeding towards the ice road. They were heading for the airport at Ugolny.

The Scotsman drifted close to unconsciousness and felt as if he was in some nightmare fairground ride. He was snapped back into awareness when the bus not only lurched violently but was suddenly at a ridiculous angle. His side of the bus was higher than where Bailey sat. But the movement went on into what became a full roll. The crashing of metal against concrete was deafening. The engine was screaming again. The men with them were shouting. And then it went on again, a second roll, then a third and – Patterson lost count.

Flung around the bus as if they were in a washing machine, the six men inside the body of the vehicle crashed into each other and the floor, ceiling and sides of the bus. Limbs flayed out of control and heads crashed against metal – and against other heads. Adding to the mayhem was the sound of smashing glass as the shell of the bus distorted and the windows burst. The upright pillar of the windscreen detached itself from the rest of the vehicle's body and, as the driver was thrown around in his cabin, acted like a lance when the drugged man crashed down on it. It poleaxed him and he died instantly.

At last the agonising, torturous havoc stopped and the noise subsided into a weird silence broken only by human moans and the sizzle of hot fluids hitting frozen ground. The bus was upside down and its human cargo physically shredded as if it had gone through a mincer.

He had no idea how long he was unconscious. It was probably only minutes. When awareness fully returned to Bill Patterson he was shocked and amazed to realise he still lived. Breathing was difficult but he soon understood why. He was being suffocated by someone lying on top of him. With an extreme effort, he extracted himself from a confusion of bodies. There was some moaning but nobody else moved. Mabel was nearby, eyes open and staring blankly upwards. Patterson was no medical expert but it took no expertise at all to see his colleague was dead or near to it, his neck broken perhaps? Certainly his head was at a strange angle to the rest of his body.

Minutes passed and still nobody stirred. Gathering as much strength as he could, Patterson made his way across the carnage to the rear door of the bus which had lost its glass and burst partly open. He was able to kick it further apart and fall out onto icy undergrowth. He immediately could see and understand that the old bus had fallen down a small ravine onto the bank of a frozen river.

Still no voices came from the bus but his worries were not for those inside it but anyone who was now heading towards them. Instinct told him this was a chance to escape. From what he had no idea but there was no doubt in his mind they had been kidnapped and were under close escort and in some danger. On their way to where, and why, were matters to be resolved later. For the time being escape and survival were the priority. And now that also meant escape for himself. There was no way he could go back into the bus and try and extract Mabel. Anyway, from what he had seen Mabel might already be dead.

Looking up at the side of the ravine into which they had plunged he saw it sloped, decreasing in depth until a few hundred metres away the roadway from which they had fallen was at the same level as the frozen river. He slipped, slid and crawled his way from the crash scene, eventually making it to the road. He had no idea which direction to go but the more distance he could put between him and the crashed bus the better.

Looking back he was surprised to realise he could not see the overturned vehicle. It was in the ravine, totally hidden from sight. That was good news. The crash might remain undetected for some time.

How far he travelled he had no idea. He stumbled along the road, falling at times and lying there until enough strength came back to him to stagger on. At times it was as if he was walking yet asleep, so near to unconsciousness was he. Close to complete exhaustion, he reached a high security fence. On the other side he could see derelict and dilapidated buildings. Unknown to him, he had stumbled upon Anadyr-1. The wire mesh was bent, buckled and broken in several places and where a large hole had developed Patterson squeezed through and stumbled his way to one of many buildings scattered around. Inside he found an oil stained sackcloth which he wrapped around himself in the hope he could gain some body heat.

Now sitting on the floor, body propped up against the wall, Patterson realised that time was not on his side. He felt seriously ill and unquestionably the crash had sapped more strength from him. It was late morning now. There was some suggestion of warmth from the sun. But night time would see the temperature plummet. He doubted he would survive until the following day. Somehow he just had to get to the airport before the day ended. If he did not, it would be the end of him.

He made an effort to get up from the floor and was kneeling when he was startled by a noise from the direction of the door to the building. He looked up and was astounded by what he saw. There, perhaps 50 feet away, standing staring at him, rooted to the spot in a state of sheer terror matched only by his own, was a throwback to the times of ancient man. Some five and a half feet tall, he had a dark, red and weather worn face, eyes wide and bright with fear, long, ragged, black matted hair and wore what looked like an ancient coat made from animal skins and clutched a wooden stave. Patterson was taken aback – shocked. The new arrival was obviously similarly startled by the encounter. For a moment they were frozen in mutual fear.

Patterson could see it in the other person's eyes and the wooden stave now pointed at him in a defensive gesture. He noted its arrowhead fashioned from stone. He felt he was confronting someone from an early civilisation rather than from the remnants of a nuclear town. With the initial shock fading it slowly dawned on Patterson he was looking at not a man but a woman and maybe a young one at that. Then, as quickly as she had arrived, she turned her back on him and fled. He stared after her in total disbelief.

Chapter 2

Gene Bond had chosen this journey quite deliberately. The only other concession to make this a different day to any other was a breakfast of homemade porridge enriched with a generous helping of whisky impregnated raisins. Then, rather than sit and mope alone in his retreat cottage on his birthday, he chose to drive the 60 or so miles along the north coast of Scotland to the Kyle of Durness. In itself that was enough to take anyone's mind off niggling troubles. His cherished but now venerable Porsche 911 Carrera which he religiously kept as if to hang tenuously onto links to his increasingly distanced youth, growled as he drove it aggressively. The tachometer needle regularly nudged the red line. The back end of the car frequently slipped away as he fought moments of oversteer. He pressed it fast through the many tight, narrow and twisting bends, then felt it leap as if released into freedom when they reached the few long, traffic free stretches of straight road. It was exhilarating and uplifting for his heavy heart.

He stopped twice on the journey, both places being of very special rugged beauty. On the causeway the other side of the village of Tongue, he pulled onto the small car park and sat for a good ten minutes just staring at the vast Kyle of Tongue, full of water at this time of day. It never ceased to amaze him that as low tide arrived, millions and millions of gallons of water would empty the Kyle to leave a vast area of sand. To his left and high above the shoreline stood the small but prominent Castle Varrich, while the scene ahead was dominated by the distant high mountain ranges. Nearby, the gentle sound of water lapping on the shore line mixed with calls from fishing gulls and the always busy oystercatchers. Echoing across the immense openness, the unique sounds of a curlew gave a measure to how otherwise silent this massive scene was. After a short stop he drove on, wondering not for the first time why the energy of the huge movement of water in and out of the Kyle each tide wasn't captured. He had stood many a time on the causeway bridge watching the fast running water pass below. Just a couple of turbines would do the trick.

Some miles on he stopped again as he always did at this point at the top of the hill overlooking Loch Eriboll. It was a crime to do otherwise. The view to the sea loch way below him and extending out into the distance, with its salmon farm and surrounding mountains, is outstanding – extraordinary. As he stood there in the sun with a blustery wind sweeping in from the sea, anger swelled within him that she was not with him to share his day and the beauty and romance of this place. He should be holding her now, feeling her body close to his as they delighted in the vast openness of this wonderful part of the world. She would have inevitably responded to him and they would have embraced with a long, lustful kiss. It would not have surprised him if she had, there and then, alongside the main road and high above the loch below, pulled her jumper over her head to reveal her bare breasts to the world and to be exhilarated by the fresh wind on her nakedness. It was the sort of thing she did. This dramatic environment would stimulate her. Inhibition was not a characteristic of the lady he sometimes called Naughty Nagriza.

As if to demonstrate his mood and his resignation to the fact she was now dead, he kicked at the grit of the layby and slammed the door of the Porsche before angrily accelerating fast down the long and steep hill that takes the road to the water's edge. He drove at speed round the far end of the loch, tyres sounding loudly as if in rebellion to the strain he was putting them to. Then the single track road was climbing again and he floored the throttle aggressively in second gear, engine unnecessarily noisy at high revs, exhaust thundering. Fast, but without being reckless on the bending and twisting single track main road, the Porsche progressed through the rock strewn wilderness of a landscape towards Durness. He drove through without stopping and soon reached this spot he loved so much.

Though this was not his ultimate destination, he sat on the dry stone wall for more than an hour just looking at the view, hoping to see the local otters in the entwinement of seaweed lapping the shoreline. Inevitably they failed to appear. The stunning scene across the enormous expanse of the Kyle of Durness with its numerous sand banks exposed before the incoming tide covered them, with the mountains of the Western Highlands in the distance, was, to him, one of several tranquil and exceptional places he knew on the north coast of Scotland.

In his opinion, the real Scotland starts north of Inverness. From thereon everything just gets that much bigger – the mountains, the lochs, the huge sweeping valleys. The whole area has an overabundance of magnificent scenery but this corner of Scotland he rated as being as good as it gets. He savoured the quality of the air, pureness personified except for the hint of peat smoke from some distant chimney.

With the Kyle now filled he slowly drove the short distance to the car park near the ferry. The word ferry is a generous overstatement for what in reality is an oversized, outboard engined rowing boat capable of carrying only a handful of people. Its boatman is someone to have faith in! There are only two ways to access the farthest north westerly point of the country by land and these are not always open as the area is regularly used as a military bombing range. The least popular route is via a long and testing, unmarked trek over rough, open and often boggy moorland from Blairmore on the West coast.

The much preferred route starts with the ferry. Yet crossing to the other side of the Kyle is treacherous and renowned for its shifting sandbanks. So travellers need to have faith in the boatman. That is not easy when the man at the tiller spends the whole crossing angrily and noisily remonstrating as part of an ongoing spat he is apparently having with one of the drivers of the buses that will take his passengers on to Cape Wrath. Bond was less concerned than some who sat in the boat around him. He had encountered this before and he knew John the boatman, eccentric and outlandish though he might be, could almost do this journey blindfold, local knowledge and years of experience telling him where the sand banks lay at any time just below the surface of the choppy waters.

They reached the far side of the Kyle safely and boarded the minibus. Bond was prepared for what came next. He had undertaken this many times before. The road journey across the eleven or so miles to the lighthouse on the high lump of rock that juts out into the sea close to where the Atlantic meets the North Sea is as manic as the boat journey. The small bus jumps and bangs quickly along narrow, severely potholed roads with frequent significant drops both sides, sometimes at the same time. Progress is not slowed by the roughness of the road. The bus seems to bounce over the uneven surface and Bond, like all his fellow passengers, hung onto his seat with grim determination and felt as if his bones were being shaken to bits.

It was a relief to reach Cape Wrath. The effort to get there is rewarded by unparalleled views to the east of the rugged north coast of Scotland with its towering stacks and high cliffs disappearing into a hazy distance. Ahead lies an expanse of sea that extends to the horizon and onwards to the Arctic Circle.

The area is dominated by the lighthouse built in 1828 by Robert Stevenson. Not for the first time Bond marvelled at the men who not only engineered the near 70 feet high structure but how they got blocks of granite to this extremely remote and difficult location.

It was a wonder of the ingenuity and determination of construction engineers of that age.

Bond knew he would not be able to approach the edge of the cliffs as some visitors were now doing so they could see seals on the rocks far below. The highest cliffs in the UK presented his poor head for heights with more of a challenge than he wanted to confront. He was content to sit on the grass and take in the sheer, breathtaking, colossal scale of this natural wonder. It was awe inspiring. He took his ancient, battered, silver flask from his jacket pocket and sipped and savoured his favourite single malt, the Douglas Laing's Big Peat from the Isle of Islay, more than 200 miles south of where he now sat and north of what he thought to be one of the most romantic place names in the UK, the Sea of the Hebrides.

Of all the places on the planet, he knew this was the one where he could clear his worried and confused mind. The sheer scale of the natural, gigantean environment at Cape Wrath seemed to make puny his own challenges and difficulties. It put them into perspective.

His mind strayed back for the umpteenth time to a desperate moment some eighteen months ago. No sniper however skilled can be sure absolutely everything is within his control the moment pressure is applied to the trigger. So it had been when a Tajikistan military sniper thought he had a 100% clean shot at a terrorist holding Nagriza in Tajikistan in Central Asia.

For the second time in as many years Gene Bond had become unwillingly embroiled in the world of terrorism and political intrigue. This time it was partly to do with the threat of a 21st Century water war spreading across the Ferghana Valley, fuelling tension and military movement involving Tajikistan, Kyrgyzstan and Uzbekistan. The borders of these former states within the Soviet Union have been unstable and uncertain since the demise of the political colossus of which they were all once part.

It was more by chance and good luck for the terrorist rather than a defensive move. It was certainly bad luck for Nagriza. At the very moment the high velocity bullet left the rifle at near sonic speed, the terrorist twisted his body, bringing Nagriza from behind him to be in line with the shot. At the time nobody – the sniper, the elite squad of Tajikistan marines, those watching events unfold from London via head-set cameras worn by some of the marines, was sure if the terrorist or Nagriza had gone down in the seconds immediately after the shot. Tragically it quickly became obvious Nagriza had died in the attempt to rescue her.

Gene Bond was mortified. It compounded the frustration of being dragged into what he thought to be an unreal world, utterly alien to the one in which he normally lived. A professional environmental entrepreneur, Bond earned his living promoting the principles of sustainable development in which the values of economics, social care and environmental responsibility are treated equally. He was involved in a number of projects turning theory into practice.

The life changing moment responsible for him becoming a passionate advocate of sustainable development came when he first encountered the story of the Aral Sea in Uzbekistan. Once the world's fourth largest inland sea – the size of England – today it has been described as a "toxic sump" – a pool of residual waste, chemicals from agricultural additives, and anything else people have dumped into it. It is so reduced in size that Munak, once a thriving port employing 40,000 people in fishing and related businesses, is now separated from the polluted waters by 60 miles of sand dunes scattered with keeled over, disused, rotting fishing smacks.

Bond had been appalled when he first discovered the demise of the Aral Sea was caused when Soviet engineers diverted its filler rivers to provide irrigation for rice and cotton growing. It was, he thought, as bad an example of economic ambitions dominating without thought to environmental and social consequences. As it happened, the ill thought out actions of policy makers and engineers alike caused chaos not only to the environment and to the health and wellbeing of people living near the sea, but ironically also to the economy of the area which was devastated with the collapse of two major industries. Vast numbers of people were made jobless. Munak has subsequently fallen from prosperity to now being a near ghost town.

It was a defining moment for Bond. Already concerned by examples of manmade disasters that impacted negatively on the delicate and complex nature of the planet's environmental infrastructure, the Aral Sea story epitomised everything that was wrong.

"What on earth are we doing to our planet?" he thought when he read of what had happened. "And what on earth are we doing to ourselves?"

It had served as the trigger that saw Bond commit his

life to trying to do something about what he thought to be man's rape of the planet – a road to self-destruction. He became a sustainable development warrior but interpreted through a one man consultancy that sought to stimulate projects that would put some wrongs to right.

It was an extraordinary coincidence that linked the woman he had so deeply loved with the place that had inspired his environmental passion. Nagriza, he eventually learned, was born in Munak, daughter of a fisherman made redundant by the collapse of the industry as the sea receded before him. As a teenager she became involved with a Belgian scientific group researching the Aral Sea story. They eventually offered her a job – a menial one but a chance to escape poverty. Getting the necessary permits to leave her home country was challenging. After days sleeping rough in Tashkent, the capital city, and trying desperately to obtain the paperwork she needed, she was befriended by a civil servant who took a liking to her, particularly sleeping with her. It transpired he worked for the SNB – the Uzbekistan National Secret Service and he eventually secured a secretarial job for her there.

"Once in," she later told Bond, "I worked hard, I learn quickly and I find out a lot. I find things out about some of my superiors and I get a better job. Then I start working on projects for them and that took me to meeting Georgi."

Far out at sea Bond could see a large tanker beating its way west through a heavy swell. It reminded him of the first time he had seen whales. He had been sitting on more or less the same patch of grass some years ago, just staring out to sea as he now was or marvelling at the flying skills of the sea birds as they use the upward thermals from the huge cliffs to soar effortlessly across the wide open space of the Cape. His mind was brought back from wherever it had wandered by a shout from another visitor to the headland.

"Whale!" The cry had alerted everyone and sure enough in the dim distance a pod of whales could be seen at about the same distance from land as the tanker now was. They too were heading west, majestically powering their way through a sea of massive waves. Bond had stood to get a better view and found himself sharing the moment with a total stranger, an elderly man. Irrationally, he thought afterwards, together they had shed a tear. Why, he had no idea. Perhaps for some primeval reason it was a very emotional moment – a rare connect between one species and another and a feeling of affinity. Yet again it caused Bond to reflect on the wonders of the world in which he lived.

Georgi Patarava, to whom Nagriza had eventually gone to work for in London, had much to answer for, Bond pondered. A longstanding friend and a special drinking partner, they initially met when Georgi was a First Secretary at the Soviet Embassy in London. Through quite regular business meetings they had got to know each other well, enjoying each other's company and consuming large quantities of brandy from Georgi's home country, Georgia. As the friendship grew, so Georgi more frequently made cynical comments about Gene Bond's name.

"007 with a girlie name," he would say, winding Bond up which on this subject was not difficult.

"Piss off, Georgi," Bond would reply. It was a matter of some sensitivity to him. He detested Ian Fleming's choice of his family name for his now infamous spy hero. "There can hardly be anyone less Bond-like on the planet than me."

These were to prove to be ironic words.

And as for his Christian name, as Bond told Georgi until he was tired of doing so, he had no involvement or responsibility for his father being a Johnny Cash fan and taking some sort of weird satisfaction in emulating what Cash did in the song 'A Boy Named Sue' and giving his son the feminine sounding name of Gene.

With the ending of the Soviet Union and the Embassy closing in London, contact between the two of them was lost until a few years ago when fate brought Georgi and he back together again. A shooting on the north coast of Scotland in a pub Bond knew well led him to help Georgi confront a plot to encourage California to leave the United States of America. It transpired that Georgi now headed up the communications division of something that officially does not exist, the European Secret Service. Though based in Paris, its communications centre is in London. Georgi headed a sizeable team there including Nagriza. It did not take long before Bond had become utterly infatuated with her.

The California plot was devised by a South Korean, Sum Taeyoung, who called himself a chaos entrepreneur. This encounter with Taeyoung ended with what became known as the 'Battle on Lake Geneva' with Bond saving the life of the Governor of California and many others by throwing a bomb off a lake ferry just before it exploded. When the media realised Bond's name they had a field day, much to Gene Bond's embarrassment and consternation.

As if to compound the difficulties of becoming involved in Georgi's work, the reluctant hero became entrapped in a second battle with Taeyoung, all to do with water. Bond and Nagriza ended up in Central Asia where Bond met her family in Munak before she went on to Tajikistan and her ultimate death whilst he took the opportunity for the first time to see for himself what had caused the Aral Sea disaster.

Now, sitting on the grass of Cape Wrath, she came into sharp focus. He recalled when he first saw her in Georgi's London apartment. She took his breath away as she entered the lounge from an adjacent bedroom. Nearly six feet of staggeringly sensual femininity with hazel hair and brown eyes, she wore a brightly coloured full length silk gown in red and yellow patterns. The thin flowing garment was tied casually at the waist by a band. Above and below the band its effectiveness in keeping the two halves of the gown together was questionable and gaps frequently appeared to offer the briefest of glimpses of the nakedness that lay beneath.

And Bond remembered her legs. Oh those legs! They seemed to extend forever and were shaped fit for a Goddess. In fact, this vision of beauty who radiated sexuality was, thought Bond, something out of this world. Georgi eventually introduced her as "Nagriza Karimov, formerly of the SNB, better known as the Uzbekistan National Secret Service."

Once over the shock of finding she was an active member of Georgi's team of espionage experts, and especially discovering the coincidence of her being born on the shores of the Aral Sea, over a period of time the affection between Nagriza and Bond grew and they found occasions in their hectic lives to make love. It was beyond anything he had experienced before. She was generous in her love making and they both found delight as much in giving as they did in receiving.

She was a tease, a flirt, and, Bond constantly told her, "very naughty." Both had the ability to take the other close to the brink of explosive ecstasy but then to back off so their passion could be maintained. Their love making was uninhibited, sometimes physically wild and raucous but at other times gentle, soft and caressing. Now, all this time later, he could still sense her, almost taste her.

But she was gone. No sooner had this Goddess-like woman crashed into his life than she was taken from him by a sniper's bullet. He was having great difficulty coming to terms with it.

Sensing movement around him Bond realised people were progressing back to the minibus. The return journey was uneventful and, in a more tranquil and thoughtful mood, he cruised the Porsche back towards the cottage located on the north coast some 25 miles west of Thurso. An hour later he was passing through Portskerra and, having decided to visit its small store, drove onto the first of the two harbours serving the small village community. He planned to park the car by the memorial to lost seamen then walk across the headland pathway with its small but steep-sided hill to the other harbour and back. It would be a good and physical end to the day.

The sun was now dipping towards the horizon and a rich red sunset was promised. If his timing was right the walk back would be well rewarded. He set off down the track towards the small hill that separates the two harbours, then started up the steep incline where at the top the sea and coastline would come into full view as would the setting sun. To his right, out at sea, there was a constant two way traffic of sea gulls going out to the fishing grounds and returning with their catches to the cliff nests surrounding the harbour to which he now headed. It was another favourite place of his, somewhere from which to watch the sea birds and, in stormy weather, to spectate as huge seas crashed up the rocks. On one bitterly cold winter day, with the temperature reading minus 15 degrees in the Porsche, he had been amazed to witness the sea spray frozen. It looked like a huge ball of glistening crystal mist held static in a gravity defying mid-air act above the rocks over which the sea was crashing. It was wonderful and quite uncanny. Bond had never seen or even heard of such a thing happening.

Now he was reaching the top of the steep climb. Voices came to him from the direction of the second harbour. Though he could not yet pick out what was being said, there was a certain aggression to their tone that made him slow down, now to walk slowly and warily to the top to try and catch a view of what was going on before anyone saw him.

As soon as he caught a clear view he ducked down again. In the briefest of glances, perhaps not even lasting a second, he saw a large black van with darkened side windows and at least six men. Five of the men were all dressed the same. The sixth seemed to be under their care – or was it under their guard?

Checking behind him to ensure nobody could see what he was doing, he crawled on all fours back up to the crest of the hill and peered over the top. It seemed as if they had all arrived in the van and were now leading – or virtually dragging – their prisoner – for that is what Bond took him to be – towards the slipway heading to the harbour water and out from his sight.

"How very odd," thought Bond. He crawled back down the hill to make sure he was not seen and now sat and waited.

The occasional voice drifted towards him then the gurgling sound of a powerful marine engine. Minutes passed and the noises drifted off. All he could hear now was the sound of waves against rocks and the multitudinous mix of calling sea birds, the unique cries of the oystercatchers dominating.

It was a full ten minutes before the boat came into view. For some reason it took him by surprise and he moved quickly to ensure he was not in sight from the sea. Sneaking a look, Bond saw a long, black hulled boat, perhaps some 24 feet long and seemingly quite narrow, like an oversized canoe. It was being steered by a man standing at a wheel located in the centre of the boat's length. Towards the bows sat two men in black jackets plus the man Bond took to be their captive.

The boat creamed fast through the water. It was an unusual craft, thought Bond, with a powerful motor.

A military boat perhaps? He could hear it clearly from where he lay on the hill. He watched as it sped parallel to the coast heading towards the bay at the head of which stood a solitary building, the formidable structure Bond knew to be The Mansion. Right opposite him but at some considerable distance Bond dared to take a picture of the craft on his iPhone.

"How very odd," he thought to himself again as he made his way back down the hill towards the Porsche, any idea of completing the walk now abandoned. He was unsure if the van was still there and whether anyone was in it.

On the drive up the lane from the harbour back towards Portskerra and the main road, Bond thought about The Mansion. This large and imposing property stood in its surrounding grounds at the end of a road that went nowhere else. The property's history in the last few decades was very chequered and Bond had lost track of who now owned it. An overwhelming curiosity to find out what was now going on saw him turn the Porsche off the main road and down the single track road leading to some of the expansive beaches that are a feature of the Scottish north coast and to The Mansion. Bond had not been down this lane for years. He had no reason to. Unless the objective was to visit someone in the solitary building at the end, or to walk on the beach, there was no point in doing so.

The Mansion, Bond recalled, stood imposingly in its own substantial walled grounds and boasted a fine, impressive if somewhat opulent wrought iron gate. He was not sure what he was going to do when he got there but any planning would have been wasted. Since his last visit a barrier had been established across the road, some two or three hundred yards from the entrance to the property. It was down. Bond quickly noted a security entrance phone by the barrier but, more importantly perhaps, a CCTV camera on a pole alongside the barrier. Assuming it was live and manned, his arrival would have already been seen and noted. Bond stopped as soon as the barrier came into sight. He hardly paused before turning the Porsche round and heading back the way he had come.

"Curious. Very curious," he thought to himself. But what to do about what he had seen? If the odd man out in the boat was indeed some sort of captive, then Bond had something of a moral citizen's responsibility to report it. But was that what he had seen? Was the man in any way a prisoner? Or, thinking about it, were they helping him? Were they dragging him to the boat or giving him assistance? Bond was not at all sure. All he knew for certain was that what he had seen was odd.

The idea came to him slowly. He accepted it with great reluctance. There was one person who might be able to help. But the last thing Bond wanted was yet another escapade with him. Two had been enough. He paused. And paused. But eventually, driven by curiosity that outweighed caution, he reached for his phone and sent a text – and the photograph of the boat – to Georgi.

Chapter 3

Alexander Fitzpatrick looked enviously from his window down onto the bustling roads of Berkeley Square and at people going about their ordinary daily lives in the oasis of green and seeming tranquility in the central area of this famous London square. The high midday sun exaggerated colours and gave a rich greenness to the expanses of grass through which cut many pathways with their wooden bench seats, trees, sculptures and statues.

Fitzpatrick's day – and perhaps his life – had been turned upside down with the arrival of news that actions he had instigated in Siberia had gone disastrously wrong and instead of potentially helping resolve a problem now escalated it to heights he could not have dreamed of. He confronted a living nightmare beyond anything he had experienced before. He wished he was amongst those outside in the Square – living their hectic but, in relation to his own, simple lives, and coping no doubt with numerous pressures but none on the scale he confronted.

It all began days ago just after the office opened at 0800. He had never before received a handwritten envelope from Siberia. The writer had written his name and address on the front just underneath the address of Imperial Mining. It was from Pavel Galdin, Senior Administrator, Medicines, Anadyr Hospital. Fitzpatrick had never heard of him. He was intrigued. He opened the envelope not knowing what to expect. What he read was astonishing.

Dear Mr. Fitzpatrick. I write in the most serious of confidences. My subject is of great sensitivity. It is of grave concern to me, my city, my country and the industry in which you operate. Only one other knows of this letter and it is he who suggested it. He is my superior to whom I report. I therefore extend the serious request that this letter is treated with total security.

I am Senior Administrator, Medicines, at the major hospital in Anadyr, Eastern Siberia. We have confined in our establishment two employees of yours, William Patterson and Jack Bailey. I regret to inform you they are both seriously ill. We are unsure at this time as to what is causing their poor medical state.

Our concern is this. The permafrost that covers much of Siberia and the northern extremes of our planet is melting. It is believed to be the result of climate change. The impacts of this are many but one is of immediate concern to us and is why I write. It has been widely reported that not long ago a highly contagious virus dating back to the Neanderthal period of some 30,000 years ago was released from the permafrost in Siberia. Fortunately it only infects single-celled organisms and doesn't closely resemble any known pathogens that harm humans.

However, the scientific and medical community is concerned that, if climate change warms long untouched regions of Siberia, more ancient or eradicated viruses, including other Neanderthal viruses or even smallpox that have lain dormant in the ice for thousands of years, could be released.

We now have to confront an additional new threat. As you know, holes have been appearing across Siberia. It is now thought these are the result of subterranean explosions caused when melted permafrost has penetrated sufficiently deeply into the ground as to meet hot rock formations. This union of two materials of extreme temperatures causes explosions and has thrown materials into wide areas around the holes.

Your two scientists were investigating one such hole in the Chukotka territory. They were subsequently taken ill and brought to our medical institute in Anadyr. We have secured them in an isolation area.

Our problem, which is also yours, is that initial tests cannot determine what is wrong with them. Certainly they are impacted by some sort of virus but we cannot identify which.

It is easy to be too adventurous in these circumstances and ill-informed thinking can be dangerous. However, my concern, and that of the Director of this establishment, is this. If your two men have been impacted by some ancient virus released from the hole and if that news becomes widely known, it could have devastating impacts on the whole of Siberia. It could, for example, put large areas into quarantine, including where you hope to operate the gold mine on the Chukotka tundra. That could close your operation here. Other mining potential in Siberia would close. The impact on the economy of Anadyr and the whole of the nation could be severely damaged.

At the moment we plan nothing. We monitor and test the two scientists. Hopefully we will find our extreme concerns are not justified, the virus will be identified and the patients cured. But that does not look like the current prospect. We would prefer nobody to know this has happened. Ideally we hope to find an antidote to the virus. Meantime we have made the area around the Chukotka hole an isolated and militarily protected area.

We are considering our options. We would like you to do the same and to urgently advise us as to what you believe to be the best forward action in the interests of your company, the gold extraction industry of Siberia and my nation's economic wellbeing.

A handwritten signature was followed by the words Pavel Galdin, Senior Administrator, Medicines, Anadyr Hospital.

Shocked by the letter, Fitzpatrick's first action was to find more information on the viruses known to be released in Siberia, something he had not heard about before. From basic web research he found entries such as "There is now a non-zero probability that the pathogenic microbes that bothered ancient human populations could be revived, and most likely infect us as well," according to a study by co-author Jean-Michel Claverie, a bioinformatics researcher at Aix-Marseille University in France. He had written in an email: "Those pathogens could be benign bacteria (curable with antibiotics) or resistant bacteria or nasty viruses. If they have been extinct for a long time, then our immune system is no longer prepared to respond to them."

A telephone call to a friend specialising in rare medical diseases told him: "Some passive viruses have already been released from the permafrost after 30,000 years of freezing. There's no reason to think that viruses that affect humans could not do the same. Climate change is causing the permafrost and sea ice to melt quite rapidly. At the same time we have more and more drilling and mining going on in Alaska and Siberia for oil, gold and other increasingly rare materials. It is well within the bounds of possibility that this combination of activity will release other viruses – such as smallpox which was supposed to have been eradicated in the 1970s. Personally, I believe we are confronting a recipe for disaster."

The more he researched the more concerned he became. He also struggled with the decision as to whether or not to inform his fellow directors at Imperial Mining. In the event he decided not to. At this stage the fewer who knew the better. But Fitzpatrick came to the gold extraction industry straight from a career in the military and that had built within him a tendency to be decisive and to take action when confronted with a problem. He also had an overwhelming conviction that he always needed to be in charge. So as he considered his options and his plans in the aftermath of receiving the letter, he believed a fast response was required and that he should take close and personal control of the situation. It was impossible to manage this situation across such a distance. Over the course of a particularly hectic day, he assembled a plan including phoning numerous people he believed would help. He felt better now he was taking some sort of action though later even he would come to the conclusion it was misconceived from the outset. It was a typical Alexander Fitzpatrick military, gung ho, shoot from the hip response.

It was late in the day when he eventually left the office with an overnight case slung over one shoulder and his laptop over the other. His destination was Wales.

He had to undertake research to find exactly where it was and it would take him two and a half days to get there from London.

Two fingers of land point at each other from either side of the Bering Strait. On the Western side is Lavrentiya, the administrative centre of the Chukotka Autonomous Okrug or district of Siberia, part of Russia. On the Eastern side is the small reindeer hunting community of Wales in the US state of Alaska, the largest but least populated of all the American states. Less than 100 kilometres divide the two. Fitzpatrick's research showed the Strait to be a strange, geographical freak that separates two of the world's most powerful nations. A waterway that links the Arctic Ocean in the north to the Pacific Ocean in the south, he found it was first recorded in the early 1700s by Danish-born Russian navigator Vitus Bering. Navigable in the summer, it is frozen during the winter and has been crossed several times with the first recorded modern crossing in 1913 when a German, Max Gottschalk, achieved the journey by dogsled.

In 1778 the English explorer Captain James Cook named the outcrop of land Cape Prince of Wales. The Eskimos knew it as Kingigin, or 'high bluff'. They called themselves Kingikmiut, 'people of the high place.' Today the single runway airport of Wales is some two kilometres north of the desolate, ramshackle settlement. It is here, in the most extraordinary of environments and surrounds, a somewhat travel-weary, stubble faced Fitzpatrick met the team of five mercenaries from Eastern Europe he had flown in especially to undertake his plan. He knew these men from his military days and he held them in high regard for their commando skills and experience.

The team, and the pilot he had tasked with the job of flying them into Anadyr, had linked up in Calgary, Canada before flying to Wales to meet him. The aircraft belonged to a company specialising in flying people and equipment associated with the minerals extraction industry. It was known to the authorities in Anadyr and an application to land there and a flight plan had been accepted and authorised. Fitzpatrick planned the aircraft would remain at Anadyr whilst the five mercenaries snatched the two ill geophysicists from the hospital. They would be whisked away from Alaska before the authorities knew what was going on. From there they would be taken to a hideaway Fitzpatrick thought ideal for the circumstances. Control would then be with him, as would the fate of the two geophysicists. He would then feel more confident about the future.

To start the operation they met in the most unlikely of places and environments, the basic building that is the terminal at Wales, Alaska. There he briefed the mercenaries and the pilot in detail about what he expected them to do. It was a long journey to give such a brief but he considered it vital he did so personally rather than through any other form of communication. There was nobody he could trust to do it for him.

Now, looking from his London office at the tranquil scene outside, such a marked contrast to the monochrome ruggedness of Wales, Fitzpatrick reflected on how the commando raid had deteriorated into a farce. The crash of the KAvZ bus had been a disaster. Three mercenaries had been killed outright, one being the driver whose recklessness had caused the accident. The other two were both injured but capable of movement, as had been Jack Bailey, though how he still lived was a surprise to everyone. But of William Patterson there was no trace. The leader of the two surviving mercenaries had a choice – look for the missing geophysicist or try and get himself, his surviving colleague and Bailey back to the waiting aircraft. Time was not on his side. The aircraft could not wait indefinitely. He chose the latter, stealing a truck to drive across the ice to the airport at Ugolny. They had driven straight onto the runway, up to the aircraft, scrambled into it whilst heaving Bailey aboard, and flown out before the control tower spotted them moving. They were out of the country and over US air space before Ugolny ATC could inform the Russian military there had been an unauthorised departure. Later the aircraft owners would claim to the Russian authorities that their aircraft and pilot had been hijacked by armed terrorists and they had no option but to follow their commands.

Fitzpatrick looked from his London window and contemplated the disaster. Bailey was now isolated and safely secured. He was still ill, hovering on the brink of death but hanging tenuously onto life. Clearly he was still suffering from the effects of the virus caught near the hole on the Chukotka tundra. The magnitude of the gamble Fitzpatrick was taking had by no means escaped him. Indeed, it was now a constant worry. What if Bailey had got some contaminating, unknown viral disease? He had been quarantined and isolated in the hospital at

Anadyr but now he had been in close contact with the mercenaries, the pilot and, more recently, the team that had transported him to the hideaway.

And then there was Bill Patterson. Where the hell was he? Was he alive or dead? Did he too have a deadly virus that he was even now spreading wherever he was? The worst case scenario was difficult to comprehend. A lethal virus could have been released to spread and cause untold suffering.

While in London Alexander Fitzpatrick searched for new ideas to help him escape the mess he had got himself into. He explored clandestine ways of finding out precisely what Bailey was suffering from. He dared not use conventional ways like simply calling in a medical expert to examine Bailey. That would totally let the cat out of the bag. It was a nightmare dilemma.

Chapter 4

Sum Taeyoung sipped his cup of double harmony tea and contemplated his life, his business, the world in general and the green shoots of his new venture – the most ambitious escapade he had conceived – but which had already taken an unexpected turn for the worse. This afternoon he was later than usual for his daily visit to the Flying Bird Tea Shop in the Insadong district of Seoul. It was something of a religion for him to visit here whenever he was in his home city. He loved just walking down to this bustling area of pungent aromas rising from the many vibrant food carts with their chaotic kaleidoscope of colourful produce, the hoards of people, many of them tourists sucked into the area to be encouraged to spend their money. He would stop now and then to look at the tteokbokki rice cakes, bright red and smouldering like hot lava, or at the strange tornado potato swirls spiralled on sticks. No two carts present exactly the same offering but collectively they created a unique, disorderly, colourful, aroma filled street circus.

But it was the Flying Bird Tea Shop that attracted Sum Taeyoung. Somewhat hidden away down a narrow alleyway off the main tourist trap area, its clientele is mainly discerning locals rather than curious visitors. He loved the quaintness of the strange establishment with its creaking narrow wooden stairs, rickety tables and chairs, knickknacks everywhere, the pervading aroma of exotic teas, and the startlingly colourful little birds that have the run of the place. But most of all he believed his continued good health and long life would be more likely if he regularly consumed the tea room's infamous double harmony tea. Allegedly containing dried roots, ginger, ginseng, cinnamon bark, and other medicinal ingredients, its aroma, let alone its bitter taste, convinces most people of its potent powers.

Sum's business world was ticking along nicely, or at least one part of it was. He formed Sustainable Development Brokers International, usually referred to as SDBI, nearly a decade and a half ago when he realised the fast growing economies of the world needed guidance to ensure such success was not at major cost to the environment and to social wellbeing. This was not through benevolent concern. Sum saw it as a pure profit opportunity. He was aware such issues had been confronted as the Western world progressed through industrialisation and ultimately into the sophisticated computer and consumer age. Lessons had been learnt. Now they could be applied elsewhere as more and more countries moved from primarily poor communities into more prosperity. He formed a brokerage to act as middle man between those he could see needing such knowledge and experience and those who could provide it. His home country of South Korea gave him a rich home market in which to develop his new business which thrived from its launch.

Its giant neighbour, China, held even greater

prospects as the burgeoning nation rushed into a neo-capitalist and consumer era at such breakneck speed as to leave environmental and social havoc in its wake. Headlines frequently exposed the health problems afflicting people living in China's massively expanded cities. Many were caused by seriously polluted air. Water too was a growing concern with urban and industrial expansion pressurising supplies and also polluting rivers and streams.

But Sum Taeyoung is schizophrenic. Whilst his mainstream business could be identified as having benevolent characteristics, there was a darker side to Sum. Born of a South Korean mother and English father, Sum was educated at the LSE in London and the Department of Economics at New York University. Sucked into the more extreme elements of student life, Sum's split personality became even greater defined between, on one hand, his passionate interest in finance and a yearning to make money and, on the other, his loathing of the basic principles of capitalism and its imperialistic origins and antecedents. Capitalism, he grew to believe, was born through a process of brutal imperialism in which nations such as England, Portugal, France and more recently America aggressively annexed countries and raped them of their assets. Ironically, he could now see China doing the same but by using financial muscle rather than military power – so far!

And he could see the main alternative to capitalism – communism – as mainly delivered in Russia and before in the Soviet Union and now in China – to also be flawed mainly because they became hotbeds of corruption. So, it seemed to Sum that though capitalism was the more successful and proven system, it was badly in need of radical makeover.

In a world troubled by a wide variety of different challenges, Sum saw opportunity to both satisfy his desire to vent revenge for the injustices of the past as he believed them to be, and to make money. He identified that two areas of business could potentially make great profit – drug trafficking and dealing in weapons. And while the world was unquestionably experiencing a period full of challenges and difficulties, the more chaos reigned around the globe, so the more Sum's darker businesses would succeed. The more strife, the more the demand for armaments and drugs.

He worked fastidiously to ensure SDBI had a legitimacy and international reputation in brokering contacts between East and West. It provided an authentic platform for his more clandestine activities. Reflecting on the state of his businesses as he supped his tea, Sum felt the legitimate business was doing fine but, irritatingly, the same could not be said of his concealed, darker world. He was working hard at putting behind him two recent setbacks. He was trying to clear his mind of vengeful ambitions aimed at Georgi Patarava and Gene Bond who had caused his latest two escapades to fail. The cost to Sum had been substantial. The desire to seek revenge was intense. But he knew he had to focus his mind on the future. To have it fogged by diversionary activity such as revenge was potentially counterproductive, immature and even dangerous. Despite his natural instinct to balance the books with Patarava and Bond, Sum had new plans to develop, a new scheme to challenge his mind and his skills.

Two things dominated his current thinking. Gold and Ebola. Few people on the planet would connect the two. Sum Taeyoung did.

He had watched while tens of thousands of people suffered and died as the Ebola virus took hold then raged across western Africa, an area in which Sum was highly active in all elements of his business. Many thought it appalling such a tragedy was again afflicting some of the world's poorest people. Sum Taeyoung agreed but also found it frustrating that while such widespread death and suffering was mainly impacting on people already deprived of many of the basics of life, it was not striking at those he so despised in the developed world, especially America and Europe. Why should the poor again suffer, he thought to himself? Why not the rich and the comfortable?

And from this arose the South Korean's latest plot. The idea emerged as he concentrated on his latest venture. Gold was Taeyoung's new interest. He had previously thought of it as an old fashioned, even boring investment commodity. In more recent years oil had dominated the financial interests of the world. Even that was potentially on the brink of being surpassed by water, the most essential resource on the planet because it sustains life itself and which was becoming increasingly commercialised. As a result of the growing population on the planet, with millions of people emerging from poverty into consumerism, and with industry making demands on the use of water as never before, the value of water was being hugely pressurised. But gold still held some sort of raw, almost primeval fascination.

Sum watched recent developments in Russia with growing interest. In recent times it had substantially increased its gold reserves and was now the world's fifth largest holder of the precious metal. Political and industrial observers concluded that Russia's President, renowned for his unconventional and often aggressive moves, was playing a highly sophisticated global game. In Eastern Europe his hostile stance over the Ukraine had resulted in the West retaliating with a host of sanctions. Yet Russia continued to rattle war chains on the borders of what had once been member countries of the Soviet Union.

In the Middle East, the President's unexpected military intervention in the region's complex political/religious problems – initially sparked in him by terrorist incidents in Moscow – saw Russia fighting the same enemy and in the same field of battle as the American led coalition of Western countries. Yet it remained independent in its actions. The Western alliance called it "maverick." The UN thought it confusing.

It was a game of complex twists and turns and ironies in which Western Europe was dependent upon buying oil and gas from Russia whilst deploying economic and trade sanctions against it. At the same time, Russia was using that income to buy gold, creating demand and inflating its value.

In the financial world it is accepted as a given that gold is an anti-dollar investment commodity. So the more the Russian President could collect gold, the more he potentially undermined the value of the dollar. At the same time he believed he could reduce his dependency on the fragile Russian ruble.

As a product of the escalating value of gold on the global market, the viability of gold mines in Siberia was being re-evaluated. Already a mini-Klondike was developing there and, ironically given the political situation overall, some Western based mining companies including Imperial Mining had started buying up Siberian mining assets.

Sum observed all this activity with interest. Indeed, he was on the brink of investing in it himself when the mysterious Siberian holes started to appear. It caused him to stop and to undertake some extensive research into the reasons for the holes which led him to learn about climate change impact on permafrost across the extreme northern areas of the planet. What he read, particularly about associated virus problems, sowed the seeds of an idea. It was a small idea that grew to be a monstrous one. He could link to it his interest in gold and his frustrations about the modern, developed world yet again escaping something that had caused deadly chaos amongst the poor of the world. In that respect, he could achieve some justice.

His fertile but warped mind went into overdrive. He would be able to fuel the tension between the West and Russia, perhaps stimulating greater conflict in Ukraine and potentially encourage increased military action right across Eastern Europe. How good might that be for his armament business? He would be able to undermine the value of gold then manipulate its return to value. What a chance to make a financial killing!

And then there was the big one – an idea that made any that had preceded it miniscule and meaningless. At the pinnacle of his thinking, he could seek to establish a new global control and replacement for the discredited capitalism he so despised. Against the threat of the release in key parts of the planet of an aggressive virus for which there was no known cure – in Europe, America, Russia, China, for instance – he would establish a single global unit of political control based on the principles of social/economic egalitarianism. As his enthusiasm for his idea grew within him, Sum Taeyoung revisited ancient Chinese cultures he had previously read about, especially those of Xu Xing and its influence on Confucianism. Equality of the people would be the driving force but via a process that would see Sum Taeyoung become the most powerful and wealthy individual on the planet.

There were three elements that made up the basis of his plot – the growing demand for Siberian gold, the appearance of the mysterious holes and now a third element based on him learning that two British geophysicists had been taken ill whilst researching one of the mysterious holes on the Siberian tundra. He immediately linked that to what he had read some time ago about ancient viruses being released as the permafrost melts. It was an element of the jigsaw in his mind that was missing. Now, knowing the two had been taken to Anadyr hospital, if he could find them and encapsulate or hide them, he could fill in the gap in his plan. He sowed the seeds of his scheme with care.

Through various intermediaries he made contact with Pavel Galdin of the hospital in Anadyr and eventually secured a deal. Most people, Sum believed, have their price. Pavel Galdin was no exception. But his plot had gone seriously wrong. Someone jumped the gun on him with the raid on the hospital and the disappearance of the two geophysicists. Taeyoung was shocked to hear the news from Galdin.

"Who would do such a thing?" he asked the Senior Administrator at Anadyr Hospital who had phoned him to break the news.

"I have no idea," responded the medical man who was genuinely perplexed and confused about the whole incident.

"Was it the police? Or the military perhaps?" asked Taeyoung.

"They were not police or military. But they did have some sort of uniform."

"What do you mean?" Taeyoung said, anxious to gain any glimmer of understanding as to what had happened at Anadyr Hospital.

"They wore black clothing and there was some sort of yellow emblem on their jackets," Galdin told him.

"Did they show any authority for the taking of the two geophysicists?" asked Taeyoung.

"No," was the curt answer.

"Could they have been Russian secret service people? Or Siberian?"

"We have no idea," an obviously bemused Galdin responded.

Clearly Galdin had no more of an idea than Taeyoung as to who had orchestrated the kidnapping of the geophysicists. All they were left with was a smashed up bus and several unidentified bodies. The only certainty was that the two geophysicists were not among the dead and nobody now seemed to know where they were. To add to the uncertainty of everything, Galdin also reported that laboratory tests on whatever illness the two geophysicists had succumbed to still remained inconclusive.

All this utterly compromised Sum Taeyoung's scheme. Clearly if they were not under his control the geophysicists threatened his plan. Whilst under his control nobody would know whether or not the illness they had was related to an ancient and virulent virus. It would not matter either way. Sum was quite prepared to play a dangerous game by providing fabricated evidence that the geophysicists had died as a result of exposure to a virus with no known antidote. But that assumed he controlled the geophysicists. Now he did not and whilst they lived his plan was dead.

He looked into his near empty cup of double harmony tea and in frustration swept away with the back of his hand one of the tiny colourful birds that had deigned to land on his table.

Chapter 5

Before Bill Patterson could implement any embryonic plan that would, one way or another, see him escape Anadyr-1, reach the airstrip at Ugolny, somehow smuggle himself onto an aircraft to get out of Siberia to Western safety – or, more likely, die in the attempt, his own fate was taken from his hands.

To say he had been shaken by the arrival of the Neolithic-like figure some fifteen minutes ago was a massive understatement. Weak in both body and mind as he was, the apparition of this caveman-like figure now floated round and round his mind like some fantasy he could not comprehend. In his attempts to rationalise what he had seen, he began to wonder if his poor physical and mental state had caused him to fantasize or hallucinate. Whatever had happened, his nerves and awareness had been heightened by the incident and he was now in even more an alert state than he had been. Which is why the second visitation did not take him as much by surprise as the first, though this was even stranger and apparently more threatening.

Three figures arrived at the doorway of the dilapidated building in Anadyr-1 plus an animal on a thick rope. It was the animal that caused Patterson the most concern though the arrival of the group sent the fear of God through him. The mongrel, a mix perhaps of husky and wolf, was a huge and powerful beast, straining forcefully at its rope lead. Its front legs were off the ground, pawing at the air. It foamed at the mouth, heaved at the restraining rope and showing every keenness to get at the figure before him, preferably at his throat. Leaning back and using all his strength to fight and restrain the animal was a bearded figure, short and square, muscular and very obviously male. With the animal's restraining rope wrapped round one wrist, in the other hand he held an arrow headed stave and had a large hunting knife sheathed inside a scabbard hanging from his waist belt. With him was another man, taller, slimmer, frailer-looking and older. The third visitor was the woman Patterson had encountered earlier. All three were dressed in long coats obviously made from animal skins. Together the trio and the dog looked like some sort of hunting group from the age of cave dwellers. This was not what Patterson expected to confront in the remnants of a nuclear town.

Frightened stiff by this new encounter, Patterson tried to rise from where he was crouched on the floor and to retreat further into the corner of the room behind him. It would have been a futile gesture, offering no resistance or protection from the newcomers. It was purely instinctive. A defensive response. His clumsy movement failed because of his lack of strength and he slipped to become spread-eagled on the floor. There was an instant reaction from the trio before him. The man with the animal stepped a pace forward which excited the dog even further and caused him to bare his fangs and growl even louder and more menacingly. The older man and the girl moved behind their companion for protection, themselves frightened by what this strange man before them might do. But Patterson could do nothing. His exhausted body, bereft of any strength, tried to move but his legs simply collapsed under him and he remained on the floor, virtually unconscious.

The two men and the woman looked at him in surprise and puzzlement. This is not what they had expected. They huddled together and whispered, casting glances now and then at Patterson as if to assure themselves he was still prostrate and no threat. The girl fiddled agitatedly at what anywhere else might have been a string of worry beads or prayer beads but which were clearly roughly formed from reindeer teeth. A full minute passed. Patterson did not stir. And a transformation slowly occurred within the three people with the dog. From their initial anxiety which had turned to aggression when Patterson tried to move, now they looked upon his inert and seemingly lifeless body and a mood of concern and compassion for another fellow being slowly came over them. More minutes passed as they stared at the fallen scientist. The dog too fell silent, panting heavily but now lying on the floor at the feet of the man who held him. The animal was more relaxed but its eyes remained riveted on Patterson.

Eventually it was the older man who cautiously stepped forward. Inch by inch he closed the gap to where the fallen stranger lay until he was standing beside him. Patterson had still not stirred though he was breathing and obviously alive, just. The elder man prodded at him with his foot. Patterson did not respond. Another prod with the foot – harder this time – and a grunt at his companions. They joined him and all three stood around Patterson, looking down on him. The sense of concern now prevailed, replacing their earlier anxieties. What they had initially seen as a foe had become a fellow human being in dire need of help.

The woman knelt, and if Patterson had been aware of what was happening he would have been able to confirm his earlier thought. This was indeed a young woman. She felt his forehead and held his wrist. A modern doctor might have done the same but she was using skills based on instinct and inherited ethnic intuition, not science. What she detected was pretty obvious. Patterson was a very sick man.

It was now the woman who took charge of events. The elder man was tasked to take charge of the dog and the younger told to gently pick Patterson up. All four of them left the building in which the geophysicist had been hiding since the bus crash and headed further into the complex that is Anadyr-1, looking around them all the time, ensuring they were not seen by anyone who had ventured into the abandoned nuclear town.

Hours later Patterson returned to consciousness. He felt terrible. His head pounded and his mouth was dry. He gingerly opened his eyes without moving his body or making any sound. His vision was blurred. He found he was lying on some sort of crude bed, covered by hairy animal skins. He was alone. From what he could see he might have been in a prehistoric dwelling. The room was small with the floor covered by large woven mats made from reeds. That and the animal skin coverings gave a distinctly ancient, prehistoric feel to the place but, in total contradiction, the room in which he lay was made of concrete and the light penetrating into it came from a window which still had some remnants of glass in it. Where the glass had gone, someone had patched the holes with cardboard waste. Nailed to the wall was a crude crucifix, incongruous in these strange surroundings.

Then he spotted the fire. It was only a small one with a single glowing bar. But it was electric! Patterson was astounded to find such a modern device amongst this primitive community. It was extraordinary and bizarre. There was apparently still some power on the site into which someone had tapped and these people, whoever they were, knew how to use it.

As consciousness slowly and reluctantly developed he became aware of nearby voices. He strained to listen. He could hear talking but it was not loud enough for him to make out what was being said. A few words drifted to him louder than others but he could not understand the words being used. The language sounded alien to him. Was it Russian? Maybe he could pick out one or two words that sounded Russian. But it seemed much of the conversation was conducted via sounds like animal grunts.

Patterson slowly and carefully tested his body for evidence of damage but all the limbs seemed to be working fine. His head still pounded. His stomach felt as if it had been hit by a sledge hammer and he felt slightly sick. He guessed he had a temperature. When he tried to move it took a significant effort and as he attempted to sit up, he felt decidedly light headed. But he persevered, surprised how weak he felt and how much effort it took but eventually he positioned himself to sit with legs bent over the side of the bed.

He had just achieved this when three people entered the room. He knew two of them – the young woman and the younger man who had had the dog with him during their first encounter. Now they were accompanied by an older woman who held a deep bowl from which rose steam. The young man held a hunting stave and was clearly escorting the two women as their guard. They still saw Patterson as a suspicious and potentially dangerous visitor.

The old woman approached him with obvious trepidation and cautiously offered him the bowl. There was a cloth with it to protect him from the hot vessel which was dark in colour, almost like rusted metal. There was a wooden spoon with it and some sort of broth that smelt fantastic to Patterson. He realised it was a long time since he had last eaten back in the hospital and though the aroma stimulated a desire to eat, his thoroughly rotten state of health caused his stomach to rebel at the thought of food. He heaved again.

The old woman did not move. She understood the situation and waited for Patterson to settle down before tentatively offering him the bowl again.

"Thank you," he said to the old woman. She looked back at him and smiled but obviously had no idea what he had said. He tried it again, repeating the phrase but this time using one of the few Russian phrases he knew.

"Spa-see-ba."

The old woman beamed. The young girl raised her hand to her mouth and giggled.

"Как дела?" the old woman responded. Inevitably, Patterson was already out of his depth and had no way of knowing he was being asked how things were, a familiar way someone asks in Russian how someone else is. She beckoned him to try what was in the bowl which he did, tentatively and cautiously. It was meaty with small chunks of vegetables. A sort of hot pot. Patterson approached it with caution and tested it with a couple of small sips. It was splendid. Now aware how hungry he was, he tried to eat it but his stomach started to rebel again and he felt in danger of just heaving back what he had consumed.

The three stood and watched as he tried to eat from the pot but after a few mouthfuls he was overwhelmed by a need to lie down again. The old woman fussed as a mother might. The younger woman produced a small cup with some liquid concoction in it which the old lady encouraged Patterson to drink before she swung his legs back onto the bed and tucked him in. Responding to the warm food he had consumed and to the heat of the single element fire, Patterson fell into a deep and relatively relaxed sleep.

Some hours later he woke. He felt marginally improved, perhaps a little stronger but very lightheaded. He thought his temperature had reduced but his head was still thumping and his whole body ached. He tried again to sit up but there was no strength to do so and the more he struggled the more dizzy he felt with the room starting to spin around him. He resigned himself to remaining as he was.

A small table now stood beside his bed and on it was the bowl from which he had earlier had the broth. Much of it remained and his hosts had obviously left it there for him to consume if he wanted to. Now there was also a rustic looking goblet with water in it. Patterson fought to grab the goblet and slowly drank a few drops. His mouth was dry and parched and the water was a godsend.

Before he returned the vessel to the table he looked at it with growing curiosity. It was a significant piece of work, large and quite heavy. In his weakened state it took two hands for him to lift it. It appeared to be made of the same metal as was the bowl which he now realised was also a substantial piece of work. The goblet's bowl was shaped almost like a thistle and the rounded short stem led to a base which had an inset ridge running round it. He had taken little notice of the bowl when he had first been offered it. He had then been more interested in its contents. Now, slowly and as best he could in his wretched state, he examined the small goblet, turning it round and round in his hand and looking at the underneath. There was something strange. Eventually he realised his curiosity was being stimulated by what the two implements were made of. Clearly they were metal. And they were quite heavy. But what metal? They were well weathered by use and though clean, the metal had long since lost its colour, dulled by the passing of time.

Ultimately his inquisitiveness got the better of him and though he did not want to abuse the property of the strange people who were clearly now trying to help him, he managed to scratch one vessel against the other to reveal the tiniest of areas of true colour hiding beneath decades of use. For a split second he thought it was brass. But that thought was a brief one, replaced quickly with the realisation that the implements he was holding were made of gold.

Chapter 6

Gene Bond has two favourite drinking venues in London, the Russian Bar and Drifters. The former is located in a dingy, dark, partly cobblestoned East London street lined by seemingly derelict, lifeless buildings. The only brightness in the otherwise completely drab surroundings is the bar's neon sign over its castle-like oak front door complete with Gothic decorative wrought iron hinge straps, aged but still prominent. Dirt and grime ensure that even the neon light is dull and in keeping with the district in which the bar is located. The staple drink here is ice-cold – near freezing – Russian vodka chasers, served in long stemmed silver goblets with white frozen sugar rims and slammed down between gulps of dark beer. He was introduced to it by Georgi Patarava and they use it as a retreat in which to get seriously inebriated.

Bond, trying to get his own back from the jibes by his friend about his double-O name, once taunted Georgi by saying how strange it was that a Georgian should frequent a Russian bar and drink their national liquor in such volume.

"The bar's owned by Arabs nowadays," countered Georgi. "And anyway, it was the Poles who invented vodka, not the Russians!"

Drifters is based in a canal side building owing its origins to the early days of industry when canals were the highways of the age enabling raw materials to enter towns and cities where factories were located, and to take finished products away to markets. Bond has great affection for Drifters. Jazz and motorsport are two of his longstanding passions and the small waterside club serves both. Around its walls are huge pictures, all black and white, either of renowned jazz musicians or of racing cars of one sort or another, all demonstrating a four wheel drift – hence the club's name. Drifters frequently plays host to motor sport evenings to which Bond would go if they co-incided with him being in London. It also has a small bistro providing basic but good food – somewhere to which Bond was frequently attracted..

He and Georgi met in the bistro. It was a much more conducive location for serious discussion than the Russian Bar where conversation simply got in the way of the prime objective of alcohol consumption. This being early in the evening they had the bistro to themselves and, to the sounds of the resident pianist playing Oscar Peterson numbers, the two set about their respective steak meals while Georgi told him what he and his team had found.

The earnest conversation and obvious friendship between the two men concealed the vast difference between them. Work that had originally brought Bond, the environmental and sustainable development advocate, and Georgi Patarava, the Eastern European counter-espionage expert, together in the Soviet Embassy in Kensington, London was broken with the collapse of the Soviet Union. The two drifted apart and Bond all but forgot his Georgian friend and even assumed him to have been the victim of the short but bloody war between Russia and Georgia.

Fate led them to bump into each other at an international conference and Bond later found Georgi now heads up the communications division of the European Secret Service.

"I didn't know there was such a thing," Bond said when Georgi told him.

"Officially there isn't," Georgi responded. "The European Satellite Centre, the Intelligence Division and the Joint Situation Centre had all been created. It didn't take much to take bits off each and morph them into something called the EU Intelligence Service which even most Members of the European Parliament don't know exists. And while the EUIS has its HQ in Brussels, it was decided the communications side should be in the UK to be close to your GCHQ with its links to the Americans, and to MI5 and MI6. So the Comms Centre needed to be in London. But where do you put an organisation that doesn't exist?"

"I don't know," Bond responded. "But I guess you're going to tell me."

"You put it in a place that doesn't exist!" Georgi responded triumphantly. "Thirty years or so ago the old warehouses in Wapping Wall to which the clipper ships of the mid-1800s used to bring spices from distant places to be converted into things like mustard and then re-exported, were modified into luxurious riverside apartments. At that time the Thames Barrier hadn't been built and there was concern the basement areas might flood. So they were sealed off. They were largely forgotten until we wanted somewhere for our base. The Thames Barrier means the basements won't now flood and anyway today we've got the technology to help make these previously unusable spaces usable. So that's where we exist. In a place that doesn't exist! But, to the outside world, we don't exist at all."

Bond had subsequently become involved in two escapades with Georgi. He was a reluctant participant on both occasions and was deeply resolved to ensure there was not a third. But what he had seen on the Scottish coast by The Mansion had raised his curiosity and Georgi and his team were the only people he could turn to in the hope of finding out more. And anyway, despite the two unwanted adventures, he still delighted in Georgi's company.

"I've brought some stuff for you to look at," Georgi told him at the dinner table. He dug down into his hold-all bag and pulled out a large envelope which he handed to his friend.

"There's not much to go on from what you've told us. So we've looked at boats and the house in Scotland – The Mansion. And that's led us onto some other thinking. I'll tell you about that in a moment. Look in the envelope."

Bond did as he was asked and pulled out a load of photographs of varying size. They were all of boats of one shape or another but with characteristics matching the small amount of information he had given Georgi. He looked through the collection.

"If you look on the back you'll find a description of each one," Georgi told him.

And eventually Bond settled on one particular picture and turned it over and read out loud: "It says this is a seven metre long rib inflatable."

"I think all the pictures are of inflatables," Georgi told him. "They're popular. If you want a boat that's got great performance, handling and safety, they're pretty good. The military use them a lot. They say there's no better craft for transporting people and equipment – even in really bad weather."

"Are these all military?" Bond asked, thumbing through the collection of photographs.

"No, you can buy military ones second hand but some are made for the non-military markets. The one you're looking at is military."

"So does that get us anywhere?"

"Not yet," admitted Georgi. "But how many seven metre long, ex-military, rib inflatables will you find buzzing around the north coast of Scotland?"

Bond looked at his friend and smiled. He was right, of course. "Not many."

"So, we'll have a sniff around and see if we can find one," Georgi told him. "And then we'll try and find out who owns it. That's a start. Then maybe we'll discover why it was going to The Mansion."

Bond agreed it was a start.

"Then there's the house," continued Georgi, cutting into his steak with unbounded energy. "The Mansion."

"I was surprised to find it so cut off with that barrier across the road," said Bond. "I'd not seen that before. It's relatively new."

"We've found the house is owned by a minerals

extraction company as a sort of corporate hideaway. It's called Imperial Mining. Ever heard of them?"

"No," replied Bond.

"Based here in London. A shelf company until the current owners got hold of it."

"A shelf company?" queried Bond.

"That's a fully registered company with all its records up to date which hasn't been operational for some time. So it's been 'left on the shelf' until someone who doesn't want the hassle of forming a new company acquires it and uses it to his own aims. In this case it's a group of speculators in minerals extraction who believe there's wealth in Siberia in gold mining. So they formed Imperial Mining and bought up a few sites in Siberia."

"I've got some business interests in gold mining in Siberia," said Bond.

"Really!" Georgi responded with some degree of incredulity. "Don't see you in the gold business!"

"It's to do with how some people are being displaced by the mining activity. I've concerns that people's lives are being wrecked because of strategies based purely on economics and not the values of sustainable development. You have to ensure you're protecting social, environmental and economic values in how you progress development – not just one of those values but all three. We've seen it in places like China where people are just shifted to make way for government projects – like a recent example where more than 9,000 residents are being moved to make way for the development of the world's largest radio telescope. These people will be paid compensation but that's not the point. The Chinese government paid compensation to the 1.3 million people they moved to enable the Three Gorges dam to be built. But many of those were proud farming people whose lives were wrecked by the dam."

"Now we've got the same sort of thing happening in Siberia where the authorities plan to relocate an entire Siberian town because gold was found there and they want to establish a mine where the town currently is. I've been asked to do a sustainability assessment on behalf of a campaigning NGO which is concerned about the social and environmental consequences of the economically led decision to move the people of the town of Partizansk to make way for a gold mine. There have been protests in the streets but not to any effect. They're going to be shifted anyway. It's well summed up by someone from the local administration who said – "In order to be able to mine gold here, we need to move the town."

"So will you be going to Partizansk?" asked Georgi.

"Don't know yet," Bond responded. "It depends how much I can do without going."

"Gold has suddenly become big news in Siberia," Georgi added. "It's not that long ago – a couple of years – since a huge chunk of gold was found in Siberia. They called it the 'Devil's Ear' because its shape is like a pointed ear, it was found on Friday 13th and it weighed 6.66kg – the devil's number."

"We forget how big Siberia is," he continued while attacking his steak. "The eastern slab alone is almost twice the size of Australia and the quality of gold being extracted from mines such as the Olimpiada Mine is of such a high grade it makes it worthwhile to work in very bad conditions."

"And the size of the mining operations is massive. The Olimpiada deposit was first discovered in 1970. It's now the fourth biggest gold mine in the world with estimated reserves of around 32 million ounces of gold. Further east, the Kupol mine employs some 1200 people and its owners, a Canadian company, estimate it will yield up to 2.5 million ounces of gold and more than 30 million ounces of silver."

"Bloody hell," said Bond. "They're big numbers! I didn't realise Siberia had such activity. It's only been since the Partizansk story came onto my desk that I've taken any notice. I thought Siberia was just a frozen wilderness. But, where does all that take us with my mysterious boat in Scotland?"

"We don't know yet. I've authorised someone to have a look around The Mansion and see what Imperial Mining's doing with it."

"That's not going to be easy," suggested Bond.

"Why?" Georgi asked.

"Well, there are only two ways to approach The Mansion – from the sea or from the road. You'd be very conspicuous going in by sea and we know the road is blocked and covered by CCTV."

"You might be right, my friend," Georgi responded. "But the more awkward they've made it for anyone to have a look, the more concerned they must be to hide whatever they're doing. And anyway, the more difficult they make it the more of a challenge it becomes. You know how much we enjoy a challenge!"

There was a pause as they both finished their meals. It was clear to Bond that Georgi had more on his mind and that proved to be so as the Georgian set off down a new track of thinking.

"During our look at Siberian extraction activity – including oil as well as minerals, we found two things of interest. They may be meaningless and utterly disconnected. But we found them of interest. One was mysterious holes that have been appearing throughout Siberia and the other is the release of ancient diseases as the permafrost melts. It seems the melting of the permafrost is related to both. What do you know about it?"

Bond looked at his friend and sighed. "That's one hell of a question! I'm not sure where to start."

"Assume I know nothing."

"What doesn't a Georgian secret service man working for the European Secret Service that doesn't exist know about climate change?" teased Bond. "I thought you guys knew everything!"

"Not as much as double-O agents," quipped Georgi.

"Piss off Georgi. Don't go anywhere in that direction. I can't tell you how long I paused and thought before sending that picture from my phone. It was only curiosity that got the better of me – and the excuse for us to have a drink together which we haven't had for such a long time. But – and it's an enormous "but" – there's no way I'm getting into another of your ventures. No way!"

There was silence between them for a while.

"Climate change is said by some people to be the most important and perilous challenge facing our modern world," Bond eventually told Georgi. "In recent times even the Pope has started calling for more concerted action. Considering the potential consequences of what we're talking about, I'm amazed there's not greater concern or interest amongst the public. Somehow, the message doesn't seem to be getting through."

"What do you mean?" Georgi quizzed.

"Well, I'll give you two extremes of what I see," Bond responded. "I see Professor Anders Levermann of the Potsdam Institute for Climate Impact Research saying "if we get beyond two degrees of global warming we're leaving the world as we know it." Yet two people who have spoken to me recently typify the general public response. One, a retired industrialist, told me that climate change is just a natural cycle of nature. We've seen it before, he said. It goes round in circles. We'll manage it. And then there was a well-educated lady who said she loves the thought of global warming – "more time in my deck chair"!"

"Who's right?" asked Georgi.

"Well, I know who I trust!" responded Bond emphatically. "Levermann is a world leader on the subject. There's evidence around the planet that the climate is changing. We're seeing ice caps melt – the melting of the permafrost that we've been talking about – water where there has always been ice, more extreme weather, changes in plant growing patterns, and so on."

"Now you might say, as the industrialist said to me, this is a natural phenomenon, a cycle of nature. I've a very simple response to that. Either it's an entirely natural situation or its man-made, either in total or in part. If it's the former, we learn to live with it and mitigate against the consequences as best we can. But, if we're responsible or contributing to the problem, then surely – if we're the intelligent species we think we are – we should stop doing whatever it is we're doing that's making the problem worse."

"And if you care not to accept the scientific evidence and make your mind up based on your intuition, that's one hell of a gamble. If you're right, so be it. But if you're wrong, the consequences will be catastrophic. We end up with a planet that's barely habitable. What a legacy from us to our children! And if you are wrong, by the time you realise it, it may well be too late to stop the downward slide. You may well have passed the point of no return. That, my friend, is fucking sobering!"

Georgi was listening intently to every word from his friend who he recognised as being passionate about these matters. And though he accepted all Bond was saying, he still wanted to test it further.

"Two things. What should we stop doing? What are the consequences of not stopping?"

"To put it crudely, we should stop throwing shit into the atmosphere. We've had international agreements for years to reduce the amount of carbon we emit. Again if I reduce this to my simple thinking, I can't believe we can constantly throw so much stuff into the atmosphere without causing some change. So when I'm told there's a direct correlation between carbon emissions and climate change, I believe it. In 1997 the international community signed the Kyoto Protocol to reduce carbon emissions. So why, according to scientific evidence, were carbon emissions in 2013 2.3% higher than in 2012 and 61% higher than in 1990? In fact, I believe carbon emissions have gone up every year since the Kyoto Agreement was signed!"

"Haven't there been new agreements on this," asked Georgi. "In Paris?"

"Yes," Bond responded. "The international meeting there signed an agreement to ensure we don't exceed a 1.5% increase in global temperature against pre-industrial levels. It was, we're told, a legally binding agreement."

"What does that mean?"

"I've no idea," Bond sighed. "I've asked the question time and time again and never had a satisfactory answer. My question is – if a country doesn't hit its targets within an internationally agreed, legally binding contract, who goes to court? And if found guilty, who goes to prison? If the penalty is just financial, in reality the people pay. But it's the politicians who are guilty, not the people. So, if a country fails against its targets, will the Prime Minister or President end up in prison? I doubt it!"

"So it's a meaningless agreement?" asked Georgi.

"It's certainly an agreement without teeth," Bond told him.

"And the consequences of not stopping – not sending all this shit into the atmosphere as you so eloquently put it?"

"In the long term we end up with a planet on which we can't live. The planet is 1% hotter now than it was before the Industrial Revolution. The international community has set a target to ensure it doesn't go above 2%. In Paris they reduced that to 1.5%. That's good news

– if it's achieved. Levermann says "beyond two degrees of warming we're leaving the world as we know it."

"So what does that mean?" Georgi tested.

"Well, we're already feeling the results of climate change – and it can only get worse before, hopefully – it gets better. You know all about the Aral Sea from our previous exploits. But that's not the only major inland water to dry up. The Aral Sea's in Eastern Europe. Over in South America, Bolivia's second largest lake – Lake Poopó, has gone! Just plain gone! It used to cover around 3,000 square kilometres. And scientists are saying Bolivia's capital, La Paz, could face catastrophic drought this century. They're predicting inhospitable arid climates that will lessen available food and water this century for the more than three million inhabitants of Bolivia's highlands."

"Then there's the crazy story from Alaska where snow has had to be imported so they can run the famous Iditarod dog sled race! Some 300 cubic yards of snow has been hauled by railroad more than 350 miles from Fairbanks to Anchorage to enable the opening ceremony to happen! Unbelievable!"

"That's all happening now. In the coming years rising sea levels will threaten cities like New York, Calcutta and Shanghai. The Thames Barrier will need replacing otherwise your Wapping base will sink! But across the planet, climate change will impact on food supplies, water security, ecosystems, health – all creating social pressures which are bound to cause conflict. The most recent thing I've read is that more than 60% of the world's power stations could be impacted by water shortages caused by climate change."

"But it's not all bad news. For instance, shipping distances will be reduced as ships sail north from China to Europe and North America rather than south."

"How come?" asked Georgi.

"They'll sail through seas where there used to be ice," Bond told him. "It's happening already. China's biggest shipping company intends to launch regular services through the Arctic Ocean to Europe as global warming makes the route viable. It's already sent ships round the Northeast Passage rather than sending them through the Suez Canal. The journey normally takes 48 days via the Canal. It's taking 35 by heading north and going via the Bering Strait. It's 3,000 miles shorter than the usual route."

"Not good news for Egypt," Georgi responded. "Loss of Canal revenue just when their tourist industry's been hit by terrorist activity."

"Yes, but imagine the cost savings on fuel and general running costs. And there's the benefit of getting products to market quicker. It's the sort of consequential impacts we'll have to adjust to as climate change increasingly impacts on us," said Bond.

"If you're right about all of this, why isn't more being done to prevent climate change happening or prepare people for the consequences?" Georgi asked.

"A lot's happening," Bond assured him. "But by no means enough and not fast enough. So emissions continue to go up year after year, despite all the promises and commitments. And increasingly across the planet we see more and more examples of extreme weather – with floods and land slips and more and more impoverished people. That – and increases in conflict – causes people to seek better places to be. So you get mass migrations happening."

"Are you trying to tell me that the huge migration problems we've been having are related to climate change? I've not heard that before," Georgi confessed.

"You remember the Stella of the Vultures from our second skirmish with Sum Taeyoung?" asked Bond.

"Vaguely," confessed Georgi. "Remind me."

"It's an etched stone tablet kept in the Louvre in Paris. It depicts a treaty brokered by Turkey to end a war 4,500 years ago between two factions fighting over water from the Tigris and Euphrates rivers. It's thought to be the world's first water war. Fast forward to 2006 and a drought in northern Syria through which both those rivers flow. The Smithsonian Institute suggests that lack of water forced farmers to abandon their fields and migrate to urban centres. That sparked tensions between different factions. That fuelled civil war – and the rest is, as they say, history with a migration of people today on a biblical scale abandoning war ravished northern Africa and trying to escape to Europe."

Georgi thought about that for a while. "It's an extraordinary connection," he eventually suggested.

"But it may be a precursor of more to come," Bond responded. "Climate change will impact on people in so many ways. Low lying land is likely to be engulfed by rising sea levels. People in mountainous areas will be deprived of fresh water as glaciers melt. If climate change causes it to be more difficult to grow food where we've traditionally grown it, you can expect many more people to abandon their traditional homelands. And don't forget the population's growing. There's never been so many people on the planet – and they all need feeding!"

Again there was a silence before Georgi said: "And how do we connect all this to what we're talking about?"

"I don't know," Bond retorted. "It was you who started talking about what's happening in Siberia – the melting of the permafrost, the holes that have appeared and the escaping viruses. But what's all that got to do with my mysterious boat in Scotland?"

Georgi Patarava laughed. "How the hell do I know? That's what we need to find out."

Chapter 7

It only slowly dawned on Amy Kelly that she was as much a prisoner as anyone who now considered themselves trapped in The Mansion. If things had worked according to plan, only Jack Bailey was truly confined here against his wishes. But his awareness of his confinement was probably nil as he continued to float in and out of consciousness and was often hanging onto life itself by the most tenuous of threads.

In contrast, Amy fully comprehended her plight. What she did not understand was why it was happening and who was making it happen. Circumstances had changed since her arrival but she had no idea what was going on, except she could not leave the building on her own and could not communicate with the outside world. She was allowed to walk the enormous sands of the area and even scramble along the extensive rocky outcrops that stretch along the coast towards Portskerra. But she was never alone, always accompanied by at least one of the men in their black uniforms with yellow flashes on their chests. Often they had dogs with them.

The task at The Mansion was never going to be easy. As a freelance nurse contracted to Alexander Fitzpatrick's Imperial Mining company, she had responded instantly when he had called her saying he needed her on an assignment that could last a couple of weeks or so. Of her small group of corporate clients, Imperial Mining was miniscule in size in terms of numbers of people it employed but it was by far the biggest payer. So when Fitzpatrick called with a plea for help she reorganised her commitments to enable her to help him.

She was told a member of Fitzpatrick's team had picked up some sort of virus whilst abroad. He was now isolated and Amy was needed to care for him and hopefully nurse him back to good health. The whole matter was of intense commercial sensitivity and Fitzpatrick told her she must not speak about it to anyone. He did not even tell her where she was going. His instructions were for her to pack for an indefinite period away and to meet him at London's City Airport in the historic dockland area of the now modernised Royal Albert Dock.

From there they flew in an executive aircraft north to the Scottish border and onward to the airport at Wick on the east coast. Transferring to a helicopter, they headed further north on a spectacular journey along the coast to the very tip of mainland Britain, rounding the headland with Dunnet Head to their left, the swirling waters of the Pentland Firth below and the Scapa Flow entrance to the Orkney Islands to their right. It was an extraordinary flight in a mode of transport totally alien to Amy but routine to the entrepreneurial Fitzpatrick.

During the journey he briefed her about the task ahead.

"We had a scientific team out on the Siberian tundra. Our interests there are in gold mining. Imperial Mining recently acquired a Siberian company that owns several mines. But one, on the Chukotka tundra in the eastern part of Siberia, is of special interest to us. Test drilling shows the quality of gold there to be especially high and we're keen to start explorations as soon as possible. However, mysterious holes have been appearing across Siberia. It puzzles people as to their origin but the best theory we believe is that climate change is causing the permafrost to melt. That's sending freezing water down into the substructure where it's hitting subterranean hot rocks. This sparks explosions and results in these holes. Now that's only theory. We have major investors in our project who need more than theory as to the cause of these holes. They want hard facts."

"As if that wasn't bad enough, the two scientists we sent to try and secure that evidence were taken ill. At the hospital in Anadyr in Siberia it was found they'd been attacked by a virus. What that virus is hasn't yet been identified. But we're mindful that some very ancient viruses, some more than 30,000 years old, have been released as the permafrost has melted. Scientists say they're potentially infectious but what has been released so far poses no danger to humans. However, as the climate warms and Siberia thaws, mining and drilling is starting to penetrate previously inaccessible areas and how that will impact on the release of other – and maybe different – viruses isn't known."

"My worry is that this might unnerve my investors to such a degree they withdraw their support. That would be catastrophic! So that's why this matter is so important I cannot leave it to others. We implemented a plan to extract the scientists from Anadyr and take them to our own isolated location so we could better control events. We've established an isolation room there and brought in state of the art medical equipment – enough to keep monitoring the scientist and keep him alive while we find out what this virus is. So that's your job. To keep him alive and monitor him."

Alarm bells were ringing. Amy was greatly concerned and disturbed by what she was being told. And confused.

"You said there were two scientists. Now you're talking about "him" as if he's the only one. How many are there?"

"Just one, I'm afraid. The extraction from Siberia hit problems and we've lost one of them. I know that sounds ridiculous but that's how it is. We don't know where the other man is or whether he's even still alive. The circumstances in Eastern Siberia are very difficult. The chances are he must be dead by now unless the authorities have got him but aren't telling anyone."

"But," said Amy with increasing concerns. "This virus issue is a highly specialised medical matter. I don't have qualifications to deal with viruses."

"I understand that," said Fitzpatrick. "All I need you to do is to nurse this guy – Jack Bailey – and keep him alive while we find out what the virus is. I have some of the best medical brains working on that at the moment. We're paying for the work and it's being kept top secret. The Russians too are working on it. They're also keeping it very quiet. Like us, they don't want the beginnings of a gold rush in Siberia dying before it gets going because investors become frightened. "

And so they flew on along the northern coast until they reached the estuary of the Halladale River and landed on the expansive rear lawn of The Mansion. Amy was seriously impressed by the sheer size of the extensive tall building and its accompanying outhouses and walled garden. Standing in the solitude of the rugged surrounding countryside and dramatic coastline, it was conspicuously the only building in sight. It looked stately, grand, but foreboding.

They were met on the lawn by Iain Barthwait, Imperial's most senior of managers.

"Welcome to the edge of civilisation," he said, shaking her hand and taking two of her bags. Of immediate concern to Amy was the sick geological scientist and at her request they went to see him before Amy was introduced to the rest of the building. They climbed to the third floor and into what had once been one of the many bedrooms. Now it looked very different.

The room had obviously been gutted and rebuilt. The walls and ceiling were whitewashed and half the room was occupied by what in essence was a room within a room but one constructed of metal sections and see-through plastic panels. Amy saw inside there was an isolation sheet hanging from ceiling to floor which had sleeves so hands and arms could be used to attend to the person beyond but without being exposed to him.

Lying on a hospital bed was a man to whom various pieces of equipment were attached to monitor his body's vital signs. Outside the isolation area an array of technology showed the patient's state of well-being which Amy immediately scrutinised with keen interest.

Jack Bailey was alive and stable but clearly a very sick man.

Iain Barthwait took the newcomer under his wing while Fitzpatrick disappeared to attend to other business matters. He took Amy on a tour of the building and introduced her to two groups of people – the elderly Scottish couple who ran the house, and those who were providing the security screen to the operation, the latter all in the black uniform with the yellow flash on the front. She learnt they were from an Eastern European specialist unit that undertook high security work such as this. Their leader, a tall, lean man with closely cut hair and sparkling blue eyes who she guessed to be in his late 30s, was introduced to her as Janka Koldun from Belarus. He seemed little interested in Amy – dismissive of her. His mind was clearly on other things he considered more important. She realised over the following days that the more she encountered Koldun the more he was always like this – a very abrupt man who kept his thoughts very much to himself and spoke very little. When he did speak it was in good English and with great authority. Janka Koldun did not ask for things. He ordered them.

There was conflict between him and Amy almost from the start as he confiscated both her mobile phone and her laptop.

"It's the rule here," he told her. "No contact with the outside world except through our official channels."

When she protested that she would not be able to work like that – that she would need to speak to the laboratories analysing the virus – and, perhaps, to other medical advisors and specialists, Janka Koldun was adamant that any communication with anyone should be via him and through the corporate lines of communications linking the house to the outside world. In an update about the state of Jack Bailey, Amy was told he had initially had a dangerously high fever, had been in a coma and was prone to irregular seizures. The more extreme reactions to whatever was afflicting him had subsided and he now remained largely unconscious and was being fed intravenously. None of the laboratories searching to find what the virus was had yet come up with results. The task now was to monitor Bailey's status and ensure he did not deteriorate.

Amy tried to settle into a routine. It was difficult and her discomfort at her situation was compounded by her continuing poor relationship with Koldun who she found to be aloof, arrogant, of military training and who exercised his command role as if he expected everyone he was in charge of to jump the instant he barked. He had six men with him and they all responded to him as if he were a senior officer and they the lower ranks. To Amy, this all jarred against her characteristics which had been fashioned by her fiery Irish background and her free spirit. It was this make up that caused her to dislike the authority of the state medical system and why, once she had qualified and gained experience, she became a freelance nurse specialising in the corporate sector.

But now she found herself bottled up in a confined environment and managed by what she thought to be a megalomaniac and a control freak. It was not of her liking, to put it mildly. During the week that followed Fitzpatrick flew off in his helicopter leaving

Iain Barthwait in charge. Amy tried as best she could to settle into a routine centred around the monitoring and nursing of the sick geologist. But not long after Fitzpatrick departed she noted what seemed to be a change of rule and control within The Mansion. For reasons unknown to her, Janka Koldun, who previously had been subservient to Barthwait, now seemed to be calling the tune. Conversely Barthwait, from what Amy now saw, was very reluctantly responding to Koldun and appeared to be, as was she, confined to the building and only allowed outside accompanied by a guard.

What Amy did not know was that she was right. A complete juxtaposition had occurred. It all started with a telephone call to the Eastern European's mobile phone, one of the few still functioning within The Mansion. Koldun did not recognise the number being shown as the phone buzzed. It was with some caution he answered it.

"Yes".

"Please confirm I am speaking to Janka Koldun." He did not recognise the voice that had spoken in English with just a hint of an American accent.

"I am Janka Koldun," he confirmed. "Who are you?"

"Ah, Mr Koldun. What I wish to talk to you about is of the utmost importance and potentially of great value to you personally. So, please don't hang up."

Janka Koldun's instinct told him to end the call immediately. But there was something about the voice at the other end of the line that was intriguing. The man calling him sounded English, but maybe American, and yet there was a slight unidentifiable accent.

“What do you want?” he asked abruptly.

There was a slight pause before the voice said “Mr Koldun. Please confirm nobody else can hear this conversation.”

“Nobody can. What do you want?” Janka Koldun’s impatience was starting to outweigh his curiosity.

“Mr Koldun. My name is Sum Taeyoung.”

Chapter 8

Jack Bailey remained cocooned in clinical and medically sterile surroundings monitored by state of the art, sophisticated equipment and a full time and highly trained nurse. Meanwhile, laboratory scientists in research establishments in various parts of the world sought to discover what virus was attacking him. The circumstances of Jack Bailey could not be in sharper contrast to those of his longstanding colleague William Patterson. Patterson's life consisted of brief moments of lucidity but largely of vivid, colourful kaleidoscopic dreams and hallucinations in which he floated through a world close to unconsciousness. Reality and fantasy become an entangled muddle. He had some vague awareness of the family looking after him and who he had, perhaps cruelly, nicknamed the Flintstones. That did not help. Now his mind played on images of the cartoon series and jumbled them with the stone-age family that was nursing him back from near death.

Not long after he discovered that the vessel in which his broth was served was made of gold, his health deteriorated. Moments of cognizance were few and far between but when they occurred he was aware he was being fed and given some sort of medicine. As the days passed, of the Flintstones family which he knew now to consist of mother, father, son and daughter, it was the latter who seemed to have been tasked with looking after the stranger who they had initially considered a threat but who they now saw as a fellow human being in severe difficulties and needing help only they could give.

The daughter – the first of the family to have encountered him – administered various concoctions and tried to cool his forehead and chest with a cold, damp cloth. She would sit behind him, move his body to be across hers so she could spoon feed him. Through his cloudy and swoony appreciation of what was going on, he was sometimes conscious of the warmth of her body against his, her smell, her arms around him, the firmness of her breasts, the gentleness of her touch, her femininity. She was, he guessed, in her late twenties.

The first image he had had of her as she stood in the doorway, as frightened of him as he had been of her, was of a crude person of indistinguishable gender belonging to some ancient cave dwelling tribe. Now he knew her to be someone of compassion, tenderness, with eyes of deep dark blue, long black hair and a red faced complexion. Despite the craziness of the situation, when she bathed his body with a dampened cloth, he could not help be aroused by her touch, especially when she washed him around his manhood. He mentally reprimanded himself for responding in such a way. He should not be aroused by this girl. These people – this young woman – were showing great tenderness and compassion to him – saving his life no less – in return for which he was having sensual fantasies towards a complete stranger whose femininity he questioned not so long ago. It was preposterous and he felt ashamed.

Sometimes the process of being fed or having his brow gently bathed in cool water made him lucid enough to try and talk to her. But most of the time he lived through a sleep of crazy, multi-coloured dreams, illusions and hallucinations in which this girl often featured. It was difficult for Patterson to determine whether the world he was dreaming was pure fantasy or the real world. During one moment of full consciousness when she was sitting close to him, he had tried to communicate.

"Bill," he had said to her, pointing to himself. She looked at him quizzically and with a degree of fear.

"Bill," he repeated, pointing to himself again. "What's your name?" he asked, now pointing at her.

The girl's face relaxed as understanding dawned.

"Nika," she replied with a hint of a giggle. She was obviously happy to try and converse with him but still wary, very cautious and certainly shy. Her major priority was to administer food and drugs to this stranger who had so suddenly entered their previously secluded world but who had become her personal responsibility and challenge. Whilst Bailey was being kept alive through the most modern of techniques, technology and drugs, William Patterson owed his ongoing life to medicines based on traditional Siberian remedies dating back into the mists of time.

Not that Patterson was to know it yet but he was the first male apart from her father and her brother Nika had encountered in her 26 years. Entrusted by her family to look after their unexpected visitor, her initial fear of the stranger turned to compassion – then curiosity – then more. More? But what more? She could not recognise many of the emotions. This was all totally alien to her. Never before had she had a close relationship with anyone apart from the three members of her family. Now, through an extraordinary set of circumstances, she had been brought into close contact with the man who had initially frightened her but to whom she now felt some sort of bonding.

Nika administered analgesics to help him manage the pain. They were a recipe of Chaga mushrooms, various herbs and wild Siberian cannabis. Other drugs of similar historic origins were given to try and combat Patterson's fever and violently upset stomach. And whereas the treatment being administered to Bailey was guided by scientific information provided by the technology that was monitoring him, with Patterson it was based on Nika's intuition, acquired skills and the knowledge and experience of her mother.

As the days passed Patterson slowly improved. More time was spent in the conscious world than elsewhere and he began to move again, using Nika to try and help him gain a sitting position in bed. Their relationship continued to grow as did conversation.

"Reindeer?" he asked quizzically, pointing at the contents of the bowl as Mother Flintstone brought another helping of broth to her daughter for her to feed their patient.

Nika looked back at him blankly and then to her mother. Mother Flintstone shrugged her shoulders, obviously as mystified as her daughter.

"Reindeer?" the geologist repeated. And as he did he

raised his hands to his head and did his best to imitate antlers. It took several goes and quite a bit of giggling before Nika grasped what he was on about.

"Severnyy olen!" she replied triumphantly in Russian. Patterson still had no idea what language the family was speaking, Russian or any of the languages spoken in Siberia or by the Eskimos.

As Patterson slowly recovered so the relationship with Nika grew closer. She helped him take the few first steps as strength started to return to him, his arm around her shoulder, her arms around his body in support. Again he experienced reactions to her intimate closeness that he felt inappropriate but could not control. With her help, hand in hand, he moved around the room, venturing to the window to look out to the dreary sight of the abandoned nuclear town and its rotting buildings. How many days had slipped by since the bus crash Patterson had no idea. He had lost track of time completely and had no way of finding the current date. His mobile phone had been taken from him at the hospital. He increasingly felt a frustration that he was isolated and cut off from the outside world.

Over the days that followed the stronger he grew, and the more the impact of the virus faded within him, the more the irritation of his confinement exasperated him. There were consolations. He was alive. His health was improving. He was feeling stronger. His mind was now alert. And he increasingly relished the company of Nika.

The more he explored where he was the more he became puzzled about the family that had undoubtedly saved his life. They were unquestionably weird. Their lives were confined to the buildings of the abandoned town. Every step outside the buildings was made with huge caution as if they were prey and preditors might be anywhere nearby. They had selected where they lived with care. It was the farthest point from the perimeter road, as far away from the nearest civilisation as it could be, and in part of the town that was in a hollow and quite out of sight unless you were walking specifically into that area. From what he could see the Flintstone family had been here for many years and had taken over several linked buildings and converted them into their living and sleeping quarters. One building was now a massive greenhouse with the roofing tiles removed and replaced by transparent plastic sheeting scavenged from the abandoned town. The growing of vegetables and herbs was clearly the responsibility of the mother and her daughter. Father and son brought in meat from regular hunting trips out on the tundra.

The Flintstones increasingly treated him as a friend. As soon as he was able to stand and support himself and to walk without help he sat with them to eat. They opened their home to him but made it clear he should not wander out of the building. The relationship remained difficult, the problem of language ensuring there was a frustrating gulf between him and them. He was still trying to fathom the language they were using and to get used to them communicating through what he could only describe as grunts. It appeared to Patterson that without the need to communicate outside their own small group of four, words had partly become redundant as the family developed its methodology of conversing with a mixture of words and grunts.

As his strength grew Patterson explored more, often hand in hand with Nika but egged on by a curiosity to know who these people were, why they were here, and why they had drinking vessels made from gold? Scattered around the complex of buildings he found remnants of the building's former use lying around where they had been discarded. There were books, files and pamphlets, all in Russian and meaningless to the Scottish geophysicist.

The Flintstone family had their individual responsibilities and a family routine. There was much evidence of them being a religious family and prayers were said every day and at meal times. Wooden crosses hung on several walls, all carved by the family and all with small elements of gold within them.

There was no doubt they were obsessed with the need to remain concealed from the outside world. Patterson had no idea if anyone else ever entered this derelict town but clearly the Flintstones wished to remain hidden. Whenever they left the building they did so with cautious looks all around them. The son, some years older than the daughter, appeared to have some knowledge which enabled the family to tap into the electrical power that extraordinarily still ran through the site. There was no running water but he had constructed a rain water gathering facility which included a rudimental piping from the roof down to where the family cooked and ate.

Two areas were of particular interest to Patterson – the kitchen and the room in which the Flintstones exercised their religious commitments. In the kitchen, Patterson found a weird mix of containers, mugs, plates and bowls, all ceramic and presumably found from scavenging around the abandoned town. But it was the pots and pans that fascinated him. Like the bowl from which he had earlier drunk water, many of these were also made from gold. And here there were lots of them.

The commitment of the family to their God was blatantly obvious and Nika eventually introduced Patterson to a room the Flintstones had transformed into a small chapel. It was here the family prayed twice a day. And it was here Patterson found the astonishing story behind this extraordinary family.

Chapter 9

EXTREME NATURE WATCHING the advertising placard proclaimed. Jimmie Hall made a mental note of it when he found the rigid inflatable Georgi asked him to search for on the north coast of Scotland. Tall and lean, with ragged long blond hair and still good looking despite an aged and severely weather worn face, Jimmy had retired early from his unorthodox military career in the aftermath of the short but bloody war between Georgia and Russia where he fought as a mercenary for the Georgians. In its aftermath, he roamed somewhat aimlessly around northern Europe, eventually thinking he might settle to a life of fishing and rough terrain walking in northern Scotland. But he was wrong. Life after military service took some getting used to and Jimmie, like other ex-servicemen and women, found integrating back into society a real challenge. He took to petty crime, heavy drinking and a series of relationships with women who could at best be described as of questionable repute. Too regularly he was before the courts. Eventually a social worker explored his skills and experience and recognised them as a potential opportunity. A series of events led to a meeting with Georgi Patarava who sympathised with the plight of someone who had fought for his country. He eventually recruited him to become the representative of his London based espionage organisation to cover everything in Scotland from Inverness up to the north coast and the islands beyond. He paid Jimmie a small retainer then on a project by project basis.

Jimmie was delighted to be tasked to do something for Georgi. And it was easy. He found the craft Georgi was looking for where he expected it to be – tethered to a mooring post and bobbing gently on the placid waters of Scrabster harbour near the town of Thurso. As soon as Georgi mentioned it Jimmie thought he knew the boat. He lived not far from Thurso and often worked doing odd jobs in the busy harbour at Scrabster. All he needed to do was to check that it was the particular boat Georgi was hunting for and not just a similar one. So he went down into the harbour amongst the fishing smacks, cabin cruisers and yachts and there it was, pretty well as Georgi had described it. Jimmie photographed it and sent the picture off to London. In next to no time confirmation came back that he had found what they were looking for. Having photographed it during daylight, he sneaked back later in the dark and attached a tracker device so he could find out what the boat was up to.

Its owner, revealed by some simple detective work conducted mostly in the Ferry Inn, was Adam Janos, a Scottish naturalised Slovak who moored the inflatable in a tiny harbour south of Freswick, just round the John O'Groats headland east and south of Thurso and a half hour sail from Scrabster. During the tourist season Janos mostly kept it where Jimmie found it. Janos, it transpired, had married a Scottish girl some 15 years ago and they lived in a former crofter's cottage near the coast not far from Freswick.

Keeping an eye on the movement of the craft in the days that followed him concealing the tracker on it, Jimmie found that Janos was mostly what he appeared to be to the outside world, an Eastern European who had made his home in Scotland and spent most of his time taking tourists on excursions along the Scottish north coast to see the extensive bird life there. The "extreme" element of the trips referred to the high-powered, fast and tight manoeuvres Janos subjected his boat and passengers to on their way back to Scrabster. It provided a thrill dimension to the experience that other more placid and conventional birdlife trips did not offer.

But only four days after starting to track the inflatable, just as the sun rose over the horizon to launch a new day and while he was having breakfast, Jimmie saw on his computer that the inflatable was on the move. Such a dawn sailing was way ahead of any tourist activity and Jimmie watched with great interest as the high speed boat headed west from Scrabster hugging the coastline. Being based not far from Thurso, Jimmie could not resist the temptation to leap into his car and speed along the A836 in pursuit.

Monitoring the inflatable from his laptop parked on the passenger's seat alongside him, Jimmie watched as it suddenly veered away from the coast heading out towards the distant Orkney Isles. But not far off the mainland it seemed to stop – not for long – before speeding back to the coast and towards the tiny harbour of Fresgoe at Sandside Bay, virtually opposite the atomic power station of Dounreay which is now being decommissioned.

Jimmie knew the area well. He knew the car park at Fresgoe. It was memorable for its view of the sweeping, very pretty bay with its long curving beach to the right, golf course to the rear of that and the dome of the atomic power station across the water. He recalled the two contrasting signs in the car park, one giving helpful information about the wildlife visitors to the bay might expect to see. The other, somewhat incredulously, warns that atomic particles have been found in the area and people should not pick up material off the ground and especially from the beach.

Jimmie, like others, found the small sign very disturbing. How could atomic particles be scattered around the area? Clearly they had originated from the Dounreay power station which had been operational from the 1950s. But for particles to be polluting the area such a distance from the site of the nuclear reactors was very worrying. How come such a beautiful part of the world had become so polluted? Were the lobster pots still bobbing about on the waters of the bay between the small harbour and the power station also polluted? And he was even dubious about playing golf in an area where, if the warning sign was to be heeded, atomic particles could presumably be anywhere. Not that that seemed to deter local golfers who have become accustomed to jokes about their balls glowing in the dark.

It was not uncommon for van drivers and commercial travellers to turn off the main road to take a break in the car park at Fresgoe, perhaps for an early stop for lunch. Sure enough when Jimmie reached the car park there was already a white van parked there, its driver sitting behind the steering wheel reading a morning newspaper. Jimmie parked up and followed suit, opening his own morning paper. He dropped the car window down a little to take in the morning's fresh and clear air and to hear the calls of the large numbers of sea birds in the area and the crashing of waves against rocks some 200 yards in front of him. He was tempted to stretch his legs, to leave his car and walk beyond the car park and the sign saying "No Cars Beyond Here" to the tiny harbour with its few dwellings cut into the cliff face. But he thought that would make him too conspicuous so he tested his patience and waited for something to happen.

Only five minutes later the inflatable came into sight, creaming through the calm waters of the bay and heading into the harbour out of vision from where he was parked. In the brief moment he saw it he spotted Janos at the helm located about half way along the boat's length. Sitting at its stern was a middle aged man dressed in a business suit clutching a brief case.

A further 15 minutes passed before the sound of an engine heralded a car speeding from the harbour area, through the car park and on its way to the main road at the village of Reay. Sneaking a view above his newspaper, Jimmie identified the driver as the man who had only recently been the passenger in the inflatable. Almost as soon as the car had disappeared, the inflatable came into sight, heading east across the bay towards Dounreay and, presumably, onwards to Thurso.

Jimmie phoned Georgi. The day was still young but he knew the Georgian would answer his mobile.

"An early call Jimmie," said Georgi.

"I thought I'd let you know what's just happened," said Jimmie. "All a bit strange really." And he went on to report the morning's action.

"What do you make of that?" asked Georgi.

"Well, it could be that the fellow who was a passenger in the inflatable had been in it all the way from Thurso. But I just got the feeling that wasn't so. I reckon when the inflatable went offshore it rendezvoused with another vessel. I think what I've just seen is an illicit entry into the UK."

"So our Eastern European friend isn't squeaky clean?" suggested Georgi.

"Maybe not," Jimmie replied. "It just makes me wonder if he's a part-sleeper." It was a term Georgi's unit used to denote someone planted by one country into another to become part of the community but to be available on call to undertake illicit activity, like spying, for instance. A 'part-sleeper' in Georgi's jargon was a sleeper who rarely, and sometimes not at all, was called upon by his Masters.

"Possibly," Georgi agreed. "Anyway, keep on monitoring him and keep me informed. And you've got the other task in hand?"

"Yes," Jimmie assured him. "I'm tackling it tonight."

It was early evening when Jimmie drove the 20 or so miles to a point where he drove off the tarmac main road onto a muddy track he knew led down to a small loch he had fished in the past. Beyond the loch open scrubland extended for perhaps a little over a mile to the cliffs and the sea beyond. Only animal tracks crisscross this substantial, bracken dominated area scarred in patches where peat is being dug. He left his car by the small loch. Even four wheel drive vehicles struggle in this territory. The crofters use buggies. Anyway, he preferred to be on foot. With the sunlight dying rapidly to be replaced by the softer light of a clear, star sparkling night sky with a large and bright moon, he could see with relative ease and move safely across the rough terrain. In any case, he would not have dared use headlights from any vehicle. Whilst the clarity of the night and the brilliance of the night light was a help to him, he was unaware of those who were not that far away and already watching him.

Preparing for the task ahead, Jimmie took various bits of equipment from his holdall and checked they were all working properly including the link to the tapping by Georgi's team of landline phones in The Mansion. He established contact with the office in Wapping and spoke with Georgi. By now his lapel microphone, earpiece and headcam strapped to his forehead were all live.

"Can you see and hear me OK?" he asked Georgi.

In London Georgi, not having properly prepared for this link to Jimmie, scanned round the array of large screens on the walls of the Communications Centre and spotted the one covering the events in north Scotland.

"Got you," he confirmed to Jimmie. "Looks like a bright night there. And pretty rough terrain."

"You're right," agreed Jimmie. "Bright night helps moving across this ground but doesn't help with concealment. But I guess it's too much to have everything!"

So, holdall bag over his shoulder, he started to trek

the mile or so towards where the coastline cuts inland to form a wide and open inlet. Here the Halladale River spills out into the Pentland Firth. The river sweeps round in a majestic curve just as it meets the sea. In the centre of that curve stands The Mansion with the river passing it on three sides. To the east of the property the ground rises gently but significantly so the building is well sheltered from weather coming in off the sea. It was from this high point Jimmie hoped to settle down to observe whatever he might see in The Mansion.

One of the hazards of walking in this area, especially at night, is rabbit holes. After the third incident of his foot and half a leg disappearing down such a hole, Jimmie stopped and took some military night glasses from his bag. These certainly helped and progress became more certain and hole encountering moments fewer. Eyes now glowed back at him as the light sensitive glasses picked out the rabbits that were looking at him. He did not see the human eyes that were tracking him.

He headed directly for the coast so that he could follow the cliff face round to the inlet and hopefully close in on it undetected. The night remained clear and bright with just the gentlest of breezes. It was a great place to be, he thought. The coast spread out before him in a rugged black line that disappeared into the distance. To its right, the sea was gunmetal grey except where it shimmered in the light of the moon and where its waves, silvery topped, rolled onto beaches or collided gently with rocks and cliff faces to create a white, foaming strip dividing land from sea.

When it came into sight The Mansion looked foreboding, large, somewhat menacing and fortress-like. It cast long and dark shadows. As Jimmie settled down on his chosen spot to survey the building through his night binoculars, all he could hear was the sound of waves breaking on the nearby shore, and the occasional calls from sheep and birds both of which should be asleep by now he thought. Several downstairs rooms were illuminated as was one room upstairs on what he saw to be a third floor.

Of any life there was no sign at all but it had been there, close by, tracking him ever since he left his car. However much Jimmie had deployed his military stealth skills, those watching him were his equal, if not better. Jimmie died here. There was no warning, nothing for him to anticipate the end. The 20 inch carbon bolt fired silently from a military crossbow and with the aid of a nightscope and infrared laser hit his neck at well over 250 feet a second, passing right through it and shattering both sets of jugular veins. He crashed forward from the kneeling position he had been in, his head hitting hard mud. The camera attached to his forehead shattered. In London, the picture on one wall screen disappeared. Georgi was immediately informed but attempts to talk to Jimmie failed. All contact was lost.

On the coast of Sutherland, with the heather and bracken moving gently in the slight sea breeze and a starlit night with its gleaming moon casting long shadows, two figures dressed from top to bottom in black, both wearing light intensifying night glasses and one carrying a lightweight but powerful military crossbow, reached the fallen body of Jimmie. They meticulously cleared all his equipment into a bag for later inspection and analysis and tidied the ground upon which he had died. Broken glass was bagged. Blood-soaked turf was kicked over. Eventually they lifted him and carried him the short distance to the cliff top. There they launched Jimmy into space. His body, limbs dangling wildly out of control, fell like a rag doll to the sea 100 feet below where it hit a large wave as it crashed into the bottom of the cliffs. Jimmie could be seen for only seconds before his body was dragged out to sea on the backwash and undercurrents.

Chapter 10

The new, enormous and dazzlingly sophisticated strategic war room of the Russian Federation – the National Control Defence Centre – is located on the banks of the Moskva River, a mile and a half south of the Kremlin from which it can be accessed directly via one of the many tunnels that crisscross the capital city. Today its gigantic Command and Control Hall was half full. Most of the workstations on the ground floor, seven rows of some 20 state-of-the-art workplaces with computer links, audio and translation services, touchscreens and keyboards, were occupied but the two balcony areas above were virtually empty except for the most important of groups on the first floor. Surrounding the room, the massive screens, some the size of small football pitches, were filled with pictures, many of them live. Those assembled represented all the various elements of Russian military might, military academics, political and military advisors and strategists. Sitting in the middle of the very VIP group occupying the central position on the first floor balcony was no lesser person than the President himself.

The assembly had two questions to be answered – is the time and are the circumstances now right to open a third front? The programmes to destabilise Europe were now well advanced. The armed conflict in the Ukraine continued as did 'military exercises' on the borders of countries that were former states within the Soviet Union. Such activity greatly agitated both the EU and NATO. The European Union continued to be in disarray as biblical numbers of people unrelentingly tried to escape strife-torn Africa. Turkey remained in turmoil, split between factions as old as time itself as its senior politicians tried to align the nation more to Europe but in doing so antagonised traditional and religious links to the East.

Now climate change and the melting of sea ice presented a new opportunity to further protect Russian interests and pressurise and irritate America and its Western allies. Russia was watching events on one side of the planet where America and China rattled swords at each other. Strategic thinking was advocating complementing that friction in the South China Sea by an audacious plan based on the Bering Strait located just to the south of the Arctic Circle and which provides a narrow sea channel link between the Pacific and Arctic oceans. It also divides Russia from America.

On Far Eastern seas and roughly equidistant between Hainan, China's southernmost point, and the coast of Vietnam, the US destroyer Curtis Wilbur had recently patrolled off Triton Island, part of the Paracel Islands chain. This followed the much publicised activity of the destroyer Lassen that had sailed near the Spratly Islands where one of several of China's artificial islands is being constructed on top of a reef. This widespread reef-top development was in the face of ownership claims by

Vietnam and Taiwan and protests from the international community led by America.

Now new airstrips were being established on these artificial islands, a contentious activity undertaken by China for some time. The US and others claim that because the reefs are below the water at high tide they are international waters.

The messy issue of ownership is further and massively aggravated by China's official argument that it had used these island since ancient times, pre the development of international law, and that anyway China was first to discover them and the first to use them for fishing and other purposes. Even aged European maps show the islands belong to China.

Now the Russian President's political and military advisors were saying that on the opposite side of the planet precedence could be taken from China's stance in the South China Sea and Russia should claim ownership of a sea passage that until recently had been virtually unusable because it had been frozen. Now climate change meant the ice was melting, the passage was becoming navigable, and its strategic importance was growing to be potentially massive.

"Russia once owned all this part of the world but no longer does so," a senior naval officer was telling the assembly. "But, by good fortune, we still own an island right in the middle of the Bering Strait – Big Diomede, which is in the Chukotsky District of the Chukotka Autonomous Okrug of Russia. It is sometimes known as Imaqliq or Inaiq Island or even Ratmanov Island. We maintain a weather station there as well as a base for the Border Service of the Federal Security Service."

"In fact, there are two islands in this locality. About a mile away from Big Diomede is Little Diomede which is owned by the Americans. The International Date Line passes between the two islands which means Big Diomede is 23 hours ahead of Little Diomede. Because of this, they are sometimes known as Tomorrow Island and Yesterday Isle."

The naval officer paused to look up at his audience as if to judge whether this small joke created any effect on the assembly. It had not. He quickly continued.

"Little Diomede is currently occupied by a community of Eskimos. A further indication of climate changes in the area is that the Eskimo village is now having to be maintained by helicopter as the normal supply aircraft can no longer land on the sea ice. That is a far more expensive arrangement and the longevity of the settlement on Little Diomede is questionable. In addition, the Eskimos have not been able to hunt for seal as they normally do because of the dangerous conditions on the sea ice."

The President listened intently to the evidence being submitted. Below him, seated at their lines of identical light grey hi-tech desks, were the other delegates, mostly uniformed.

"The Chinese are now starting to run commercial shipping through the passage," the naval officer continued. "It is cutting significant times and costs off the journey from China to Northern Europe, Canada and America. They plan to make regular use of the route."

"In recent weeks a Russian naval expedition has passed through the area. This consisted of a destroyer, two frigates and an ocean-going tug. None of the ships had ice breaking capabilities and though ice was seen it did not constitute a difficulty or impair the passage of the ships. A report from a representative of the Defence Ministry provides more information about the area."

The naval officer shuffled his papers, found the one he was looking for, and read: "The water between the two mainlands is about 82 kilometres at its narrowest point which is Cape Dezhnev in the Chukchi Peninsula of Russia, and Cape Prince of Wales in Alaska in the United States. Its depth varies between 30 metres (98 feet) and 50 metres (160 feet). To the north is the Chukchi Sea which is part of the Arctic Ocean and to the south the Bering Sea which is part of the Pacific Ocean."

A lawyer with specialised knowledge of maritime matters, reminded the meeting of a key historic event.

"On March 30, 1867, in Washington, America, an agreement was signed to sell 1.5 million square kilometers of Russian property to America for $7.2 million, or about 2 cents per acre. At that time, an unproductive plot of land in Siberia with the same surface area was valued at 1,395 times as much. But Russia was keen to divest itself of territory it could not effectively defend and at the time there were threats that Britain might invade it. In addition, Russia needed cash. So Russia sold Alaska to America. If it had not, what we are discussing today would be irrelevant. However, it is my contention that the agreement of 1867 was a matter related only to land. It contains no reference to territorial waters. In 1893 a dispute arose between Great Britain and America when the US Coast Guard captured Canadian seal hunting ships in the Bering Sea. Britain at that time still controlled foreign affairs for Canada."

"The US claimed exclusive jurisdiction over the sealing industry in the Bering Sea, and that led to negotiations outside the courts. During this time the British also protested Russia's unilateral claim to waters 100 miles off its coasts. Whilst the issue of zones for sealing was agreed through this process, the matter of territorial rights to the waters of the Bering Strait was not. I believe we can still maintain these waters belong to Russia."

"After World War 2, the native population on Big Diomede was repatriated to the mainland in order to avoid contacts across the border. Today, unlike Alaska's neighbouring Little Diomede, it has no permanent native population, but as already mentioned, it is the site of a Russian weather station and a base for Russian Border Guard troops."

Further evidence was provided from other experts including the operational state of maritime ports in the area, what parts of the year they were open and accessible by sea with the ice melted, and what the prospects were for their development. Various ideas were muted as to how military strength and capabilities on Big Diomede could be expanded.

The need for rapid development of sea routes and ports was underlined by a speaker from the Ministry of Minerals who provided evidence of the growth in mineral extraction in Siberia including diamonds, gold, and coal as well as oil and gas. The 'Far East Development Programme' had been a top priority for some years and the value of the wealth potential of Siberia was "beyond estimate." "Indeed," commented the spokesman, "new areas of opportunity are being discovered on a regular basis, including the recent discovery of rare minerals similar to man-made MOFs used in the production of fuel cells. But to capitalise on the extraction of these natural materials we need improved infrastructure. The melting of the sea ice is bringing into play maritime routes and ports that until now have been limited in their use and value."

After a day of taking evidence and hearing presentations that both favoured and opposed the proposition that had evolved during the conference, the President withdrew to a private room with his closest aides where he tested his thoughts on them. Satisfied he had not missed any vital points that could have caused him to come to different conclusions, the President returned to his place in the war room. This time he did not sit but stood at the front of the balcony holding the brass bar before him. Cameras focussed in on him and his image filled the screens around the building.

"I have listened to all the evidence and guidance. It is my decree that our plan for the Siberian/Alaskan passage will commence without delay."

Chapter 11

In London, Georgi was shocked by the sudden disconnect to Jimmie Hall and his surveillance of The Mansion in Sutherland. It took only seconds to confirm this was no simple technical fault. Something had happened and Georgi had every reason to conclude the worst. Jimmie had been discovered and his surveillance ended before it had started. The fate of the man was, at this stage, a matter of conjecture but again Georgi was hardly optimistic. He immediately called a project team meeting together and put in a call to Gene Bond.

"We've lost our man in Scotland," he told his friend.

"What do you mean, lost?" Bond responded.

"Our link to him has gone dead. We suspect the worst. There's nothing for you to do just now but I thought I'd let you know. Apart from anything else, it means we're not making progress in finding out what's happening at The Mansion. What it does tell us is that whatever is going on there is being very aggressively protected."

Attention turned to what results were forthcoming from other activity, mainly phone tapping and electronic traffic surveillance. The answer was equally negative and equally disturbing. Landline calls to and from The Mansion had virtually dried up. So had emails. There had been a number of mobile phones and laptops functioning a week ago. Now those too had gone quiet.

"It stinks," Georgi told his team. "They must be communicating with the outside world somehow but they seem to have some unconventional means. We need to widen our search. And I don't like this zero intelligence we're getting. I think I made a mistake in not doing a better risk assessment before sending Jimmie in on his own. But the one thing it has told us is that somebody is making strenuous efforts to conceal what's happening at The Mansion. To me, that's enough to sanction a more energetic effort to find out. I want a full commando-type team up there in the next 48 hours and I'll join it. Let Gene Bond know what we're planning and leave it up to him if he wants to be involved."

In Seoul, Sum Taeyoung was developing his plot. The more he thought about it the more excited he became. But the fate of the two geophysicists was paramount. Only he and his inner sanctum should know whether or not the two men had been infected by some primeval virus for which there is no known antidote. If that is really what they eventually died from so much the better. If not, they had to die to protect the lie that it was not an unknown virus that had killed them. There was only one snag to the plot at the moment and it was pretty fundamental. He did not know where the two men were. Since learning the shocking news from Pavel Galdin of the unexplained kidnapping of the two sick men from the hospital in Anadyr, Sum had moved quickly on from his initial despair that his plot had hit a brick wall. He instigated an extensive global search of the world of terrorism and counter-espionage to see if he could find where the two men were.

Via links in Moscow and Lithuania, one of his research team heard of a gangster organisation based in Minsk which was normally involved in extortion, pornography, and computer hacking. Gangland chatter suggested this organisation had branched out of its native Belarus and was now starting to operate on a pan-European level. It was suggested it was already involved in clandestine work for some major corporates. Further delving brought up the name of the group's leader, Janka Koldun. It transpired that Janka had not been seen in Minsk for some time and rumour was he was currently in some remote part of the UK.

Of all the intelligence coming back to Sum from around the planet, the information on Janka Koldun was enough for Sum Taeyoung to initiate a concerted effort to find out more about this man and his current location. Sum wanted to know everything and he was prepared to dig deep into his pockets for information.

Which, eventually, led Sum to call Janka Koldun in Scotland.

"What do you want?" Koldun responded aggressively to the call on his mobile phone. Few knew its number. It was virtually unheard of for a stranger to phone him on it.

There was a slight pause before the voice said "Mr Koldun. Please confirm nobody else can hear this conversation."

"Nobody can. What do you want?" Janka Koldun's lack of patience was starting to outweigh his curiosity.

"Mr Koldun. My name is Sum Taeyoung."

"What do you want?" Janka asked again, this time even more brusquely.

"I believe you are currently managing an asset I may have an interest in," came the reply. "Am I right?"

Janka was curious but cautious. "What sort of asset?" he asked.

"Um, how best do I describe it? This is an asset of a scientific interest, particularly related to holes and rocks." Sum Taeyoung continued to be cryptic as he probed.

Janka Koldun knew immediately what Taeyoung was talking about. He became even more agitated and worried. "Look Mr Taeyoung. I don't know who you are. I don't know how you got my phone number. I don't know what you are trying to find out or why. Get to the point or I will cut off this call."

There was a moment of silence before Sum Taeyoung spoke again. "The matter is simple, Mr Koldun. I want to make you an offer for the asset you are managing. I want to pay you for that Mr Koldun. Whatever you are currently being paid and by whom, I will multiply that amount by a factor of four. Now, Mr Koldun, are you still going to listen to me?"

"Wait," said Janka. His mind was racing. Money was the driving motive to everything Janka did. What the mining company was paying him was no small amount. But this stranger at the end of the phone was offering four times that. He was more than a little interested but still very cautious and whoever he was talking to did not know all the facts.

"I only have one asset," he told the caller.

"I know," Sum Taeyoung replied. "I believe you lost one. Very careless."

Janka was taken aback. How could this person know about the missing Patterson?

"How do you know about that?" he asked.

"You might be surprised at what I know Mr Koldun." The response was threatening and generated a host of questions in the Eastern European's mind. But instantly he concluded that to probe further with this stranger might be counterproductive. The thought of earning four times his current rate dominated all other considerations.

"We think the missing asset doesn't exist any more," Janka tried to be reassuring.

"This is ridiculous," Sum Taeyoung responded. "This conversation has gone far enough for us to both know what we're talking about. And I assume you're interested in my proposition. Does what I say interest you, Mr Koldun?"

"Of course it does," the Eastern European responded.

"Then we need to meet to do a deal. I am not prepared to talk any more down a phone link I cannot trust. So we must meet. And fast. In London. The day after tomorrow."

Janka Koldun agreed.

Which is why a Belarus terrorist met a South Korean chaos entrepreneur in the most unlikely meeting point below the historic Methodist Chapel of Central Hall, Westminster, virtually opposite the Houses of Parliament. The unpretentious environs of Wesley's Café are located in the basement below the grandiose, spacious hall above. In sharp contrast to the more affluent establishments frequented by Sum Taeyoung, this modest venue provides cost-effective temporary work places for visitors to London and is frequently filled by an extraordinarily cosmopolitan assortment of people of different nationalities. Students, politicians from the Houses of Parliament just across the road from Central Hall, Parliamentary secretaries and office staff, business people and tourists mix together in a multi-cultured informal assembly.

Sum Taeyoung felt less conspicuous here than in many other establishments – more able to merge into this vast assortment of people. As usual the large area was busy and contained a scattering of individuals working at their laptops and one or two small groups in earnest conversations.

Janka Koldun was, as most people are, taken aback by meeting the long-haired, bearded and very large South Korean whose English would be almost flawless if it were not for the just detectable influences of America and the Far East.

"So tell me what happened. How did you lose the one asset?" Sum demanded. It was if there had been no gap in time between their phone conversation and now.

Janka Koldun recounted the story of the kidnapping in Anadyr and the subsequent bus crash. He recalled having to make fast decisions that resulted in him escaping Siberia with Bailey. In the carnage of twisted metal and bodies in the aftermath of the crash, he could not see Patterson. That was not to say he was not there. He simply could not see him. Anyway, he was torn between trying to find the second geophysicist and getting away from the crash scene as fast as he could. He could not, he told the South Korean, throw more light on what had happened to Patterson. He had not been seen since the bus crash in Siberia. Most people involved thought he was dead. He surely must be. He was a very sick man. He was last seen in an extensively mangled vehicle in open countryside in Siberia with nobody to help him. The environment was extreme – hostile and bitterly cold – sub-zero temperatures. A person as ill as Patterson was could not be expected to last more than a few hours. There had been no search for him after the crashed bus had been discovered.

By any measure Koldun had done brilliantly to get out of Siberia and to take Bailey with him. In the aftermath of his escape, officials quickly made the link to the aircraft that had made an unscheduled visit to the airfield at Ugolny. Assumptions were made that both geophysicists had been taken out of Siberia by the unidentified team of commandoes.

Sum Taeyoung's anger and irritation by what he saw to be a loose end in his plot remained with him for some time after the meeting in Westminster. He tried to instigate a hunt for Patterson but organising one in that remote part of Siberia was beyond even his abilities. He did make contact with Pavel Galdin and pushed him to get the hospital to initiate some sort of search. But Galdin was not interested. He was clearly only too pleased to wipe his hands of the whole episode now the two scientists were no longer under his wing. He had done what Taeyoung had asked him to do and had been paid for it. That the two scientists had been lifted from the hospital meant he no longer had any influence on the matter and it was, therefore, as far as he was concerned, closed.

So the whereabouts of Patterson remained a mystery. Sum Taeyoung could only hope that the widespread opinion was right. The geophysicist must by now surely be dead. That, to Taeyoung, was fine. But he wished he knew. Meantime, he secured the deal with Koldun.

Chapter 12

The stillness and tranquillity of the beautiful Halladale Estuary was blasted asunder. The noise was intense. Skuas, guillemots, gulls and shags scattered. Puffin on the flat-topped stack just up the coast from the estuary dived for their holes. Sheep panicked and, as they do in such moments, urinated prolifically. In an approach from the east, two AH7 Lynx helicopters of the Royal Navy's Commando Helicopter Force hugged the coast and screamed round the cliffs below cliff top height to arrive at Melvich Bay in such a tightly choreographed manoeuvre it co-incided with two semi-ribbed inflatables powering their way into the river from the open sea. Simultaneously, four large 4WD vehicles crashed through the road barrier at speed as if it did not exist. It was a well-orchestrated operation that went like clockwork.

"Clear!" The message to Georgi in the first of the 4WDs came from a commando in the lead Lynx as it landed on the rear lawn.

"Clear!" This time from the commander of one of the inflatables as the two boats veered off the water and onto the glittering beach. And on the road approach to the front of the building the 4WDs skidded to a halt in a cloud of tyre smoke and also met no resistance. Georgi was more than surprised. He had expected an aggressive response. But his initial reaction quickly gave way to concern and dismay.

"Clear!" The lead marine from one of the Lynx reported as he crashed through a rear door and into the building just as Georgi and a group of commandoes broke in through the front. There was much shouting, thumping of boots on wooden floors and slamming of doors. But of resistance there was none. The place was devoid of any form of life.

Two hours after the peace and quiet had exploded in the Halladale Estuary, Georgi, the only one not to have departed the house, sat on the edge of the large table in the impressive and eerily silent main hall of The Mansion. This debacle was going to take some explaining! He would be under fire from Brussels, Westminster and the various military people he had pulled strings with to put this operation together in next to no time. He might even lose his job.

He looked with almost hypnotised interest at the golden liquid swirling around the thick glass of the thistle engraved tumbler with its pebbled bottom. Finding a well stocked whisky bar was small consolation. The last swig still lingered on his pallet and not for the first time the thought crossed his mind that to add anything to whisky – other than more whisky – was sacrilege. He sat on the edge of the large table with glass in one hand and bottle in the other and reflected on what had happened. Raiding the bar was one small element of solace in what otherwise was an unmitigated disaster.

Within minutes of the raiding party's arrival it was obvious nobody occupied The Mansion anymore. A comprehensive search of the building and outbuildings revealed nothing out of the ordinary remained except for the strange room on the third floor that had been modified to be an isolation area. Georgi had all the evidence he needed that someone had been kept here. But where that person and all the rest of them now were was a complete mystery.

Janka Koldun had evacuated the premises at speed in the aftermath of the killing of Jimmie Hall. Whoever this man had been he was very well equipped and had been in contact with someone as he sneaked across the coastal bogland in the dead of night. The freelance fighter from Belarus hoped they might identify who was monitoring what this man was up to in the middle of the night in the remoteness of the north Scottish coast. But despite their best endeavours, they were unable to trace who he was connected to. But it was all enough to quickly convince Koldun that their safe haven in Scotland had been compromised.

Even before this incident Amy Kelly had become aware of a change in regime control within The Mansion. On her arrival, Iain Barthwait had been top dog, reporting directly to Alexander Fitzpatrick and everyone reporting to him. Janka Koldun, arrogant and rude though he might be, showed the sort of reluctant deference he was expected to portray to a customer, which was what Barthwait was. But only days after her arrival at The Mansion she detected the signs of some sort of palace coup. All of a sudden it was Koldun who was calling the shots and Barthwait had disappeared. Where to she had no idea.

With his new sense of authority adding to his already well embedded arrogance, Koldun took charge of events at The Mansion. Amy was not to know that Koldun had done his deal with Taeyoung and Barthwait had become unwanted baggage. He was disposed of.

The killing of Jimmie Hall changed everything as far as Koldun was concerned. Whoever Hall had been connected to, whoever he was working for, his disappearance was bound to stimulate a response. Something else stuck in Koldun's mind – something Taeyoung had said. It was about Patterson, the other geologist. He had said he hoped he was dead and that nobody would find him. That way Taeyoung could still progress with his plot. The whole key was for the outside world to believe he had both geophysicists under his control. That was the ideal. But it was not the reality. Patterson was missing, presumed dead.

In Koldun's mind if Taeyoung could play such a game so could he. Taeyoung did not need Bailey alive. He had said so. The plot would work just as well if he were dead. The evacuation of The Mansion would be that much easier if Bailey was dead. The whole situation would become so much simpler. So Koldun killed Bailey. It was not a difficult task. The man was close to death anyway. It took less than a couple of minutes for the Scottish geophysicist – known to his friends as Mabel – to stop breathing as Koldun smothered him with a pillow.

Now Koldun turned to consolidating what he had started. The elderly couple who managed The Mansion and nurse Amy Kelly had all become liabilities and had to be eliminated. They were shot. With only his team left in The Mansion, but with time running out, the Belarus terrorist applied well-practiced techniques to ensure recognition of the three dead people would be at worst slow and at best potentially impossible before their bodies were dumped over cliffs to follow the fate of Jimmie Hall. By the time Georgi's military attack commenced, Janka Koldun and his team were long gone, heading back home to disappear into the jungle of the Belarus underworld.

"Anything left in that bottle for me?" Somehow Gene Bond's voice came as no surprise to Georgi.

"Trust you! You've missed all the bloody action but not all the whisky," Georgi responded, then added, "not that there was much action. Our bird had flown."

Bond, alerted by Georgi's team in London, had been in Manchester when he heard the news. He had driven non-stop for eight hours to the north of Scotland but by the time he got to The Mansion the only immediate evidence of Georgi's activity were two marines manning a road block near the mangled barrier on the approach to the building, fresh skid marks on the tarmac immediately in front of the house, and a formidable front door now swinging at a hideous angle from its top hinges, the only ones to which it now remained attached.

"But there's plenty of whisky," Georgi reassured his friend and went on to recount the story of the raid and to tell him that the only thing they had found of interest was the isolation room on the third floor plus a full medicine cabinet.

"Where they kept whoever I had seen on the boat," surmised Bond.

"That's the conclusion you come to," Georgi agreed.

"No clues who he was?" asked Bond.

"No." was the short response.

"Or who was holding him?"

"No."

"Or who else was in the house?"

"No."

"Is there anything here of use to you?" asked Bond, desperately seeking something positive in this mess.

"No," Georgi replied again but this time added, "We'll check out all the medical stuff. We may get a lead from where the medications came from. But I've got nothing out of this so far. Basically I'm in the shit. Big time."

They fell into an uncomfortable silence in which the consumption of whisky became the only action. It took the sound of a vehicle drawing up outside to stir them out of their miserable contemplation of recent events. Georgi, cautiously, moved his hand closer to the gun he had placed on the table.

"Expecting anyone?" asked Bond.

"Nope," said Georgi.

They listened as someone made their way towards them. A man arrived at the door to the room. He was tall, slim and wore an obviously expensive suit. Before he uttered a word his body language made it clear he was a very angry man.

"Who the hell are you two?" The question was barked. It was more like a demand than a question. It certainly was not the friendliest of opening remarks.

Georgi, taking an instant dislike to the newcomer, was, not for the first time in his recent life, unsure how to answer. It was always a challenge to introduce himself when he was not supposed to exist and worked for an organisation which also was not supposed to exist.

"We're from national security," he said, offering the easiest answer he could think of. "And who are you?"

"I own this place," said the stranger with a sense of anger and indignity in his voice. "My name is Alexander Fitzpatrick. Perhaps you could explain what the fuck is going on here."

Chapter 13

Hand in hand Nika led Patterson into the one room in the Flintstone's complex he had not been into before. She was in an excited, almost girlish mood. She wore a knee length white dress with swirling red patterns. He had seen her wear this before but then a bonnet adorned her head and an apron completed what was obviously traditional attire and, in this case, homemade, of course. Today the bonnet and apron had been discarded and her black hair cascaded down onto her shoulders. She gripped his hand especially firmly and her whole demeanour told him that this room was particularly important to her and she was very keen to show it to him.

As they entered it took a while for his eyes to adjust. The lighting was dim, provided mainly through one small window. The flickering of several candles added to the room's half-light. Already the aroma of some sort of homemade incense was tickling his throat and making his eyes water.

She led him a few steps into the room and stopped so that he could look around. To all intent and purpose this was yet another concrete room in this abandoned town of concrete buildings. But this was very different. This one contained a palpable atmosphere – a presence. The main feature was an altar, some sort of table covered by a cloth that had been heavily embroidered. Two crude candles both held in what looked like handcrafted gold holders stood at either side of the altar central to which was a simply made wooden cross with gold base and three cross pieces, slightly angled. It reminded Patterson of a similar cross he saw when he visited a Greek Orthodox church in London. Flanking the cross were two small and simple floral displays. On a side table, also covered by an ornamental cloth, a deep gold dish contained an obviously homemade wick that rose from a pool of thick liquid and a collection of tiny pieces of green and brown leaves. A flame bobbed and danced at the end of the wick, reflected in the gold and sending a wisp of smoke fanning out into the room. It was from this crude incense that the dominating aroma originated.

A motley collection of a dozen differently styled and coloured chairs stood before the altar. The question immediately crossing Patterson's mind was why these people needed more than four but maybe such a number just looked too small or insufficient in front of an altar. It was not as if they were expecting more worshipers! Quite the contrary. In every respect the Flintstones were recluses.

More versions of the three-pronged cross, each with gold features, hung from the walls and displays of flowers, some looking decidedly droopy, adorned the room. On one side wall a number of metal crates had been modified to become shelves and a place where bits and pieces related to this self-built place of worship were kept. On the opposite wall more boxes had been covered with a cloth and the top was used as a simple library consisting of a few books, some files and odd loose papers and manuscripts. It was these that immediately grabbed Patterson's interest.

Thumbing through the documents the frustration at not being able to read Russian was agonizing. But slowly, picking out a word or two here and there amongst the books, magazines, technical papers and newspapers and especially examining all the photographs, the reality of this place dawned on him. The story slowly unravelled before him of a community that was in this desolate wilderness to support the functioning of intercontinental ballistic missiles. It was not difficult to put two and two together and surmise that it had been evacuated after the collapse of the Soviet Union. The name that appeared in many of the documents in one form or another was Anadyr-1 and eventually Patterson concluded that this was the name of the abandoned town.

Nika, having left his side, knelt before the altar and bowed her head in silent prayer. Patterson looked on. The golden elements of this room added to the mystery he had not resolved since discovering some of the utensils used by the Flintstones were made of the precious metal. He felt humbled by what these people had established here, all of their own volition, all with their own skills and whatever materials they could find around the abandoned nuclear town – and the gold. Whoever they were, whatever their background, here in this rotting town of former atomic power and frightening nuclear deterrents, they had assembled their own secluded area where they could pay homage to their God. It was a place of such strange contradictions and clashing cultures.

But what had been created was simple and extremely

effective. This converted concrete room had an atmosphere of serene reverence.

It was the books and documents that Patterson was excited about and he could see more on the other table. He could not wait to get a closer look at them even though he fully expected them also to be Russian and therefore pretty well meaningless to him. Though he now felt he had cracked one major question – where he was – he still had little idea who these people were. Maybe the remainder of the books and papers would answer that too. His hopes were to be seriously surpassed. But in deference he waited for Nika to end her prayers and to introduce him to the small library. So he stood in silence for the four or five minutes she remained before the altar.

Eventually she stood, bowed her head to the roughly formed wooden cross, held out her hand to grasp his again, and led him to the small collection of books and documents. She very gently and carefully lifted one book from the collection.

"Bibliya," she said to him, slightly quizzically because she did not know if he would understand her.

"Bible," Patterson responded. And they smiled at each other as a further word was added to their mutual vocabulary.

The book was old and obviously much travelled. He handled it with care and the deference he felt it deserved and thumbed through it gently in the expectation it would fall apart any minute now. It was all in Russian as far as he could tell. Whatever, it was old, beautifully produced, quite fragile and to him utterly useless.

Nika was obviously keen to show him a particular

item from the collection of stuff that had been accumulated on the table. Patterson concluded that most of it, if not all, had arrived here through foraging activity by the Flintstones in the derelict town. Most of what she showed him was old technical brochures from the military camp, old Russian newspapers, and some folders from those who used to work here. She was getting agitated at not being able to find what she was looking for but eventually, after some minutes of searching, she gave a triumphant grunt and passed a single sheet of paper to Patterson.

It was badly creased, faded and with dirt stains on it. But, and of obvious great delight to Nika and to the amazed relief of Patterson, it was in English.

He quickly realised what he was looking at was the original of a message that had been transmitted by telegraph. He had not seen such a message for years. The letters were on a white strip and that was glued to a light brown thin cardboard. It was dated July 20, 1919 and from a George Symons to Commander Berkley, BSSB, London. It was much later Patterson found that BSSB stood for the British Secret Service Bureau, forerunner to the modern intelligence services, and that Symons was one of its spies. The place of transmission was noted as Yekaterinburg. It was a place that rang a distant bell in Patterson's memory.

Patterson read the message with growing fascination and incredulity.

"Romanov family executed by Bolsheviks STOP Heading Siberia after bullion STOP Am with persecuted Old Believers STOP"

"Good God!" muttered Patterson. He read and re-read the message. The place name Yekaterinburg now came back from distant memory cells. It was notorious in history as being the place where the Romanov family, father, mother and four daughters – the royal rulers of Russia – had been executed by the Bolsheviks. He dimly recalled recent rumours that at least one of the children had escaped. Anastasia! The name came back to him. There had been great speculation and even books and films about her but also about the alleged large amount of gold bullion the family had travelled with. Now here he was, holding a piece of paper that linked him directly back to that infamous moment in history.

He read it again. It told him much but equally it raised a host of new questions.

The Old Believers. This meant nothing to him but as Nika and her family before her had treasured this old telegraph message – seemingly almost as much as they did their bible – presumably its origins lay with her forefathers. Presumably they had been the Old Believers George Symons had been with. Standing as he was in this concrete room turned into a place of religious worship, it was easy to assume the Flintstones provided a continuance of the Old Believers story.

He picked up the bible again. The word Staroobryadtsy was embedded in faded gold into the cover.

"Staroobryadtsy," he said as best he could to Nika who looked at him quizzically. "Old Believer," he said. "I think this tells me you and your family are Old Believers. Some sort of religious group. Persecuted says

George Symons. So maybe hounded out of Russia and over nearly 100 years you've found your way further and further into the Siberian wilderness and eventually to this hideaway."

Nika looked at him in anguish as language continued to stand between them and any sense of understanding. The frustration was unbearable.

If, thought Patterson, they were persecuted then, as George Symons reported, were they still being persecuted? Or had they hidden away from the rest of the world for so long they simply did not know? How long since they had met a stranger such as he? And how long had they been hiding in Anadyr-1? From what he could see of the home they had established here it must have been for some years. There were just so many questions and he had no idea how he was going to get answers. The telegraphed message in a way just increased the mystery of the Flintstones.

And then there was the reference to bullion. Patterson dimly recalled the Romanovs were supposed to have escaped Russia with a vast fortune in gold bullion. He had always supposed that to be in gold bars. But slowly an idea emerged. Maybe it was not in bars at all. Or maybe it was a mix of gold items and gold bars. Is that why some of the utensils used by this reclusive, primitive family were gold? Had these been passed down from the Flintstones' forefathers – Nika's grandparents? Were the origins of these items with the Romanovs? It seemed preposterous. But – his mind was racing – if they had such gold items, did they also know where the gold bars now were?

Patterson looked at Nika with so many questions in his mind. The telegraph had told him much but it opened up so much more he did not understand. Their hands met and she again clasped his, not just for the security it offered but as an expression of the pent-up frustration she felt. This man who had entered her life in such an extraordinary way was the first she had met other than her brother and father. He represented a new relationship, something that her inbuilt femininity responded to, something that triggered hormones that until now had remained dormant within her. Instinct took over. She responded to the moment by doing something she had never done before. She kissed the man standing before her.

Chapter 14

Sum Taeyoung was amazed and initially dismayed to learn that events seemed to be overtaking his plans. Whilst laboratories in various parts of the world who had been contacted either by the hospital in Anadyr or by Fitzpatrick's mining company continued to investigate what the virus was that had impacted on the two geophysicists, Taeyoung took independent action. He wanted just one thing – confirmation from a laboratory that the virus was previously unknown, had no known antidote, was highly virulent and deadly. And, as far as he was concerned, it mattered not whether all that was true or otherwise. He just wanted evidence.

Throwing the matter into a conversation with his new recruit, the Belarus terrorist Janka Koldun, he asked him if he knew of any laboratories that would have the skills to undertake analysis of the virus and which would be corrupt enough to provide him with what he needed.

"Biological stuff is all over this part of the world," Koldun told him. "Belarus was a major manufacturer of biological warfare materials when we were in the USSR. There were laboratories everywhere. But our government's been trying to abide by international treaties and has been closing these places. Some of the scientists have moved into unregistered manufacturing resources in places like Donetsk. There's a healthy black market for such shit."

"Donetsk?" queried Taeyoung, not too sure he knew where that was.

"It's the self-proclaimed independent state on the eastern side of the Ukraine," Koldun told him. "It borders onto Russia and is supported by Russia. It broke away from the Ukraine in 2014. It's still an area of conflict."

"And you think you can find a laboratory that will give me what I want," asked Taeyoung. "Someone we could trust. Someone we can buy."

"No doubt about it," a confident Koldun told him immediately thinking he could cut himself a percentage on any such deal.

Taeyoung agreed to let the Belarus terrorist broker an agreement with a suitable laboratory. By doing it this way he remained at arm's length just in case anything went wrong. If it did, he would leave Koldun holding the baby.

Only a week passed before Koldun reported he had secured just the sort of deal Taeyoung was looking for. But it was not long after that matters got out of control.

The last thing Taeyoung needed was a real virus with no known cure pre-empting his own plot. But reports were coming to him of dozens of deaths and hundreds of people suffering from respiratory problems in several Eastern European countries including the Ukraine, Belarus, Moldova and even western border towns in Russia such as Belgorod and Valuyki. It was hard to get any real news or hard facts. This is not an easy part of the world to find out anything. Rumours were rife. Western news sources were headlining the story but with no substantive evidence and no detail.

An idea common to many of the reports was that the disaster was caused by a virus escaping from a secret chemical research establishment in Shelkostantsiya, 30 kilometres from the city of Kharkov, Ukraine's second largest city located in the north east of the country. According to one unofficial report, the laboratory was thought to be run by US military scientists. Others said it was a CIA establishment. An official statement from the Ukraine government said *"as yet the virus cannot be subdued by any medicines. The epidemic is sweeping through the eastern Ukrainian city of Kramatorsk — and the conflict smouldering nearby is making the situation even worse."*

Doctors had been unable to identify the exact strain of the virus. A further complication had apparently arisen because information about an antibiotic potentially capable of treating the suspect Shelkostantsiya bug was in a laboratory located in the separatist-controlled, self-proclaimed Donetsk Republic that was breaking away from the Ukraine. It was virtually impossible to access it because of the ongoing conflict.

Parallel to this a man who so far remained unidentified but apparently of Eastern European origin, was under arrest in Los Angeles having made threats against the White House. He told officials he had built a "microbe bomb" containing a virus that had been produced in the Ukraine and for which there was no known antidote. He said he had planned to explode the bomb in the vicinity of the White House.

Taeyoung called Koldun to see if he knew anything. It was not good news.

"It's impossible to find out what's true," he told Taeyoung. "There are rumours everywhere. But the centre of the problem seems to be exactly where we've asked research to be undertaken."

"You're joking!" Taeyoung thought the whole thing was incredulous. "Are you telling me that the place you arranged to research our sample involves the Americans?"

"Yes," said Koldun. "But a deal is a deal is a deal. In that part of the world there are people all over the place who are just after making their buck. It doesn't matter who they are."

"And how bad's this outbreak?" asked Taeyoung.

"It's not good. It's hard to find the truth but I have heard that 20 people have died and several hundred are ill. I have two men down with it and I must admit I've not been feeling too good."

"With this bug?"

"Maybe," Koldun replied. "As far as we can tell."

"How bad are your men?" Sum Taeyoung asked.

"Bad. They're in hospital and taking oxygen. It's breathing that's the problem."

"How long have they been like this?"

"It's got worse over the last two weeks," Koldun reported. "But I have some real worries."

"What?" asked Sum cautiously. He did not want any more bad news and he was trying to be careful what they said over the phone.

"I wonder where they caught it?" said Koldun. "What if they didn't catch it here in the Ukraine but perhaps on their recent journey? Perhaps the spread of the bug started with them not a release from a laboratory."

Sum Taeyoung knew immediately what the man from Belarus was talking about.

"It would mean," continued Koldun, "they caught it from the two assets we sort of acquired. You follow?"

Taeyoung knew exactly. The snatch of the two geophysicists from the hospital in Anadyr.

"It would mean what you thought you would have to fake is real," said Koldun, unnecessarily spelling out the obvious to Taeyoung. "But if that's what it is, it's already released and causing chaos. I might even have got it. I tell you I'm shit scared."

Sum Taeyoung had already thought about that. It was a shattering possibility.

"But I do have some good news," the Belarus terrorist added. "I've got your report."

"Does it say what we want it to say?" asked Taeyoung, excitement now rapidly replacing the gloom the conversation had cast him into.

"Yes," Koldun assured him.

Two days later the report was in the South Korean's hands. With this piece of the jigsaw now in place, Sum Taeyoung formulated his master stroke. Now he would be able to progress the formation of his single global unit of political control based on the principles of social/economic egalitarianism. The cards were now, he felt, falling into place.

He assumed the two geophysicists were dead. One he knew was. The other could clearly be assumed dead by now. And that would be the news broadcast to the world. The two had died as a result of exposure to a virus some five or six times older than civilisation. And he had laboratory evidence to prove it.

He would even hint that the virus was already spreading – in small numbers in and around the Ukraine. That, he would tell people, was a test programme to check how deadly the virus was. People could see from the evidence now before them that it truly was lethal.

He penned his Declaration to be delivered to the heads of state of the 193 member countries of the United Nations. It read:

Declaration Of Intent

The Problem

We, the dominant species on Planet Earth, are at a crossroads. We have been here for about six million years, about 200,000 years in our modern form, and only some 250 years as a global industrialised society. We now face an unprecedented convergence of challenges, many of them with a capability of ending our time here. Sophisticated and extraordinarily capable though we now may be, we do not have a global mechanism by which to respond to this simultaneous, multi-dimensional crisis. The problems we face include:

- *The largest population of humans the planet has known*
- *An emergence from poverty into the consumer society of vast numbers of people*
- *Growing pressure on critical resources*
- *Continuation of polluting activity with growing impact on our seas and our atmosphere*
- *Rising consequences of climate change*

- *The largest movement of people ever seen on the planet caused by war, loss of water and food shortages*
- *Rising differential between those who have and those who have not*
- *A revolution in our ability to communicate with each other*
- *Weaponry of ferocious capability*

The Need

There is urgent need for a new approach. Communism has failed, mainly because of corruption. Capitalism has widened the gap between those who have and those who have not. It has run its course. The only global unit, the United Nations, is an organisation without teeth.

I have turned to ancient history for a new solution, to the Han dynasty, the second imperial dynasty in China that erected an Altar of the Great Unity; to Confucius who emphasised the need for personal and governmental morality, correctness and justice and sincerity; to Bahá'u'lláh, founder of the Bahá'í Faith, who envisaged a world commonwealth in which all nations, races, creeds and classes are closely and permanently united, to Hwanung who founded Sinsi, the City of God, and others.

The Solution

I am creating a totalitarian approach – the creation of a set of objectives capable of responding to the nine challenges listed, and more, with solutions to be delivered undeterred by parochial, national interests, vested interests of any kind, the introverted ambitions of individuals, the doctrine of religion.

The Inducement

I have in my possession a lethal virus of unprecedented

contagiousness. This originated from one of the holes that have appeared in Siberia where the melting of the permafrost has sent ice cold water down into the earth to meet hot rocks. The subsequent explosions released viruses of more than 30,000 years of age.

Two British geophysicists succumbed after exposure to an especially aggressive virus released on the Chukotka tundra, an area now sealed off and under military control. Both geophysicists have subsequently died – in my custody and under strict medical isolation. The virus that attacked them is unknown to modern science. No antidote exists. It is thought to be extremely virulent with a capability of spreading extremely quickly and mutating.

To test the virus a tiny sample has already been released and is proving to be deadly and without cure.

I am supporting this Declaration with an extensive scientific/ medical report. I am not exposing the source of this analysis but anyone of scientific standing will quickly appreciate its legitimacy.

This Declaration is being delivered to the heads of state in key countries around the world.

The following is required within 60 days of this Declaration being circulated.

Without agreement the virus I hold will be released in each of those countries. The impact will be horrendous. My conscience is clear because I am offering the international community a way forward without which the human species will surely perish.

My demand is:

30 days from today, the day this Declaration will be delivered to heads of state around the world, £1,000,000,000 dollars will have been deposited in a bank as per details accompanying this Declaration.

45 days from today, each national leader who has received

this Declaration will have agreed, in an individually signed written Bond, to the conditions of the Declaration.

There will be no attempts to arrest and detain me.

60 days from today, the United Nations will be disbanded and replaced by a new, global institution which I will lead.

61 days from today, if none of the above has been achieved, or if I have been arrested or harmed in any way, the virus I have within my control will be released in the capital city of each of the nations whose leaders have been sent this Declaration.

Signed
The Spirit of Hwanung

Chapter 15

"Are you from Imperial Mining?" asked Georgi, recalling the name of the company shown in various records as being the owners of The Mansion.

"I'm its Chief Executive," responded an obviously agitated Alexander Fitzpatrick who had now walked further into the room to stand before Georgi and Bond. "National security, you say. What the hell does that mean? Who are you two? Where are your credentials? Where's your authority? What are you doing here on my property? Why are there marines outside? Why's the front door hanging on by a single screw? Where is everyone?"

Georgi did not take well to this hostile approach from the mining executive. He had taken an instant dislike to him. His hand was still alongside the gun that lay on the table, adjacent the now nearly empty whisky bottle.

"I think you have some questions to answer too, Mr Fitzpatrick. What's been going on here? Why the medical centre upstairs? Has someone been held here against their will?"

"This is my property," Fitzpatrick responded angrily, his voice rising. "I have no idea who you two are. I haven't a clue what the fuck has been going on here. I'm answering none of your questions until I know who the hell you are and under what authority you're here."

"Don't raise your voice at me, Mr Fitzpatrick," Georgi answered calmly but with authority. "That'll get us nowhere. And I think you should understand your position. There is evidence and substantive indications of wrongdoing here. Illegal activity. And, like it or not Mr Fitzpatrick, I have the authority to caution you that anything you say now might be brought before the courts as evidence if any legal hearings arise from this."

Alexander Fitzpatrick was near to exploding. Far from lowering his voice it went up in volume. The anger was undisguised.

"Was that a formal caution? Don't you bloody threaten me! I don't know who the hell you two are. I don't know what's happened here. I see you're armed. There are armed marines outside. My staff have disappeared. And this is my property and you're here without my knowledge or permission. Take this to court at your peril!" Fitzpatrick took a deep intake of breath. "And again, I ask – who the hell are you?"

"And again," Georgi responded with a calmness that Bond found surprising. His friend was renowned for having a short and fiery fuse. This performance was commendable. Georgi continued, "I ask you – what's been going on here? Why the medical centre upstairs? It's an isolation room isn't it? Who's been contained in it? And why?"

"These are private premises," replied Fitzpatrick. "What goes on in here is none of your business."

"It is if it's illegal," Georgi told him.

"What evidence have you got? What are your

'substantive indications' of wrongdoing as you put it?"

Georgi looked at Bond and shrugged before turning back to the mining executive.

"I can tell you that this property's been under extensive surveillance for some days – both physically and electronically. We believe a very sick person was brought here, probably against his will. We believe he was put into an isolation chamber – the medical room upstairs. We believe a security cordon was thrown around this building to keep people from knowing what was going on. What I can tell you is we have evidence from our work here that substantiates what I've just said. And that all indicates illegal activity. And if I'm right, my friend, you are in the shit big time!"

News that The Mansion had been under such surveillance obviously took Fitzpatrick by surprise.

"I need to know who you are," he told Georgi, his tone now far less aggressive. "I can't tell you anything until you explain who you are – and until you tell me what on earth has happened here."

Encouraged by the less aggressive attitude of the mining executive, Georgi took a card and his mobile phone from his jacket and passed it to Fitzpatrick.

"Phone that number. Use my phone otherwise you'll not get an answer. Ask them to confirm the person you are standing in front of is Georgi Patarava. Ask them who I work for. You can also ask them about him," he nodded towards Bond. "This is Gene Bond, a friend of mine. Though he sometimes also works for me, he's the most reluctant member of the security community you'll ever come across, despite his name. Gene also happens to live near here – sometimes. Anyway, phone that number."

Fitzpatrick looked at the card, then back at Georgi, then again at the card. Eventually he dialled the number. It rang three times then the line went dead.

"Wait," commanded Georgi knowing full well what was happening. Fitzpatrick looked at him quizzically but before he could speak Georgi's mobile rang.

"Answer it. But tell them I'm here right by you."

Fitzpatrick answered the phone. The conversation that followed did not last long.

"They want to talk to you," Fitzpatrick said, passing the phone to Georgi.

The room fell into silence as Georgi listened. After a couple of minutes Georgi said, "OK. Get Adam to put my personal code into it then divert it to the printer in my car. And do it now. Right?"

And with that he ended the call.

"I'm going to have to leave you two just to get something from my car. I've a hunch it has something to do with what's happened here."

And with that he picked up the gun from the table and walked quickly from the building.

There was an uncomfortable silence between Fitzpatrick and Bond, broken suddenly when the mining executive said "the least I can do is drink my own bloody whisky." And with that he departed the hall, returning a few minutes later with a glass for himself and a decanter full of whisky. He poured a liberal drink for himself and replenished the glasses of Bond and Georgi.

"Patarava said you lived around here?"

"Not quite right," replied Bond. "I own an old

crofter's cottage not far from here. I use it as a retreat – to get away from the pressures of life."

"You work for Patarava?"

Bond shook his head. "Not really. Not if I can help it. He's an old friend and sometimes I get dragged into his business."

"So what else do you do?" Fitzpatrick's voice betrayed that he wasn't really that interested. His mind was elsewhere and this was just a way of filling in time until Georgi Patarava returned.

"I'm a sustainable development consultant," Bond replied.

"Oh God," responded Fitzpatrick. "Another bloody consultant. And what has a sustainable development consultant got to do with the world of national security which is what I gather Patarava's involved in?"

There was a cynical tone to Fitzpatrick, almost leering. But before Bond could respond Georgi returned clutching several sheets of paper.

"Look, Fitzpatrick, this whole business has suddenly gone ballistic. It was serious enough before. Now it's mega."

He grabbed his replenished glass and took a large gulp of whisky.

"I have already cautioned you. But in the light of what's happened I think you need to co-operate with us now rather than wait to be taken to court. Let me be absolutely clear, you can be totally certain you are heading for court and big time trouble unless you co-operate with me now. If you agree I'll tell you what's just happened. If you don't, I'm empowered to arrest you and to accompany you to London where you will be put in the cells until your court hearing. So, which is it to be?"

Fitzpatrick peered into his whisky glass as if looking for tea leaves in a tea cup that would answer the question. Eventually he gave a sigh and an answer.

"I guess I've no option," he said reluctantly. "What do you want to know?"

"Tell me what's been going on here?" Georgi responded.

Another sigh – then Fitzpatrick told his story. He started slowly with reluctance but got quicker as he progressed, as if the more he told the more he realised he was beyond a point of no return and these people might as well know everything. He also felt some burden being lifted from him as, for the first time since the geophysicists fell ill in Siberia, he shared his problems with someone else.

"What's happened here in the last few days I have no idea," he concluded having told Georgi about the way he hired a team to lift the geophysicists out of Siberia because he wanted to protect his interest in the developing gold extraction business there. "I had a senior manager here. He was in charge of the whole situation. But I've not been able to speak to him for some days. That's why I'm here."

"He was Iain Barthwait, I assume?" asked Georgi.

"Yes, how did you…" Fitzpatrick did not complete the sentence. He recalled Georgi having said The Mansion had been under surveillance.

"And the nurse?" added Georgi.

"Amy Kelly," replied Fitzpatrick. "And there was a housekeeper and her husband. A local couple. They lived in too. But I guess you know that too."

"And which one of the two geophysicists did you say was here?" quizzed Georgi.

"Bailey," Fitzpatrick replied.

"And you've no idea what happened to the other one after the bus crash?"

"No."

"Have you had any further contact with people in Siberia about the missing man? Like Pavel Galdin at the hospital. Have you heard from him?"

"No," answered Fitzpatrick.

"And how ill was Bailey when you last saw him?"

"He was pretty poorly," Fitzpatrick told him.

"And have you had reports from the labs about the virus?"

"No. If any came in to Barthwait or the nurse they didn't tell me. They had no reason not to tell me. So I guess there haven't been any reports."

"And the man who headed up the security team here. What was his name – and was he the same guy who headed the team that extracted the geophysicists from the hospital in Siberia?"

"Yes, he was the same man. Janka Koldun."

"How did you know him?"

"From my military days, especially those in Eastern Europe. Koldun is from Belarus. A mercenary."

"Do you trust him?"

"I pay him enough," Fitzpatrick told Georgi.

"That's not the same thing," said Georgi.

"Of course, I know that," Fitzpatrick retorted. "And no, I don't trust him. But then there are not many people in this business I do trust."

"And Barthwait was in charge of this lot?"

"I've told you that already."

"And you've no idea where everyone is. Barthwait, Amy, Bailey, the housekeepers and Koldun and his team?"

"None at all," Fitzpatrick was demonstrating weariness with this questioning.

Georgi, detecting Fitzpatrick was reverting to his aggressive self, said: "Don't forget you're under caution. And don't forget it's at my discretion as to whether you're going from here to jail or not."

Fitzpatrick stared at his whisky, almost sulking.

"When was the last time you were in contact with this place?" Georgi continued.

"A couple of days ago," Fitzpatrick told him. "I talked to Barthwait."

"And everything seemed to be as it should be?"

"Yes," said Fitzpatrick, head still bent, eyes still on his whisky.

Georgi moved to be close to Gene Bond and passed him the papers he had brought from his car. Bond looked through them quickly.

"Bloody hell!" he exclaimed to his friend.

"Quite so," Georgi responded. Then for the sake of Fitzpatrick he explained what the papers were about.

"Today – an hour ago or thereabouts, a document was delivered to heads of state of major countries around the world. It purports to be a Declaration. It seeks a substantial amount of money, a billion dollars to be precise, and the passing of global control to a new superpower. It sounds preposterous. But – and here's the major point – the threat is that unless this is accepted, in 61 days a particularly aggressive virus will be released. It is the virus that was released through the mysterious explosions on the Siberian tundra and which they say has killed two internationally respected geophysicists. It will be released in the capital cities of each of the countries to which the Declaration has been delivered."

"Fucking hell," muttered Fitzpatrick.

"Quite so," agreed Bond.

A silence fell upon the group until Georgi pointed at the bottom of 'The Declaration' and said to Bond: "Recognise that name?"

"Hwanung? Don't think so."

"A friend of ours used that name as a pseudonym when he talked to students in Paris about his plans to attack strategic dams around the world. Remember? From his Acionna Projects?"

"Christ!" exclaimed Gene Bond, a chill going down his spine. "Sum Taeyoung! Not again!"

"None other!" responded Georgi. "And as you say. Not again!"

Chapter 16

When Bill Patterson first caught sight of Nika he had been scared out of his wits by the sudden appearance of this Neolithic warrior-like person standing in the doorway and apparently threatening him with a flint headed spear. She too had frozen in fear when she had stumbled unexpectedly upon this intruder. Nobody ever came into Anadyr-1. Just by being there this man threatened the security of her family. He was, as far as she could remember, the first person she had ever encountered outside her family. They lived in daily fear of being discovered and stumbling on this man shook her to the core. She had been terrified.

Since that first encounter an intimacy had grown between the two. He fully believed she had nursed him back from the brink of death. He owed his life to her. That did not detract from the contribution Mother Flintstone had made. She clearly had the experience and the skills but the administration of the medication had been conducted by her daughter. Nika's compassion and gentleness was extraordinary. Her commitment to him was total. She was tender and caring beyond anything he had ever experienced before. And as he grew to know her better and her defences melted he realised how attractive and alluring she was. His initial vision of a weather-beaten female warrior standing before him in animal skin clothes faded into history as he realised she was young, with a complexion that betrayed a life often spent outdoors in extreme weather but which was far from being harsh and leather-like. Her skin was smooth and reflected her comparatively young age. He guessed she was in her late twenties. Her big eyes were a dark blue – almost a black/blue and her hair, which flowed down well over her shoulders, was jet black.

That kiss in the Flintstone's place of worship took them both by surprise. Nika held Patterson with a hand on each side of his head and kissed him firmly on the lips. It was a spontaneous and intuitive act. She had never kissed anyone like this before. She knew it had taken him as much by surprise as it had her but then she felt his arms extend round her, pulling her towards him as the kiss lingered. Dormant senses were awakened within her. Years of isolation from anyone apart from her family had denied her what most young women encounter as part of the experience of life. Her metamorphosis from adolescence to womanhood had been starved of any close encounter with the opposite sex.

Their relationship blossomed from that moment on. She became infatuated with the Scottish scientist. He became overwhelmed by her affection. It was an unstoppable romance but in the most incredulous of circumstances. Patterson was fully aware how ridiculous the situation he was getting into was and how untenable. But he found her irresistible. She was intriguing. So naïve. So unaware. So keen to explore what to her was the unknown territory of a loving relationship, so excited by experiences she had never before encountered. How he touched her. How they explored each other's bodies. How he could take her to mountainous heights of passion and crescendo moments of pure ecstasy.

Patterson was aware that the family knew this relationship had developed. There was a distinct division of attitude with clear hostility to the romance from Nika's father and brother but maternal though cautious support from her mother. And as far as parental responsibilities to the daughter were concerned, this was clearly a matter where maternity ruled in the Flintstone household.

Patterson was by now more or less recovered from whatever illness had attacked him. And as fitness returned, so curiosity about the Flintstone family grew including the intriguing use of gold utensils and the reference by the British spy George Symons to the gold bullion of the Romanov family and the persecuted Old Believers. Patterson could not get it out of his mind that if the Flintstones were using gold utensils in their daily lives, maybe the bullion – which he imagined would be in gold bars – was also nearby.

It was also growing in his mind that somehow, sometime he would have to find a way of leaving here. Clearly Anadyr-1 held no long term prospect for him. He needed to escape back to civilisation, back to a proper life. But how to do that and how would Nika fit into such a plan?

With the questions refusing to go away and remaining unresolved, Patterson expanded his area of exploration of the abandoned town as far as Nika, or more pointedly, her father and brother, would allow him to do. That they were paranoid about being discovered was an understatement and the last thing they wanted was for the newcomer to compromise their security.

With Nika, Patterson investigated how much of the Flintstone's utensils were made from gold. It was no easy task because the family had assembled a motley collection of pots and pans over the years plus plates and other kitchen and tableware. Using the one he had originally scratched to reveal its metal origins, the Scottish geophysicist tried to see what Nika knew.

"Gold," he said slowly to her, pointing at the shining surface his scratching had revealed.

"Zoloto," she responded.

"Zoloto?" he queried.

"Da!" she nodded enthusiastically.

He sketched as best he could a drawing of gold bars.

"Zoloto?" he asked her. "Is there anything like this around here?" And he gesticulated to try and indicate he was suggesting there might be gold bars somewhere nearby.

She shrugged and shook her head. "Niet."

Now he was left with a puzzle. Had he made any progress? Did her negative answer mean there were no such gold bars nearby or did it mean she did not know what he was talking about? He turned his attention back to the kitchenware and over a period of a few days found that the Flintstones had at least two dozen items made from gold. But the question remained. Was this collection of gold items once owned by part of the former royal family of Imperial Russia and if it was, did that mean that the bullion was nearby too?

As the days passed, family routine became re-established with mother and daughter maintaining cleanliness, tidiness of the dwellings they had created and preparing meals whilst the menfolk disappeared on hunting expeditions, scavenging around the abandoned town or busying themselves with maintenance and repair activity. Patterson helped where he could but was increasingly left to his own devices. This gave him an opportunity to slip away from the family to explore his environment further.

This strange town was vast with its rotting brick and wooden buildings and cracking roadways. An abundance of green growth and yellow-headed weeds could be seen everywhere as the town and its structures gave way to the unstoppable reclaim of nature. Surrounded by high, rolling hills, many still snow-capped despite it being midsummer and with patches of snow and ice to be found everywhere across as much of the site he ventured into, Patterson could not fail to liken this place to the famed Marie Celeste ghost ship. Anadyr-1 was indeed a ghost town.

Three storey high apartment blocks, mostly in red brick, single storey workshops and storage areas, some whitewashed but now fading and looking decidedly grubby, shops, stores and schools, even what looked as if it might have been a cinema – all stood in various degrees of decay, some with collapsed or partly collapsed roofs. Evidence that one building had once been a supermarket came from the line of well marshalled but totally rusted and rotted trollies. Fences were falling to the onslaught of nature and weather and giant advertising hoardings lay decaying where they had been ripped from their fixtures by high winds.

Always with a cautionary look around to ensure there was no sign of life, Patterson scampered from building to building. He found storerooms full of rotting, rusting materials, empty cans of food – hundreds of them, lying scattered over the floor of one. Another had clearly once been a canteen. In another, military helmets, now red rusted, filled the floor. Hundreds of them. Maybe over a thousand.

Everywhere across the site were long, box-like wooden structures. Some stretched as far as he could see. Closer inspection revealed they contained communications cables and pipes. Clearly the ground was too frozen to bury them as would conventionally happen elsewhere.

What he failed to find was anything like gold bullion or rocket launching facilities, not that he could necessarily have known what the latter would look like. He did find numerous large, round concrete structures that might have been the tops of concrete tubes penetrating deep into the ground but steel access doors to these had been welded shut. Their secrets were well protected.

Only once did he reach the perimeter fence which brought back what seemed like distant memories of him scrambling through a hole in the mesh after the bus crash. The fence here was more or less complete and he wondered if its original purpose had been to keep people in or people out. On the opposite side the public road showed no sign of recent use.

He was exploring what looked like some sort of

dormitory, perhaps for local military troops, when a voice spoke to him from a nearby door. It made him jump.

"Chto ty zdes' delayesh?"

He spun round in surprise to find Nika leaning against the door frame. He wondered how long she had been there.

"Vy ne dolzhny byt' zdes!"

He had no idea what she was saying but clearly she was not happy to have found him here. Though he could not understand the words the tone of her voice clearly denoted displeasure.

"Just looking around," he said casually, walking towards her and then holding her hand.

"Vy ne dolzhny byt' zdes!" she repeated.

Attack being the best form of defence, he kissed her, a gentle touch of the lips as if to test her mood, test her reaction.

Her hand tightened around his. She kissed him back. But this was nothing like a gentle caress. Her free hand was at the back of his neck, pulling him to her in a passionate embrace. Everything about her expressed a hunger for him. His arms were now round her, pulling her tightly to him. He could feel her breasts rising and falling hard against him as passions rose. Her hand was now down between them, undoing clothing then searching, finding, holding and guiding. Her touch was exquisite. She flinched and screeched as he entered her, then her legs were around him and her nails were digging into the back of his neck.

She shrieked in delight. Her lack of inhibition was

in such marked contrast to her original shock when she first discovered him, followed by a transition that passed through cautious curiosity to compassion as she nursed him, then affection which matured into lovemaking. Now she seemed seized by an abandoned moment of unadulterated passion.

Distracting him from their moment of sexual delight, in the distance he thought he heard a noise, a sort of pounding. It was hardly discernible and like nothing he had heard here before. Silence normally dominated Anadyr-1. He was torn between their love making with his head buried into her now naked chest, and being concerned about this intrusion. And though he had hoped it might just go away, it clearly was not going to and instead was now a distinct sound, a sort of thump, thump, thump and getting louder.

"Can you hear that?" he said to Nika who looked at him quizzically but he instantly realised she had heard what was bothering him. And the sound was growing by the second.

They hurriedly re-dressed before cautiously peering from the doorway. Nothing immediately came into view but the noise was dominating everything and Patterson now knew exactly what it was. Sure enough, seconds later, and to the accompaniment of a deafening racket, a large helicopter in green/grey camouflage colours rounded a nearby building at speed, heeled over at a sharp angle with its rotor blade ends barely off the ground. The side doors were open and Patterson could clearly see combat uniformed soldiers – many of them. Towards the rear of the aircraft was a very large red star. There was now no doubting what this was.

The Mi-8T touched down less than 500 yards from where they were and disgorged a squad of Russian special force commandoes, each armed with suppressed assault rifles of armour piercing capability.

Patterson looked at Nika. Her black blue eyes were wide open like those of an animal caught in headlights. Her body trembled. She was white with shock. He grabbed her by the hand and moved deeper into the building, his mind in a whirl as he sought what to do. Did this present a threat to him, to the Flintstones, or was it a potential escape route for him from Anadyr-1?

Chapter 17

"You've missed a turning," he told the taxi driver.

"What's that?" the rather chunky taxi driver asked.

"We're too far north. I've just seen a sign to the North Pole. So you must have missed a turn."

The driver chuckled more out of politeness than anything else. He could not count the number of times this old joke had been uttered to him.

"But at least we're not in danger of sinking if the ice goes!" he responded. "You can't say the same of the North Pole. So people come here to see Santa at our North Pole in Fairbanks. They've been posting letters to him here for nearly 70 years."

The condition of the ice at the North Pole was something Bond had not thought of before so, as the taxi sped down the conifer lined highway cutting through the rolling countryside, he searched the internet on his iPhone for a status report. He found an article published in The Independent newspaper with the heading:

Arctic could become ice-free for first time in more than 100,000 years, claims leading scientist

The article was largely based on the findings of Professor Peter Wadhams of Cambridge University. It said he "predicts the Arctic ice may well disappear, that is, have an area of less than one million square kilometres by September of this year."

The article reported that provisional satellite data produced by the US National Snow & Ice Data Centre showed there are now just over 11.1 million square kilometres of sea ice compared to the average for the last 30 years of nearly 12.7 million square kilometres. This difference – more than 1.5 million square kilometres – is about the same size as six United Kingdoms.

As usual, such published opinion had stimulated a barrage of responses both from those who supported it and those who criticised it. And for the umpteenth time Bond thought if we believe those who say the evidence is wrong, and it turns out they are wrong, what then? How do we go back beyond the point of no return? Clearly, we would not be able to.

The taxi was crossing the Chena River now. It was not far from the airport to the International Arctic Research Center, a 15 minute drive at the most. It was a clear, sunny day and the comparatively flat view from the taxi showed a countryside well covered by conifers and gently rolling hills in the distance. They turned off the main highway onto a secondary road that climbed uphill to the Center, the first sight of which was the rotunda end of the imposing, smart and clean looking building.

It was now pushing towards 24 hours since Bond had left Georgi after they had flown back down to London from where Bond had gone on to Chicago and ultimately Fairbanks. Georgi had been shocked by Bond's reaction to what they both took to be the work of South Korean havoc entrepreneur Sum Taeyoung even though "The Declaration" was signed by The Spirit of Hwanung.

"There's a lot here I would agree with," Bond told his Georgian friend after scanning through the documents Georgi had brought from his car. Alexander Fitzpatrick was reading them now.

"You're joking!" responded Georgi. "The man's a lunatic – a dangerous international terrorist and an extortionist – now with what is clearly his most ambitious plot so far. He wants to take over the bloody world – and you agree with him!"

"I didn't say that," retorted Bond. "Of course I don't agree with his threats. The man has clearly got some brain cells out of position but his list of reasons for what he says we're failing to do as a global community is spot on."

"But you can't support the ideology of a demented madman!" argued Georgi. "And his threat. Do we take that seriously?"

"Can we afford not to?" Bond answered. "The insane arrogance of the man is such we just have to take this seriously. So what the bloody hell do we do?"

Georgi obviously did not know what to say. Bond shrugged. What was this to do with him anyway? Here we go again. Being dragged into the world of Georgi's counterespionage. He had said time and time again he was not going to get involved a third time.

"I'm going to Alaska," he finally announced, breaking a prolonged silence and changing the subject.

Georgi looked surprised. "What, now! Now we've

received this threat. Where are you running off to? Lavrentiya after all?"

Bond was impressed and angry in equal order. There was not much Georgi did not log in his grey cells but this reference to "running off" was out of order.

"Bollocks!" he retorted. "I don't know precisely where I'm going. I'm off to Alaska – not Siberia where Lavrentiya is. I'm going to talk to people about the melting of the permafrost and the escape of viruses. I want to hear what they know about the new gold rush in Siberia and its effect on the ordinary people there, especially the goings on in Lavrentiya. But getting into Lavrentiya isn't that easy. So I'm heading to the International Arctic Research Center in Fairbanks and the University of Alaska and its Permafrost Laboratory. I may go on to Lavrentiya from there, that's if I can and if I still need to after meeting the university people."

It took two days of meetings in Fairbanks across a variety of buildings and different organisations – all contained in a vast area of woodland and open spaces with modern, glassy buildings and manicured lawns everywhere. By the end of it all Bond had a kaleidoscope recall of different people, mostly professors of one sort or another, many from different parts of the world, who had provided him with an encyclopaedia of information. He tried to whittle it down into some key statements of evidence.

"The impact of permafrost thaw is already being felt on the ground in Alaska where the changing surface temperatures are causing the earth to shift and disturb buildings and road foundations. Alaska's temperatures are rising about twice as fast as in the contiguous United States," one scientist told him.

In one laboratory he saw the image from an electron microscope of a section of a Pithovirus particle inside an infected Acanthamoeba castellanii cell. The length of the particle was about 1.5 microns with a 0.5 micron diameter. Researchers told him they had revived the virus, which is more than 30,000 years old, after finding it in the permafrost of northeast Siberia. That was of particular interest to Bond as it suggested it might come from somewhere in the Chukotka tundra where Fitzpatrick's geophysicists had been.

The virus particle he saw was no ordinary virus. It was the biggest ever found on Earth, the scientists told him, and thought to be part of a new type of giant virus that can be larger than many bacteria or even cells, and is visible under a normal microscope. They said that with climate change warming the planet and taking the perma out of permafrost in many polar regions, they may begin to unearth more previously undiscovered viruses, not all of which will be as benign as this new one, dubbed *Pithovirus sibericum*. This one, they said, posed no danger to people, infecting only one-celled creatures known as amoebas.

"Back to Sum Taeyoung," thought Bond. The South Korean was claiming to have scientific evidence that the virus he was threatening everyone with was lethal.

As cautiously as he could he asked if such a deadly virus had already escaped. The answer indicated it was unlikely. If one had done so the scientific community would surely know all about it. There was a caveat to that in so far as there was no way of totally knowing what was going on within the boundaries of Russia. As far as Bond was concerned that meant the answer was inconclusive.

He was shown one report from a scientific team in the Aix-Marseille University in Marseille, France, and thought it should be of particular interest to Fitzpatrick and his mining company, especially its shareholders. It read:

"Sixty percent of the new virus' gene content doesn't resemble anything on earth. The virus may have been a parasite to life forms more common in earlier days of life on earth. We are worried about the implications of this type of discovery for present-day life on Earth. It is a recipe for disaster. Once you begin industrial explorations, people will start to move around the deep permafrost layers. Through mining and drilling, those old layers will be penetrated and this is where the danger is coming from."

"Perhaps it already has!" Bond thought to himself.

He met another scientist, this one from the independent scientific group, Climate Central, who told him "Arctic sea ice shrank to its lowest level in 38 years last month, setting a record low for the month of May and creating conditions for what could become the smallest Arctic ice extent in history. We didn't just break the old May record, we're way below the previous one," he said. "Compared to normal conditions, the Arctic ice cap was missing a Texas-sized slab of ice in May. It spread across 4.63 million square miles of the Arctic Ocean, Hudson Bay and adjacent areas of the North

Atlantic – an area 224,000 square miles smaller than the previous low record for the month set in 2004. May's record low follows four previous monthly record lows set in January, February and April."

Another institute provided him with an update on the relationship between the melting of the permafrost, the arrival of the mysterious holes in Siberia, global warming and climate change. Scientists there told him that according to measurements made by Russian scientists, methane concentration at the bottom of one of the holes was thousands of times higher than in the regular atmosphere. A more thorough recent expedition identified "dozens" of new holes, all of which apparently formed in the last year or two.

"The Siberian holes," said the scientists, "draw into question the near-term stability of Arctic permafrost which traps enough carbon, if fully unleashed, to double atmospheric concentrations and potentially push global warming into a frightening new phase. We are quite certain it will take at least a century for that to happen in a worst-case scenario, but it's clear that the release has already begun."

It was all gloomy news. There was nothing here Bond did not already know but the visit provided far more detail than he had had previously. But his attempts to find out more about people being dislodged from their homes to make way for mining in the Siberian town of Lavrentiya came to nothing. His enquiries revealed that such activity was not unique and he discovered examples of people's homes making way for new or extended gold mining at a variety of locations around the world including South America, Scandinavia and even in Canada. He was also surprised to find how much of Siberia's gold mining industry was Canadian owned.

It had been an interesting trip. He liked Fairbanks and especially the area where the university and research institutes were located. But he resigned himself to abandoning the visit to Lavrentiya and going home. He returned to his hotel at the end of day two exhausted. His main thought as he reached his room and opened its door was to book his flight tickets back to the UK. But even before he turned the room lights on a voice made him jump.

"I've raided your mini bar for a whisky but at least I've poured one for you too."

"Bloody hell!" Bond responded. "What the hell are you doing here?"

"Waiting for you," Georgi told him as he sat on the edge of the bed, nearly empty glass of whisky in his hand.

"I can see that, you bugger. But what the hell are you doing in Fairbanks?"

"Have you seen the news?" his Georgian friend asked him, ignoring the need for any niceties and getting straight to business.

"No," Bond told him.

"The Russians have thrown the world into chaos – again," said Georgi. "It's gone mad!"

"What on earth has happened?" asked Bond, wishing Georgi would come to the point.

"They've declared the Bering Strait to belong to Imperial Russia, chucked the Eskimos off an American owned island there and installed a missile battery on another."

"Bloody hell," Bond responded.

"All aircraft movement in the area has been grounded to provide freedom for military responses. And – you're never going to believe this… we've been monitoring the chatter in the ether even closer in recent days and what the Russians claim they've found in Siberia will blow your mind!"

Chapter 18

Children screamed in terror and ran in panic anywhere to escape the bedlam. But there was no escape. There was nowhere to go. Nowhere to hide. Mothers desperately tried to gather their children around them and those who succeeded hurried with their flocks to their meagre homes in the naïve expectation there they would find some protection. They did not. Those men present in the Iñupiat mini township stood dumbfounded, frozen in moments of fear and hopelessness. Their instinct was to fight – to stand firm on land they and their ancestors had occupied for more than 3,000 years. To protect their families. But they were overwhelmed. There was absolutely nothing they could do.

The helicopters arrived without warning over the township of Little Diomede just as they had done at Anadyr-1. One minute normality prevailed. In the next they had appeared suddenly above the tops of the island's high cliffs. At ground level, rubbish whirled up by the rotors turned a homeland into instant chaos as dozens of well armed and highly trained commandoes abseiled down ropes, sophisticated armament at the ready. The noise was intense, obliterating the sounds of the screaming, terrorised children and a high sea swell crashing into the bottom of the towering, sheer sided cliffs. One after another, helicopter after helicopter unloaded its commandoes before settling on the comparatively flat albeit rough terrain of the island's plateau top waiting to be called down for the second phase of their mission.

In the face of shouted protests, crying children and the remonstrations of the township's mayor, slowly but surely a community of nearly 150 people was herded towards the helipad, a concrete surfaced structure standing on a round pile of huge rocks adjacent the tiny, seven square kilometre island in the middle of the Bering Strait. In less than two hours the tiny township of Little Diomede was evacuated and its people ferried to the Siberian mainland to be united with those who had been forced from Big Diomede in the aftermath of World War 2. Some 400 plus people, many of them directly or indirectly related and who had through the course of time been divided into two communities, were now reunited – whether they liked it or not.

Recently the world has become accustomed to occasional surprise tactics by those who run the Kremlin. This move in the Bering Strait was on a par with the occupation of the Crimea; the support given to help establish the self-proclaimed state of Donetsk, splitting it out of the Ukraine; the intervention in the Middle East, siding with the Western Alliance to oppose ISIS yet supporting Bashar al-Assad in Syria – all evidence of an unpredictable Russia. The action in the Bering Strait ranked equal to these. It was, unquestionably, unpredicted!

Simultaneous to the forceful evacuation of Little Diomede, a junior member of the Russian delegation to the United Nations made a statement to a meeting in Washington. It came as an unwelcomed shock despite Western intelligence being fully aware of a rise in Arctic military activity by Russia's Northern Fleet. This included tracking by satellite the recently renovated, nuclear powered Kirov-class battlecruiser, Pyotr Velikiy, and her accompanying support flotilla, apparently on exercises in the Arctic Sea.

"Developing the Arctic and defending Russian interests in the region are priority tasks for Russia's Northern Fleet," the Fleet's Commander had recently declared. "One of the priorities of the Northern Fleet is the development of the Arctic and the protection of state interests in this strategically important region. In the coming year the Northern Fleet will continue performing long distance campaigns with warships and submarines."

Whilst the President had his own strategic agenda for these actions, the media was told that the "protection of state interests" had much to do with the developing gold rush in Siberia, the President's continued interest in gold, and the need to develop an infrastructure in Siberia that would improve the transportation and shipping of extracted minerals. In the West all this activity had been taken to be no more than sabre-rattling but the statement read in Washington by a young and nervous junior civil servant changed all that. The implications were immediately felt right across Western Alaska and North Eastern Siberia.

He read: "Prior to 1867, Russia owned land which is now both Siberia and Alaska. Through it runs the Bering

Strait, 82 kilometres wide at its narrowest point. The sale in 1867 of 1.5 million square kilometers of Russian property to America for $7.2m was related only to land. We contest the Bering Strait has never left the ownership of the Russian Federation."

"The Strait is named after the Danish born explorer Vitus Bering who, whilst in the service of the Russian Empire, in 1728 sailed through what was thought then to have been an unknown strip of water. It is now known that he had been preceded by a Russian, Semyon Dezhnyov, who navigated the Strait as early as 1648."

"Russia today retains ownership of the island called Big Diomede, also known as Ratmanov Island, which stands about half way across the Bering Strait and is in part of the Chukotsky District of the Chukotka Autonomous Okrug of Russia. It is the site of a Russian weather station and base for border guards of the Federal Security Service. There is no indigenous population on the island. Since 2012 this whole area has been a closed Russian military zone."

"As of immediate effect, the sovereign state of the Russian Federation declares expansion of that military zone and ownership of the Bering Strait. We will now restrict the passage of vessels only to those which have been granted prior permission so to do. As of immediate effect, the Bering Strait is under the protection of the Russian Northern Fleet and other military defences have been or are being installed in the area."

Even as UN protests winged their way towards Moscow, Western Intelligence surveillance systems already identified that the Pyotr Velikiy flotilla was active in the Arctic Sea in the vicinity of the Bering Strait. Perhaps even more disconcerting was photographic evidence that on the island of Big Diomede Russia had installed a 3M-51 Alfa coastal version anti-ship cruise missile launcher. How it had been transported to the island and installed without Western intelligence spotting it was now a matter of urgent review.

Right across the coast of Siberia, from the Chukchi Sea to the north of the Bering Strait to the Bering Sea in the south, even going as far as a few miles off St Lawrence Island, part of the US State of Alaska, elements of the Northern Fleet explored and compiled an audit of what 'assets' Russia owned. Ports such as that at Pevek, some 1,000 km west from the Bering Strait, one of the few ports capable of accommodating the needs of modern ships, were scrutinised to evaluate what role they could take as Russia intensified its strategic activity in the Arctic. It was this 'asset evaluation' that had resulted in the helicopter incursion into Anadyr-1.

As the news of this action spread, so the international NGO fraternity flew into an apoplectic rage at what they saw to be a diabolical violation of human rights. The USA, pointing out that Little Diomede was officially part of the Unorganised Borough of the State of Alaska, lodged a formal protest with Russia over "an aggressive and illegal act." Moscow countered with a statement saying a small force from its Northern Fleet had undertaken the "humanitarian repatriation" of the population of Little Diomede as their homeland had become "untenable and unsustainable." This, the Moscow statement said, was because the melting sea ice could no longer provide a landing facility for the island's supply aircraft and the local population's seal hunting activity on the ice had been compromised. The Eskimo community had been 'resettled' with families from Big Diomede who had been forcibly evacuated from the larger of the two islands just after World War 2. The Russian statement noted that there were considerable "inter-family relationships" between the two communities and their unification would aid their long-term survival.

In Washington the President convened an extraordinary emergency joint meeting of his War Cabinet including, amongst others, the Defence Secretary and Chairman of the Joint Chiefs of Staff, and senior members of the Senate Armed Services Committee. The UN Secretary General called an emergency meeting of the North Atlantic Council and in the UK the Prime Minister brought together the crisis response committee COBRA, so called because it meets in Cabinet Office Briefing Room A.

In Seoul Sum Taeyoung bemoaned the fact that his global master plan had hit a wall of silence. Not one response had been received as yet to his Declaration of Intent. It was as if it had not happened. Ten days had slipped by. The attention of world leaders was now clearly on activity in the Bering Strait. If they had shown concern at the message from Taeyoung it certainly had not sparked any answers. It was time, he thought, to up the game.

Chapter 19

"Russians!" Patterson had shot the word at Nika as he saw the large red star predominant towards the rear of the approaching helicopter.

"Risskiye," she had confirmed, spitting out the word with some venom. She had never encountered a Russian. But her family history had embedded within her an instinctive hatred.

The building in which they stood was substantial with doors leading to rooms deeper in the complex. As with everywhere else in Anadyr-1, discarded stuff was everywhere. They hid behind a large pile of empty boxes, drums and broken wooden pallets. She held his hand tightly and together they strained to hear anything that was going on outside. There was much shouting and scraping of military boots on rotting concrete roads outside. In the distance they could hear a dog barking – Nika's dog. Then there was the sound of a single shot – and no more from the dog. Nika heard it all. There was no doubt what had happened and her hand went to her mouth to suppress her cries while tears poured down her face. Close by they could hear that some soldiers had now entered their building. They could hear brief words being exchanged before they departed. It had been a scant survey of the building, by no means a search. Patterson reasoned they were not being looked for. These soldiers did not know they were here. They were checking buildings, not looking for people.

After half an hour any noise from the intruders was now at a distance. Though she did not say anything, Patterson was fully aware of Nika's concern for the rest of her family but there was no way they could try and see what was going on without compromising their own safety. And though the natural inclination had been to hide from this military force and to be delighted and relieved they had not been found, Patterson could not escape the thought that these Russians might potentially be his way of escaping Anadyr-1. But if he did, what would be the fate of Nika? What would happen to the family? Were they still seen by the Russians as belonging to a persecuted religious order? He owed his life to these people, especially to Nika to whom he now also held a deep affection. No, he was resigned to stay and help them and to protect Nika.

After an hour they heard the helicopters' engines fire up and soon the noisy visitors had departed. Patterson felt a surprising disappointment at their going, severing this link to the rest of the world to which he was sometime bound to return. There was no reason he could think of for the Russians to leave anyone behind at Anadyr-1 but their exit from the building in which they had been hiding was undertaken with the utmost caution.

Slowly they made their way back to the complex of buildings in which the Flintstones' home was located only to find it deserted. As they walked towards it a shape lying on the concrete road before them was unavoidable. They both knew what it was as soon as they saw it. Nika cried out loud. Patterson held her hand tightly. A small pool of blood had gathered near the dog's head. Nika knelt and held the animal to her body, trembling, mortified by her loss. Patterson did what he could to comfort her but she was distraught and virtually inconsolable. It took a while before he was able to encourage her to move. Sadly her anguish did not end here. Almost equally distressing, the living quarters had been badly vandalised and the small religious room utterly wrecked. Of the other three members of the family there was no trace.

Nika was hysterical at the sight of her shattered home and the absence of her parents and brother. She broke down and sobbed, burying her head into Patterson who held her tightly as he wondered what on earth had happened to the others. Had they flown the buildings and escaped Anadyr-1 into the nearby hills, or had they been taken away by the Russians? He suspected the latter. If the Russians had discovered the buildings converted into the family's dwellings, surely they would have wanted to find the people who lived there. If they had not found them surely they would have searched, but there was no evidence from their own experience of hiding behind the pile of rubbish and hearing soldiers undertake a very cursory visit. If they had been searching for anyone, surely they would have found them. They had found the three members of the family. That, apparently, had satisfied them.

Nika eventually regained some degree of control and set about trying to undo the shambles left by the soldiers.

Despite her best endeavours to maintain her control and dignity, to be split away from the rest of her family was something she had never experienced before. She was distraught. The burial of her dog did nothing to help. At fairly regular intervals she sobbed as she continued to try and keep busy. But every now and then the situation overwhelmed her and she would find Patterson and dampened his shoulder with her uncontrolled crying.

Patterson did his best to survey the home buildings and those in the immediate vicinity to see if there were any clues as to what had happened to the rest of the Flintstones. He found nothing. By the end of the day they were resigned to the thought that the family had been taken into captivity and flown off site by the Russians.

Their assumption was right. Father, mother and son had been taken by helicopter to the tiny island of Big Diomede which had seen major transformation in a matter of days. Military construction and logistics teams had expanded the personnel quarters to provide barracks for those involved in the build and installation of the ground-to-ship missile system. The Northern Fleet had established a new Operations Centre here and the total numbers of people now on the island had been massively expanded. The nuclear-powered icebreaker Yamal and several military ships were anchored off the desolate island.

The reclusive family was virtually imprisoned on the island. Their discovery at Anadyr-1 had come as a complete surprise to the military group who had landed there as part of their 'asset assessment' activity of the area. They had no expectation of finding anyone there and no contingency for how to handle this situation. So the three were incarcerated while the military command on Big Diomede awaited instructions. The capture of two elderly people and one younger male, none of whom could speak contemporary Russian and who seemed to speak to each other through a language of their own consisting of few words and many grunts, was an unexpected and unwanted additional problem for the Russians.

Speculation as to who they were ran rife amongst the military presence on the rocky island in the middle of the Bering Strait. But instructions were clear. There would be no release of news about their discovery until orders had been received as to what to do with them.

Forty eight hours after their imprisonment on Big Diomede, a senior member of the GRU Generalnovo Shtaba, Russia's main intelligence directorate, flew onto the island together with a language specialist. They were a formidable team and the Flintstone family were no match for them despite their determination to conceal from their captors their daughter's presence in Anadyr-1 and that of the Scottish geophysicist. But eventually a combination of fatigue, constant interrogation and trickery let the cat out of the bag. The existence of Nika was let slip as was the existence of a man who, because they knew no better, they simply described as a foreign stranger who they had nursed back from near death.

Patterson was just outside the Flintstones' home quarters cutting up the carcass of an animal father and son had trapped a few days before when that unmistakable thump, thump, thump sound came to him again. His heart leapt with immediate fear as to where Nika was and he shot into the building to be out of sight. The helicopters had returned and he had no idea where she was. He peered out from the doorway to see two red starred military helicopters landing not far from a rotting, trackless armoured personnel carrier some 500 yards away. This was a slower, less dramatic arrival than the one of three days before. The aircraft sedately touched down and rather than disgorging soldiers, this time it was a far calmer affair with some senior personnel climbing to the ground accompanied by a handful of commandoes.

Patterson scoured what he could see of the rotting township for any signs of Nika but there were none. To his consternation, the newly arrived group was heading straight towards where he was, clearly well briefed as to the location of the Flintstones' home. Maybe, he thought, they were part of the same Russian expedition that had visited before. The Scottish geophysicist moved deeper into the building, knowing there was no other door to this part of the complex but there were windows and he climbed through one, continuing to look for any signs of Nika as he did so and closing the window after him.

Outside, the Russians were now the other side of the building to where he stood, looking around desperately for Nika. Still there was no sign of her. His heart was sinking. This was all surely going to end very badly.

A squall of rain and sleet descended from the nearby hills transforming what had been a bright day into a dull one with visibility suddenly reduced. Patterson cursed silently to himself that he had left his jacket behind in the building. He was quickly sodden and very cold. The wind was getting up and was icy. This was no time to be out in the open but he had no option. Or had he? Yet again the choice of simply giving himself up to the Russians crossed his mind. It would lead him to escape this dead town and eventually enable him to get on with life. But that would be without Nika. And that was not an option.

"Where the bloody hell are you?" he muttered to himself while making the decision to run to another nearby building to escape the weather. He ducked down and sprinted but had only just launched himself into the open when a voice shouted out.

"Stop!" came the command, shouted in English but thick with Russian accent. As Patterson ignored it and just kept running it was followed by another shout.

"Stop!" but this time the command was followed by a burst of automatic gunfire that echoed round the empty buildings.

Patterson skidded to a halt, arms raised high. He had already realised that the shots had been into the air but the effect on him was what the soldier with the gun had wanted. Patterson stopped in his tracks and remained motionless, the rain and sleet pouring down his face and the now high and gusting wind pulling at his sodden jumper. He turned very cautiously, arms still raised, to see who had accosted him. Only a couple of hundred yards away a young Russian soldier stood motionless, his assault rifle aimed at a spot on Patterson's head. Other

Russians had now come into sight and were walking guardedly towards him.

"British," Patterson called out. "I'm a British scientist."

With the young soldier not moving an inch and his weapon seemingly locked onto Patterson's head, two Russians approached him.

"We know. We were expecting you," said one in excellent English. "But where is the girl?"

Of course, Patterson thought. They know everything.

"You will call her to us," said the Russian. "And I suggest you do it quickly before you freeze to death."

There was even a hint of humour in the voice.

Patterson had no options. The game was up and there was no point in arguing or disagreeing. As requested, he shouted.

"Nika. I don't know where you are. If you can hear me, come out. There's no point in hiding any more."

She would not understand the words but the message would be clear enough.

It took two more calls before she appeared, emerging from a nearby building and walking slowly and resignedly towards them through the torrent of rain that was falling with such force it was now bouncing up from the broken concrete of the road. Her black hair was soaked and her saturated clothes clung to her shapely body. She looked forlorn and bedraggled, with body bent against the weather and head down. She reached them and grabbed Patterson's hand. Clearly she was frightened by what was happening and was shivering as much from fear as she was from the weather. More soldiers had arrived to swell the numbers in the group, two bringing coats which they gave to Patterson and Nika who gratefully covered themselves in protection from the now appalling weather.

It was all over in minutes. Still hand in hand, Nika and Patterson were escorted onto one of the helicopters and with the weather just on the limit of them being able to fly, the group left Anadyr-1 and headed east.

Chapter 20

On a nice summer's day it could be a sparkling, exciting, interesting, peaceful and certainly different place to be. The wooded location with neat paved pathways and wide variety of statues and sculptures, once described quite accurately as 'an open air blacksmith's art museum', still attracts tourists despite the perilous circumstances of this city of around a million people.

The Park Of The Forged Figures in the centre of the city of Donetsk in the self-proclaimed Donetsk People's Republic this evening felt far from being a peaceful safe haven for art lovers. It was dark and miserable with black clouds scurrying overhead driven by a ferocious wind. Near horizontal rain swept across the area and sounds of battle – artillery and mortars – were not far away. Occasionally the work of snipers echoed around the city. That evening Donetsk International Airport, or what was left of it, just seven kilometres from the park, was the scene of bloody fighting as an eight month battle between Ukrainian forces and Russian-backed separatists came to an end in favour of the latter. Both terminals and the control tower had been completely wrecked and now stood in testimony to a conflict that to date had killed more than 10,000 people.

He was forced to close his eyes to mere slits as the

rain drove straight into him with some force. It stung his face and dripped down and inside the upturned collar of his long and now sodden raincoat. Janka Koldun splashed his way across the park as he strode towards his meeting and silently cursed Sum Taeyoung for getting him to do his dirty work for him.

The paved pathways glistened with puddles that reflected the park's lighting and were made lively by the torrent of rain and the wind. In the dying light of the day the surrounding trees looked menacing, like legions of tall warriors. His mind was on the task and he swore at the weather. The Belarus mercenary had no time to consider or even appreciate the numerous skilfully forged figures and sculptures scattered around the park to which they gave their name. Indeed, its name had inspired the code word he would use at the meeting he was on his way to.

"Metallicheskaya figura" would ensure who he met was who he was supposed to meet though it had long since crossed his mind that nobody in their right minds would be out in the park on an evening like this unless they absolutely had to be. Clearly all sane people were indoors. The park was deserted.

It had been a taxing and frustrating journey to get here. Normally he would have simply travelled south, crossing Belarus and the Ukraine towards the Sea of Azov and its holiday resorts. But the local war changed all that and instead he crossed from Belarus into Russia, headed south and eventually crossed the border into the Donetsk People's Republic some 100 kilometres east of the city of Donetsk. Entering the country from Russia was by far the easiest and safest route but even that was fraught with challenges.

Now he was reaching the beginning of the Signs of the Zodiac Alley with its sculptures high above the pathway, some forming bridges. And there, sure enough, stood a solitary figure, dim in the dying light and the pouring rain. Janka assumed it to be a man. If so, he was small but beyond that Janka could tell little. The diminutive person was hooded and stooped making it impossible for Janka to see his face. Though it seemed no more than a theatrical gesture because nobody in their right mind would be standing here this particular evening, Janka uttered the pre-ordained words – "metallicheskaya figura."

There was a barely discernable grunt from the other person who simply handed a large and bulky package to Janka and then walked off without a word. It had been the briefest of encounters. Janka watched the other person disappear into the dullness of the evening, worried now that the sooner this matter was out of his hands the better. He retreated from the park, dodging the one or two check points he encountered, skirting round an area where the sounds of automatic gunfire bounced off buildings.

The journey home was as tedious as it had been in the opposite direction and he stopped only in Minsk centre to post the package. Throughout his actions he wore gloves, not only to prevent his fingerprints transferring to the envelope but to ensure he was in no way contaminated by their content. He had been reassured he would come to no harm unless he broke open any of the envelopes contained in the package. Nevertheless he was relieved once he had posted it.

The package found its way safely to its destination in Paris where some students who had worked before with Sum Taeyoung simply opened it then posted the six brown envelopes it contained. A Parisian postal stamp was far less likely to stimulate any great interest. One from Minsk would have undoubtedly done so.

At six locations around the world – in the USA; Russia; China; Germany; UK and Brazil, unsuspecting mid-ranking civil servants opened the letters addressed to them. Sum Taeyoung had based his scheme on an incident in 2001 when letters containing powdered anthrax spores were distributed through the US postal system. Some 22 people were targeted in that attack. Five died. All six civil servants targeted by Taeyoung were to die. The letters they received had been impregnated with an especially virulent form of anthrax developed by the rogue bio-weapons manufacturer in Donetsk.

The attack was followed immediately by another message, this time sent to all the leaders who had received Taeyoung's infamous Declaration. It said:

"Ten days ago I issued my Declaration of Intent. This has been received by a wall of silence. I remind you that you now have just 20 days to agree to my terms by first depositing the funds I have demanded. You now have just 35 days for each of you to sign your copy of the Memorandum of Understanding committing you to the terms of the Declaration. There are now just 50 days before a new World Order will be established.

As an indication of the seriousness of my intent, your lack of response has resulted in the death of six civil servants. The blood of these people is on your hands. Your silence has stimulated this action which was directed at soft targets and using old biological warfare techniques. My threat in the Declaration of Intent is based on a much more lethal virus with no known antidote that will be released on a global basis if you do not cooperate.

My Declaration warned that 61 days from the day you received it, if none of my demands have been achieved, or if I have been arrested or harmed in any way, the virus we have within our control will be released in the capital city of each of the nations whose leaders have been sent this Declaration.

You now have 50 days.

Signed
The Spirit of Hwanung

Chapter 21

Bond was still reeling at finding Georgi in his Fairbanks hotel. And that was before Georgi dropped his bombshell.

"What the fuck are you doing here?" he exclaimed to his Georgian friend.

"That's nice," Georgi responded. "I come all the way out here and that's the greeting I get!"

"Bollocks," said Bond. "So, what are you doing here?"

"We think they've found Patterson!"

"Who?" Bond asked.

"What do you mean – who?" Georgi's impatience was blindingly obvious.

"Who's found him, of course," Bond replied, equally shortly.

"The Russians," Georgi told him.

"The Russians! You're joking!" Bond responded. The news was preposterous. "Patterson was supposed to have died ages ago."

"Apparently not," Georgi continued. "As you can imagine, with the Russians having invaded territory owned by America and declared ownership of the international waters of the Bering Strait, every listening device we've got has been directed to their northern activities. And amongst all the audio chatter we hear about a UK scientist who has apparently been found in an abandoned nuclear town in Siberia. Can you believe that?"

"No," Bond agreed. "It's totally unbelievable. How do you know it's authentic?"

"Why shouldn't it be?" Georgi asked him. "Why should the Russians be talking about it if it hasn't happened?"

"Are you sure it's Patterson?" Bond queried, still having difficulty taking in Georgi's news.

"Of course it's Patterson." Georgi's tone was impatient. "Who the bloody hell else would it be? Come on Gene. Wake up. Has the cold got at you?"

Bond ignored the remark. "So where is he? And what's this abandoned nuclear town you're on about?"

Georgi told him about Anadyr-1.

"We think he's now on a small island in the middle of the Bering Strait called Big Diomede. That whole area's become a political maelstrom. Like I just told you, the Russians have declared ownership of the Bering Strait. They've kicked off the Eskimo community that lived on the other Diomede island, Little Diomede which the Americans own and which is only about two miles away from Big Diomede. They've declared the whole area under their military protection."

"Bloody hell," Bond muttered. Georgi continued.

"The American's have gone ape. They've declared the whole thing illegal. They're assembling a naval group to head off to the Bering Strait to challenge Russia's declaration – and, they say, to retrieve the island they rightfully own. Little Diomede might only be a little bit of fucking rock sticking out of an often frozen sea and in part of the world nobody in their right mind would want to go to, but right now it's become the most important bit of real estate on the planet. This has all the makings of becoming the biggest military crisis since Kennedy confronted Khrushchev over the Cuban missiles."

"Good God!" said Bond.

"Quite so," said Georgi. "The Royal Navy's involved too. By coincidence, someone somewhere had done some good forward thinking. The Royal Navy's been saying that because of the melting seas in the Arctic the area's going to become more 'strategically and nautically important.' How prophetic! How bloody right! So they've been running Operation ICEX – a fully blown ice exercise which included the nuclear submarine HMS Astute sailing through the Bering Strait and heading north just before the Russians declared they owned it."

"Astute's been involved in the first under ice action by a Royal Navy sub for more than 10 years. Now she's linked up to an American nuke that's also sailed under the ice, the USS Seawolf. They're at a place known as Ice Camp Sargo, 150 miles or so north of the Alaskan coast. It's supposedly a research base but it's got a serious military side to it too. But there are problems there. Because of climate change the ice is cracking around the camp and navy people and researchers are having to move."

Bond thought for a moment. A suspicion was growing in his mind.

"That's all fascinating, Georgi. But why are you telling me this? Why have you flown all the way to Fairbanks to tell me this?"

There was a short pause.

"Because I need your help. I..."

"Oh no! No you don't," Bond cut his friend off mid sentence. "Not again! No! No! No! I told you before I wasn't going to get involved again in any of your escapades. So, whatever you're thinking, forget it."

"It's up to you, my friend," Georgi sighed. "You're going to be stuck in Fairbanks for some time. There's a blanket ban on all non-military flying in an area covering a 500 mile square to the East of 65° N and 168° W. Check it out. Fairbanks International is closed down. And if you think of training it out of here and catching a plane somewhere else, forget it. Travel right now is chaotic and impossible. You, my friend, are going nowhere."

Bond was horrified. There was nothing wrong with Fairbanks but it wasn't somewhere he would elect to stay for any great period of time. And the thought of just putting a stop on life until the international crisis ended had no appeal.

"So that means you're stuck here too?" Bond challenged.

"Well, er no," Georgi sounded slightly embarrassed. "I've got a lift out of here with the USAF. I've got to be at Fairbanks International about an hour from now otherwise I'm also truly in the shit."

"And you can't get me on that flight?" asked Bond, knowing full well what the answer was going to be.

"No." The answer was emphatic.

"Are you offering me an option?" he asked tentatively, again guessing he knew what the answer would be.

"Yes," Georgi said but added with cynical laughter in

his voice. "But you just said you didn't want to know."

Bond sighed. "OK. What do you want?"

"I'm offering you an opportunity," his friend responded with a hint of triumph in his voice. "You've been on about the melting of the permafrost, what's happening in the Arctic, the impact on the Eskimo community. I'm offering you a chance to see all of that yourself. First hand!"

Four hours later when Bond met up with Sam Noack, his feeling that he should never have agreed to the 'opportunity' Georgi Patarava had presented grew further in his mind. It was a dull afternoon with heavy clouds overhead, flurries of snow in the air and a cold wind blowing in from the north. Bond found Fairbanks Independent Air Services in what looked like an old WW2 hanger, now painted white though the paint was badly faded and patchy. The front of the building had the name of the company in large blue letters and numerous advertising panels, many in poor repair and some hardly readable. There was nothing to suggest that Fairbanks Independent Air Services had at any time in its past seen better days. The bored young girl in the front office took Bond through into the building where amongst a chaos of workbenches, old fuel drums, a couple of dilapidated cars and general mess stood the establishment's proprietor alongside the company's major asset, a four seater Cessna 172. Wearing less than pristine overalls, fancifully decorated boots that once might have been attractive, with long fuzzy hair that fell to his shoulders, and smoking a half burned Cuban cigar, it was difficult to decide which was in the worse condition, the aircraft or its owner.

It was also impossible to guess the man's age. Anything from 30 to 60. He could have been a youngster well battered by life to look more like 60. Or he could have been 60. The odds, Bond thought, were on the latter.

"Sam Noack?" Bond asked, hoping for a negative answer and that the man and the aircraft he wanted were somewhere else and presenting a more reassuring picture than the one that stood before him.

"You bet," the aviator beamed, exhaling a cloud of smoke and dropping an oily rag to the floor to move forward to grasp Bond's hand in a bone-crunching handshake. "I've been expecting you. We're all fired up here and ready to go."

Bond looked at the aircraft. His expression must have given his thoughts away.

"Now don't you worry about a thing," Noack told him. "Old Betty here has been with me a long time and never let me down. She's a Piper Cessna 172 Skyhawk and there's been no other aircraft made in more numbers than the Skyhawk. They've been made in such numbers because people buy 'em. And people buy 'em because they're reliable. Betty's reliable. So have no worries."

Bond almost expected Noack to complete the sentence with a turn of the head and a spit into a hidden spittoon. But the hillbilly character did not go quite that far. Despite the reassurances, Bond found it less than easy not to worry. He knew Georgi had done a cash deal with Noack. God knows for how much. Probably more than Noack would normally earn in a year. But then the task was a bit more than your normal jaunt in a single engined aircraft.

"I want you to go to the Nome Eskimo Community down on the shores of the Norton Sound in the south eastern part of the Bering Sea. It's just over 500 miles from here." Georgi had told Bond. "I've spoken to them at the right sort of level and explained our problem. They're up in arms about what the Russians have done to their people on Little Diomede so when I came along with a request that helps them get a little of their own back, they were only too keen to help. So you'll fly down to Nome and pick up someone who's going to help the navy. Then you'll fly up to a place called Wales and meet up with the navy folk there. Piece of cake!"

"Oh yeh?" said Bond. "A piece of cake. Nome then Wales? Wales? That can't be right."

"It's 109 miles north west from Nome to Wales – mostly north," Georgi responded. "You'll love Wales! It's the closest place in Alaska to Russia. And you'll be able to see what climate change is doing to these places. Right up your street! You should be thanking me for this!"

"And how do I get there?" Bond dreaded the answer.

"I've commissioned a private aircraft. The pilot will have to fly low to avoid the military flying black out. I've tried to get approval for this and it should be alright. But it will be better if the pilot flies low."

"You're joking! What do you mean – should be alright?"

"It'll be fine," Georgi reassured him. "So long as you keep low."

Bond took a deep gulp of whisky. He needed it. "And why aren't you doing this? Why me?"

"I can't leave the shop for any length of time," Georgi told him. "I've got the crisis with the Russians and don't forget Sum Taeyoung's threat."

"What's happening about that?" With everything else Bond had nearly forgotten about their arch enemy's threat. "Now it seems Patterson's alive, doesn't that mean Sum Taeyoung's virus threat is dead?"

"I don't know," Georgi confessed then told Bond about the death of civil servants around the world, the virus spreading across the Ukraine and Taeyoung's new message.

"We've been tasked to track Taeyoung down and take him out once and for all."

"Any progress?" Bond asked.

"No," said Georgi with a tone of despair. "We've got nowhere and we've only got about a month now before he carries out his threat. We don't know if the virus he says he's going to use is from Siberia – though that seems unlikely now – from a secret lab in Donetsk that's trying to break away from the Ukraine, or something else. We think he used anthrax to kill the civil servants. But who knows? With that mad bastard anything's possible."

"Bloody hell!" Bond muttered, refilling his whisky glass. "I feel like getting seriously pissed."

Chapter 22

It was mid-afternoon when the explosion ripped through the grey, concrete four storey building, demolishing it completely in a huge cloud of cement dust and smoke, causing a major accident on the adjacent Ganbyeonbuk-Ro, the Riverside North Road, and stopping traffic on the nearby Hannam Bridge. The explosion echoed across the busy commercial districts. Seoul officials declared it to be a "catastrophic explosion caused by a gas leak" but Georgi Patarava, Sum Taeyoung and a few others knew otherwise. This had been a deliberately targeted attack on the rogue South Korean. It had completely wiped out the offices of Sustainable Development Brokers International, the business owned by Taeyoung. With the building reduced to a pile of smouldering rubble, the death toll would take some time to determine, but those who had perpetrated the attack were not to know for a while afterwards that, contrary to their intelligence, Sum Taeyoung had not been on the premises when they blew it up.

Anticipating such an event, Sum Taeyoung had instigated a set of actions designed to protect himself from his enemies. It was not the first time he had undertaken such precautionary measures. He moved his personal operations from the SDBI offices to other premises in a less prestigious part of the massive city of Seoul and a considerable distance from the River Han. The small private apartment became extensively equipped with counter-surveillance technology and provided a perfectly adequate base for his terrorist activities. From here he was plotting the delivery of his next warning to the world community. He had changed his personal physique, crashing several stones off his previously obscene body weight, cutting his long flowing hair, then shaving his head but leaving a moustache, and swapping his normal colourful Eastern attire for modern New York jeans and jackets.

His plan to dominate the management of the planet was teetering on the threshold of collapse. He would abolish the United Nations and replace it with an organisation and become its Chairman. It would be supported by all leading nations because they were fearful of the threat of an attack by an ancient, highly active and unknown virus.

He continued to hear news from the Ukraine about what was being described by local officials as an outbreak of swine disease but in truth was still causing much head scratching as to what it really was. The deadly virus was running rife across the country and adjacent territories. Fingers of suspicion still pointed at the secret research base at Shelkostantsiya, some 30 kilometres from Kharkov, which rumours persistently said involved US military experts and even the CIA. The reality was that more than 20 Ukrainian soldiers were known to have died and some 200 were hospitalised. The Donetsk People's Republic intelligence reported "Californian Flu is leaking from the same place where research into this virus has been carried out."

Maintaining a watch on this but from a distance – from Seoul, Sum Taeyoung continued to wonder if the truth was that the virus he had brought in from Siberia for analysis in a laboratory in Donetsk was the cause of the outbreak. If so, the subterfuge he had developed around his fictitious virus was being outmanoeuvred by real events.

Meanwhile his messages to the world's leaders were still being met by a wall of silence. What he did not know was he was far from being ignored.

In London, in the communications centre of the EU Intelligence Service at Wapping, Georgi Patarava found himself at the centre of an international reaction to the threats of the South Korean. Part of the reason for this was that he had encountered the man before and twice been successful in destroying Taeyoung's plots. American and European agencies knew this so the team at Wapping became central to a developing activity involving national agencies in Washington, Brussels, even Moscow and the UK Government's Communications HQ in Cheltenham.

"I guess if it hasn't killed him then the action taken against the SDBI HQ in Seoul might at least have warned Taeyoung that we have linked him to the so-called Spirit of Hwanung. I doubt he'd know that for certain. We're not the only ones interested in blowing his building up. Taeyoung has quite a lot of enemies around the planet. Anyway, my guess is he still doesn't know that Patterson is alive," Georgi told his team.

Assembled around the project table were Jane, the only English representative in Georgi's multinational team, Olivia from Belgium, Leonie from Switzerland and Jacub from Poland. Also with them was a guest, Graeme Samsom from the UK's CONTEST programme.

"We also know that Taeyoung's threat has some element of being flawed. He said the lethal virus he's got is from the hole in Siberia that killed two British geophysicists. We know it didn't because we now know Patterson is alive, according to the Russians. We therefore know that the virus he was exposed to from the hole in Siberia is not as lethal as Taeyoung is making it out to be. We also know that what killed civil servants around the world wasn't some mysterious 30,000 year old virus that escaped the melting ice in Siberia. It was anthrax, albeit a newly manufactured anthrax concoction."

"So that raises the question – do we take Taeyoung's threat seriously? We know he is a nutter – an extremely clever one who has connections around the world. We know he is capable of putting very complex plots together – though we have twice stopped him delivering them. What we don't know is, is the virus he alleges he got from a Siberian hole the same one he alleges – wrongly – to have killed off two British environmental geophysicists? Or has he got something else? And if he can use a new anthrax based virus to kill off people at various locations around the world, has he access to more of the same, or something different and equally lethal?"

These were, of course, rhetorical questions. Nobody in his team or anyone else knew what Taeyoung was up to. Feeling as if his briefing had taken them up a cul-de-sac, Georgi invited their visitor to introduce himself and explain what his interests were.

A slim neat man, bald but with thick dark eyebrows, Samsom spoke quietly but with authority.

"CONTEST," he told them, "is the UK strategy for countering terrorism and has a particular focus on issues to do with CBRN."

"You please excuse the interruption," broke in Jacub. "What is CBRN?"

"Sorry," apologised their guest. "It's too easy to slip into the jargon. CBRN – chemical, biological, radiological and nuclear. Our work is to protect the nation from CBRN attack by terrorists."

"Our objectives," he continued, "cover three work streams – Pursue, Protect and Prepare. The objective is to stop terrorists from carrying out an attack. We work closely with the police and various intelligence agencies at home and abroad. Their task is to identify who might be intent on acquiring or using CBRN. A serious amount of resource goes into ensuring as best we can that we get early indications of any terrorist plan to deploy CBRN in the UK. We also track the illicit trading of CBRN and keep an ear to the ground for any evidence of state CBRN programmes anywhere around the world where security has been compromised."

"Are attacks using CBRN common?" asked Olivia.

"Fortunately no," Samsom replied. "The best known attack – well, best known to the public anyway – was an act of domestic terrorism perpetrated on March 20, 1995 in the Kasumigaseki Station of Tokyo's subway system.

It was undertaken by members of the cult movement Aum Shinrikyo. It killed 13 people and left more than 6,000 sick or injured."

"How did they do that?" asked Olivia.

"They used Sarin contained in plastic bags which they then punctured with penknives and left on the floors of trains."

"And what is Sarin?" probed Olivia.

"Sarin was created by accident – an accident many have subsequently come to regret. It was a by-product from work being done on compounds created from insecticides at the notorious IG Farben chemical company in Nazi Germany. In 1938 they hit on the Substance 146 by accident. It's a formula that causes catastrophic damage to the nervous system. The chemical they created had the grim distinction of being many times more lethal than cyanide!"

"It's quite easy to make Substance 146 but it's difficult to make it without killing yourself in the process. It's that lethal. And having made it, it's even more difficult to use it. Under the Chemical Weapons Convention it's listed as a Schedule 1 substance, making it one of the most restricted chemicals in existence."

"So I take it from that that whatever Taeyoung proposes to use if he is going ahead with an attack around the world, it's not going to be easy?" Georgi responded.

"No, very difficult," Samsom told him.

"And difficult to detect?"

"I guess that depends," Samsom replied, thoughtfully. "It depends what he intends to use, how he intends to transport it, how he intends to deploy it, and where."

"Where would you look?" asked Jacub.

"I've no idea," was the honest reply from their guest. "Without knowing what he's going to use and where, that makes it very difficult."

"Assume it's a virus," Georgi said. "A highly contagious virus with no known antidote."

"In a way it doesn't matter what it is," Samsom told him. "With CBRN we assume from the outset we're dealing with deadly materials. Deadly materials are enormously difficult to transport around the world but equally they can be almost impossible to detect. And if you don't know where the targets are, that makes it even more difficult. It's like looking for a needle in a haystack when the needle's made from hay!"

"So what would you do?" Georgi asked.

Samsom reflected on the question for some time. Eventually, with a sigh, he responded.

"You have to get rid of the central perpetrator," he told the group.

"Kill Taeyoung?" replied Georgi.

"Yes," said Samsom.

"But we've already tried that and failed."

"But that wasn't an attack aimed specifically and individually at one person. You attacked a building you thought he was in. What you need is a more targeted action."

"So you're talking about assassination," said Olivia.

"I'd call it state sanctioned homicide," replied Samsom.

"Difficult to get sanctioned," Georgi reflected.

"But not impossible," Samsom responded.

"Maybe," said Georgi.

"It's easier if you have a situation where the target is guaranteed," Samsom told them. He seemed to know much more than just about CBRN. "You need to build a scenario where the target is an absolute certainty. That's a long way from bombing a building in which you think your target is located."

"Point taken," admitted Georgi. Fortunately his team had had nothing to do with the bombing of the SDBI offices. Indeed, Georgi had cautioned against it from the outset on the very principles Samsom was now voicing.

"We need to lure Taeyoung into a position where there can be no doubt who he is and where he can be a clean and uncomplicated target," said Georgi.

"Quite so," agreed Samsom.

There was silence around the table for a while.

"I think I have a plan," Georgi eventually told his group.

Chapter 23

Bill Patterson had no idea where they were except that it was perhaps one of the wildest, remotest, most desolate of places he had ever seen but somehow it held a raw and basic beauty. They had flown from Anadyr-1 for more than three hours, Nika huddled up to him the whole way. They refuelled at a military fuel dump in the middle of nowhere before arriving on a small rocky island surrounded by a sea speckled with ice. There had been the most emotional of reunions as Nika was reunited with her family.

Patterson, relieved to find the senior officer on the island spoke good English, launched into an attack, demanding his repatriation and the release of Nika and her family. His efforts hit a brick wall.

"I am awaiting instructions as to what to do with you all," the officer told him.

"You're holding us illegally," Patterson argued.

"No, no. Quite the contrary," the officer responded, smiling and being almost excessively polite. "You were trespassing on Russian military territory. That is punishable in law. But I wait for instructions. Nobody at the moment seems to know what to do with you. You were not expected – not in our plans. So I wait to be told what to do. You must wait also."

"If you are formally holding us for trespassing then you should charge us," Patterson told him. "To hold us without charging us is illegal. And, you have to agree, to hold us on this barren rock of an island in the middle of a sea is almost inhuman. It's probably in violation of international law. And, anyway, where the hell are we?"

"You're on Ratmanov Island in the middle of the Bering Strait," the Russian officer told him. Then in the spirit of the friendship he seemed keen to encourage, added, "If you climb to any height here you can see Russia in one direction and America in the other. The two superpowers are closer here to each other than anywhere on the planet."

Patterson felt frustrated, angry and yet relieved to be away from Anadyr-1 though Ratmanov Island was hardly representative of a hugely positive step.

"What brought you to Anadyr-1?" the Scotsman asked the Russian. "You were clearly not looking for us. You admit we were a surprise to you."

The Russian officer considered his reply before saying "we were there as part of a wide-ranging asset audit of the area."

"Is that anything to do with gold?" Patterson asked.

"Yes," the Russian admitted. "But it's about other minerals too – and precious stones – like diamonds. Our President is concerned to improve our ability to extract these materials from this difficult part of the world. So we are looking to improve the infrastructure."

Patterson was curious. "That sounds like something for civil engineers, not the military."

"Ah yes," said the Russian, still clearly thinking what

he could say and how much he told this foreigner. "But there are many reasons why this area is becoming more strategically important. It's not just about gold."

"Why?" asked Patterson.

"Oh!" responded the Russian. "Now we are going further than I can."

And that was the end of the first conversation Bill Patterson had with the senior Russian representative on the island. That changes were happening here was obvious. A conglomeration of buildings were huddled together at this end of the island underneath the towering colossus of an enormous cliff. Clearly located here to offer some shelter from the prevailing weather, it was quite apparent that some buildings had been here for years and others were new. It was also easy to discern some soldiers had been here for a long time while others were recent arrivals still trying to become accustomed to the raw conditions of the island. Patterson noticed that every day at first light, whatever the weather, a group of soldiers departed their quarters and climbed a crude and steep flight of wooden steps until they were out of his sight. He wondered why and where the steps took them.

Whilst the senior Russian officer was clearly being cautious about what he was telling Patterson, it was equally clear there was no hostility here. Far from it. He seemed keen to foster a friendly relationship and was as curious as Patterson to know more about the background to Nika and her family.

"My name is Vladimir Antonov," he told Patterson at their second encounter. "Lieutenant General Antonov." And he provided an English speaking soldier as a translator so, at last, Patterson could hear Nika's story. It also provided Patterson and Nika the first opportunity to talk extensively to each other though, through the translation of a Russian soldier, sometimes with difficulty, at best uneasy.

"What's going .... to happen to us?" Nika asked, holding his hand firmly as they sat together with the Russian soldier. She talked with hesitancy, still not used to conversing much with anyone.

"I don't know," Patterson told her. "I'm trying to get us freed but there is no sign of that happening yet."

"Don't let them split us," she pleaded.

"I'll do my best to keep you all together," he promised, not at all convinced he would be able to.

"I meant ..... you and me," she said, tightening the grip on his hand and leaning over to give him a short kiss, embarrassed by the presence of the Russian who obligingly turned away from them with a smile.

Out of personal interest, Lieutenant General Vladimir Antonov sat in on some of their questioning sessions with Nika which were held in as informal an atmosphere as the prevailing circumstances could allow. They were all keen to hear her story. It was, after all, remarkable.

Patterson marvelled at how the young Nika, dropped into a totally alien world and now crowded by people, coped with what was clearly a testing ordeal for her. Confirming what he had already discovered, Nika's family, she told them, were members of a fundamental Russian Orthodox sect, the Old Believers, who had a style of worship dating back to the 17th Century.

Traditionally at odds with the establishment since the days of Peter the Great, the arrival of the Bolsheviks only made matters worse and families of Old Believers fled from persecution, some eventually finding themselves driven further and further north, eventually into the great forests of Siberia.

By the time Nika was born her family had become totally isolated. Incredulously, until they arrived at Anadyr-1, she had not seen another human being other than members of her family.

There were so many questions to ask it was difficult not to overwhelm her.

"Did you know Russia had been involved in a mighty war?" they asked her. "A war against Germany?"

"No," she replied. She did not know where Germany was.

"How much do you know of the rest of the world? Have you ever heard of America?"

Only from what she had read at Anadyr-1, she told them. Taught by her parents how to read, the magazines and other printed material the family found there had been a revelation to them, showing them a world they previously did not know existed and much of which they did not understand.

Before reaching the abandoned nuclear town, the nomadic family lived wherever food was available. They scavenged materials from the forest to build their own shelters, moving on from place to place when food supplies dwindled or when dwellings needed replacing. Frequently they were on the edge of famine being reliant on what animals they could trap which provided not only nourishment but skins for making clothes.

Those listening to the story were amazed at the skills and capabilities Stepan had developed. His story was almost incredulous. He could hunt through forests and across the tundra barefooted, sometimes being away for days and sleeping in the open in 40 degrees of frost. The only way he had of capturing animals was through trapping and those were skills he had been taught by his father. When he was successful he often had to carry the dead animal for miles back to where they lived. He frequently trekked for more than a day with the dead weight of an elk over his back. When there was no meat, they lived off what they could grow – mostly carrots and potatoes. Potato patties mixed with ground rye and hemp seeds were a frequent item on their menu.

They had few possessions but treasured the pots and pans Patterson had discovered them using at Anadyr-1. Whilst they could make their own clothes and shoes, they had no ability to create any metal objects so the pots and pans were of enormous value and treasured because they were irreplaceable and not because of what they were made from.

It had been her brother on one of his hunting trips across the tundra who discovered Anadyr-1. He viewed it from the nearby hills for some days without seeing any signs of life. In comparison to the shelter in which he normally lived, the solid buildings of the empty nuclear town were luxurious beyond his wildest dreams. He had difficulty in persuading his parents to the idea but eventually they moved in.

"How long ago was that?" Patterson asked.

Nika did not know but it was obviously some years back. The family became conscious that the older and well inhabited town of Anadyr was some distance away but nobody seemed to come to this area of dilapidated buildings, some of which they slowly developed to become their home.

Patterson tried to test Nika again on the subject of gold, but without giving the reason away to the Russians. It was impossible and his cryptic questioning got him nowhere.

"Does the name George Symons mean anything to you?" he asked, changing the direction of questions. It seemed like a long shot but worth a try. He was not surprised at her answer.

"No," she told him.

But Patterson wasn't content with that and asked Nika to ask the other members of her family if the name meant anything to them.

"Yes," she replied after consulting them. "George Symons was someone my parents knew. He travelled with them for some time." Which confirmed what Symons had said in his brief message that Patterson had read.

"George Symons?" queried Vladimir Antonov. "He has also been here."

"On Ratmanov!" Patterson could hardly believe what he was hearing.

"I remember seeing the name in old records. It was so unusual to see an English name. I remember it," the Russian told him. "Russian military came here first in

1917. There's a reference in the record that talks about 'Russian bosses coming from Chukotka in 1917 as part of the Revolution'. The references are hard to read and strange but they had an Englishman with them called George Symons. He was a spy."

Patterson was amazed. How on earth had Symons got to this Godforsaken place? And why? And now it turns out he's a spy.

"How do you know he was a spy?" he asked Antonov.

"Because documents here show our people did some research on him. It was so strange that an Englishman should have got to Big Diomede. And they found he worked for the BSSB which was the British Secret Service Bureau today known as MI5 and MI6. What do you know about him?"

"Nothing really," Patterson responded. "I saw his name on a document at Anadyr-1. It's such a coincidence to have seen his name there and now to encounter him here."

"What sort of document?" clearly Antonov's curiosity had been aroused but Patterson was concerned not to tell him too much.

"It was a copy of a message from him to his home. It was one of the few things at Anadyr-1 written in English," he told him.

And Antonov left it at that though Patterson felt the Russian was hardly satisfied by the answers given.

In the days that followed Patterson and Nika's family were given a fair degree of freedom by Antonov. They were allocated rooms with Patterson sharing a bunk room with Stepan and Nika sharing with her parents.

Patterson and Nika, sometimes with Stepan, explored the tiny island. There was not much of it. Antonov was confident there was no way they could escape and nobody anywhere nearby for them to signal to or any means by which to do so. So the Russian did not lock them up. In any case, he had no personnel available to act as guards for every hour of the day.

There were one or two areas out of bounds to the detained visitors. One was the wooden steps the soldiers took each day. They started near the huts in which they lived and disappeared sharply uphill and out of sight. At risk of upsetting Antonov and taking advantage of one particular moment when the area near the steps was deserted, Patterson ran up them, counting 197 as he did. At the top was a fence and a locked gate, the other side of which was a concrete pathway leading to a bunker-like building. The view from here was sensational with the mainlands of Russia and America clearly in view and, to the east, another small island perhaps no more than a couple of miles away. It was not difficult to conclude that the bunker-like building was an observation post of some sort which, from the way soldiers regularly went up and down the steps, was constantly manned. Patterson had a moment of sympathy for the soldiers having to beat their way up and down those 197 steps, especially when they were deep in snow and ice and with a howling, snow filled wind cutting into their faces.

The other area out of bounds was obviously a new installation and though Patterson knew nothing about such things it did not need expert knowledge to recognise it as a multiple rocket launcher. Antonov had said something about this area becoming "more strategically important." That a missile launching facility had recently been established here endorsed that beyond any doubt.

It was whilst rummaging around in an old wooden hut that Patterson made two discoveries. The first was a rough, torn and faded map of the Bering Strait with two islands shown on it, Big Diomede and Little Diomede. Marked on the bigger of the two islands that was clearly what Antonov called Ratmanov was the flag of Russia. On the smaller island was the flag of the USA. Patterson was excited by the thought that he was only a couple of miles away from American territory. This was information Antonov had kept from them.

There were all sorts of markings on the walls of the hut, mostly initials from soldiers or explorers who had been in it at some time or another. He was surprised to find one more than 100 years old but then realised that in such a cold climate as here timber buildings survived extraordinary lengths of time. This hut was possibly one of the earliest buildings on the island. He wondered about the people who had lived here before the Russians took it over.

There was one etching into the timber that really caught his interest. It was very old, faded and needed some careful cleaning before he could read it. It read

Au 65°4531.071 -169°711.1318 GS

Chapter 24

It was, to put it mildly, four and a half hours of flying the likes of which Bond had never previously encountered, not that he had flown in a four seater aircraft before let alone anywhere like Alaska. Fighting a persistent northerly wind that was encouraging the aircraft to drift south all the time, Noack's navigational skills seemed to be limited to following rivers, on this trip first the Tanana then the Yukon which together fortunately covered most of the journey west from Fairbanks to Nome. Keeping to instructions from Georgi Patarava, Noack flew appreciably below 2,000 feet which gave Gene Bond a fantastic view of the spectacular scenery with the twisting and turning rivers cutting through vast areas of forest and frequently through steep-sided gorges. It held Bond mesmerised to the window and the time passed surprisingly quickly.

Nome, it transpired, is designed on a grid basis. They overflew the small and neatly laid out township before landing at the airport adjacent Norton Sound, an inlet off the Bering Sea. Nome had all the signs of what Bond thought a frontier town should look like with a motley collection of building styles, wide streets, open spaces and its airport right on its fringes. Consequently it was only a mile long taxi drive to where Georgi had booked him into a hotel right on the shores of Norton Sound. The nearby street was separated from the beach by a line of enormous boulders acting as a defence from the sea.

It was over a generously large whisky that Bond heard the story of the town's name from the bartender.

"It's a mistake," the man told him. "The story goes that a British cartographer copied an ambiguous annotation made by a British officer on a nautical chart while on a voyage up the Bering Strait. The officer had written '?Name' next to the unnamed cape. The map reader mistook this for 'C Nome' – or 'Cape Nome.' And the name stuck. Now I don't know how true it is but it makes a good story."

Bond agreed, it was a good story. He finished his drink and retired to bed, shattered from the journey.

If Peter had a surname, Bond never got to know it. How Georgi Patarava had found him and made contact would also remain a mystery. But at breakfast in the hotel on the shores of Norton Sound, Gene Bond, the English sustainable development consultant, met Peter, the young Inuit who somehow had been cajoled into helping the Royal Navy stage a rescue mission on Big Diomede to snatch Bill Patterson away from the Russians before they sent him off to their homeland. With short cut dark hair, bright eyes, stubble beard and standing a few inches short of six feet, Peter's solid handshake matched his fit and athletic looks. It was obvious from the outset that he was keen to help.

"What the Russians have done on Little Diomede is disgusting," he told Bond with no disguise to the passion within him about what had happened on the tiny island in the Bering Strait.

"They say they did it for humanitarian reasons," said Bond. "They 'evacuated' the Eskimos from an untenable situation."

"Inuits," Peter corrected him. "The people living on Little Diomede were Inuits. Eskimo is a more collective term and now seen by some to be offensive. My people are Inuits."

"I'm sorry," Bond responded. "I didn't mean to offend."

"No offence taken," Peter reassured him. "You weren't to know."

"I fully agree what the Russians did was wrong. It was a forceful evacuation. But I guess life couldn't be that easy there," Bond suggested.

"It wasn't," agreed Peter. "And no doubt about it, it was getting more difficult. But life for Inuits across Canada, Alaska, Greenland and Chukotka in the far east of Russia is getting more and more difficult. Many are having to reconsider their traditional lifestyles."

"Why?" asked Bond, guessing he knew the answer anyway.

"We have survived for hundreds of years in harsh environments," Peter told him. "They've been our traditional homes in which we've developed our own life styles. Now climate change is threatening everything. The weather is increasingly unpredictable. We have skills inherited down generations and we know when the land looks and feels different. We can't hunt as we used to. We cannot travel safely because the sea ice is changing. It's so bad and so incredibly dangerous now. We've even lost experienced hunters through the ice. The melting of our glaciers in summer is now such that it's dangerous for us to get to many of the traditional hunting and harvesting places."

"How many people are impacted by this?" Bond asked.

"There are about 155,000 Inuits across the areas I mentioned."

"And climate change is threatening them all?"

"Yes," Peter told him. "I thought you'd ask about these things so I brought a copy of this. It's an article by Shiela Watt-Cloutier who's internationally respected as an Inuit activist and humanitarian." He passed a photocopy of a magazine report to Bond. It read:

"Climate change is not just a theory to us in the Arctic, it is a stark and dangerous reality. Human-induced climate change is undermining the ecosystem upon which Inuit depend for their cultural survival. The Arctic is not wilderness or a frontier, it is our home. Ways of life that have allowed the Inuit to survive for hundreds of years in what is for most people a harsh environment are now threatened by changes induced by humans far south of the areas where the Inuit live.

The human rights of the Inuit to decide their own life-style and habitat have been threatened as a result of these changes in nature. For generations uncounted, Inuit have observed the environment and have accurately predicted the weather enabling them to travel safely on the sea-ice and hunt seals, whales, walrus, and polar bears.

Inuit do not hunt for sport or recreation. Hunters put food on the table. People further south on the globe go to the supermarket, Inuit go on the sea-ice. Eating what Inuit hunt is at the very core of what it means to be Inuit. When they can no longer hunt what is on the sea-ice their entire existence as a people is threatened."

"This is frightening and disturbing stuff," said Bond, passing the article back.

"But the evidence is everywhere," Peter responded. "Melting permafrost causing beach slumping and increased erosion. We're seeing increased snowfalls, longer sea-ice free seasons and species of fish and birds like barn owl, robins, pin-tailed ducks and salmon have been observed in northern areas where they've never been seen before. There's even been an invasion of mosquitoes and black flies. Alaskan Inuit tell me their natural ice cellars in which they store food are melting."

Bond had good feelings about Peter. They were on the same wavelength despite the enormous differences in their cultures, backgrounds and way of life.

"It reminds me of the Butterfly Effect," he told his new friend.

"What's that?" Peter had never heard of it.

"It's a theory which basically links causes and effects. In its simplest and often quoted metaphorical example, the fluttering of a butterfly's wings in one part of the world will eventually cause some sort of effect on the opposite side of the planet. What I hear you telling me is that the way we conduct our daily lives in our modern world is impacting directly and very negatively on the lifestyle of Inuits across the extreme northern parts of the planet. We, in effect, are prejudicing the sustainability of your communities."

Peter nodded. "That about sums it up," he agreed. "It's tragic."

They fell into a reflective silence until Bond changed the subject.

"OK, tell me about the Diomede Islands."

Chapter 25

While Georgi Patarava had a plan so also did Sum Taeyoung. His was focussed on the distribution of a deadly virus and its delivery to certain strategically important locations around the planet. Central to his plot was a world-wide group of people who, one way or another, were at odds with their circumstances. His plan had been inspired by the so-called Arab Spring of 2010/2011. Here was a revolution that spread like a raging forest fire and at astonishing speed across several nations, ignited by the dissatisfaction of youth in their respective governments and fuelled by the power of social media and digital technology. It was a flame of revolution sparked by widening rifts between the haves and the have-nots, widespread corruption in political seats of power and youngsters without hope.

To kick-start his plan Sum Taeyoung turned to a group of people he had deployed before, capitalising on their disillusionment with the establishment as a whole. In his previous exploits with them he had used the name Hwanung – the mythological first king of the Koreans, to conceal his real identity. He did the same as he returned to Paris to meet the group of youngsters he had first engaged with on what he had called The Acionna Projects. It was a project that went sadly wrong because of the intervention of Georgi Patarava and Gene Bond. The plan had been to attack three strategically important dams in different parts of the world as a demonstration as how vulnerable the global community is to shortages of its most essential natural resource – water. Because of Patarava and Bond the plan was never delivered but the publicity it generated across the planet unquestionably raised the issue to the general public.

The group of young Parisian rebels was at the heart of his new plan. A multinational group, Paris Guerriers Urbains – or PGU for short – attracted youngsters from the banlieue – the impoverished areas of the city outside the famous eight lane Périphérique that circumnavigates Paris and within which is the commerce and culture that makes the French capital internationally renowned. Outside the Périphérique live the 'have-nots'.

Dating back to the1980s, PGU was formed by postgraduates, many from families with communist backgrounds who, with the collapse of the Soviet Union, did what many of their comrades did around the world – they turned to environmental campaigning. This group took inspiration from the Cult of Santez Anne with its ancient Celtic antecedents, pagan links to water worship and connections to Brittany, the French area famed for its extraordinary fountains, and the Gallo-Roman water goddess Acionna, with origins in the ancient Orléanais region of France. Sum Taeyoung 'borrowed' the name Acionna as a code for his proposed attack on dams with the A standing for the target in America, C for China and I for the Iberian Peninsular.

Taeyoung was surprised to find that life in the

banlieue had if anything deteriorated since his last visit. Discontent amongst the youngsters was rife and talk of insurrection along the lines of the 2005 riots was widespread. Back then, rioting spread across France, involving most of its major cities and causing huge amounts of damage estimated in the hundreds of millions of Euros.

Now, adding to their feelings of insecurity and concerns for the future, came disturbing news from America. The Washington Post had scooped the rest of the world's media with a story that subsequently hit the headlines everywhere. America was sending a fleet of warships into the Arctic to confront Russian claims of ownership to the Bering Strait and reclaim occupancy of the island of Little Diomede. It was, said the Washington Post, the most testing time for the two super powers since the Cuban crisis involving Kennedy and Khrushchev. In the UK and elsewhere it rekindled memories of the battle fleet sailing for the far off Falkland Islands.

"Are We Going To Hold Our Breath Again?" the Washington Post's headline asked, reminding readers how the world held its collective breath as Russian missile carrying ships headed towards a US naval blockade. With fingers poised on nuclear buttons, on that occasion Khrushchev had backed down and the world breathed a sigh of relief as it moved away from the brink of nuclear holocaust.

Now, adding to the despondent mood of the Parisian youngsters, the prospect of a confrontation between Russia and the US added to the global mess as they perceived it to be. It was beyond all Sum Taeyoung had hoped for and provided fertile ground upon which to sow the seeds of his idea. He would gain the enthusiastic involvement of the PGU, then spread the idea of the Hwanung Solution via social media to other youth groups around the world. Once the momentum had been well established, he would, if it came to deploying his threat, demonise key groups to become involved in the distribution of the virus.

The French youngsters were no exception in their loathing of their political leaders, international corporate business and the establishment in general. Around the planet discontented and disenchanted youth looked to the future with little hope. In Greece, with more than 60% of its youngsters out of work, Marxism had suddenly become the counterbalance to what was perceived to be a Germany dominated Eurozone and a system with corruption rife amongst the elite, and provided a new doctrine and ways of thinking amongst the young. In America protests about police action against young blacks were reaching epidemic proportions and the 'Black Lives Matter' campaign had gone global. Hundreds of youngsters clashed with the police in London's Hyde Park and riots were reported as far afield as Melbourne, Singapore and Scandinavia.

Deploying his usual charm, persuasiveness and cunning, it did not take long for Taeyoung to re-engage with the PGU and enthuse them towards the 'Hwanung Solution' based on his 'Declaration Of Intent'. After all, in many ways it was a mirror image of their own discontent. They too had declared capitalism to be redundant but now along came their South Korean inspirer offering a new model and one based on principles they recognised – from the Han dynasty, Confucius, Bahá'u'lláh and Hwanung.

They were totally in line with the concerns Hwanung expressed, managing the largest population of humans the planet has known; the massive expansion of consumerism; the pressure on critical resources; pollution; climate change; mass movements of people; the widening gap between those who have and those who have not; now serious unrest between the superpowers, and politicians everywhere who, they believed, had lost all connection to ordinary people.

With the PGU working for him, and especially its members who were masters of the social media and the digital world, support was rapidly gained from youth groups around the world. They were tasked with taking to the streets in support of the Hwanung Solution, raising awareness and generating commitment. What amazed Sum Taeyoung was the speed with which the whole campaign grew. Within a week, three million names had been added to a database of supporters and groups established in twelve centres around the world. It was progress way beyond his expectations.

Adding to his seemingly massive swing in fortune from his recent despair that his plan was going nowhere, now he received news that truly excited him. Via email came a message from an office within the United Nations. It told him his communication to world leaders had been received, had been considered and was being taken extremely seriously. To that end, senior members of the UN together with political representatives wished to meet him. The senior politicians could not be named and would be anonymous up until the meeting. A date was suggested. The occasion was the next meeting of the Bilderberg Group. The venue would be the Château du Lac hotel, 30 kilometres south of Brussels city centre.

Chapter 26

Back in London from his unscheduled visit to the north coast of Scotland, Alexander Fitzpatrick's life was to take yet another unexpected turn. His mine was now in the militarily guarded zone surrounding the hole in Siberia where his two contracted geophysicists were supposed to be analysing how the hole had been created. Unable to suppress the news any more, Fitzpatrick had at last declared to people in his company that Bailey and Patterson had gone missing. It was a mystery. He had no idea where they were. Siberia was, of course, a challenging and often dangerous place to be, he told them. He declared his astonishment that the hospital at Anadyr reported the two had been there and been forcibly taken away by an unknown gang of men. The wrecked bus in which they had been taken from the hospital had been discovered with several bodies in it, but not those of the two British scientists.

Fitzpatrick adopted a consistent story for both his business associates and the media. He was astonished by the whole episode. He now did not know where the two geophysicists were. He had no idea why they had gone to the hospital at Anadyr except for what officials there were saying – they had succumbed to a virus emanating from the hole they were researching. He could offer no explanation as to why they had been taken from the hospital or by whom. Fitzpatrick was totally perplexed.

In reality, the only people he knew to be aware of the truth were Georgi Patarava, Gene Bond and Janka Koldun. The first of these, because he did not officially exist and worked for an organisation that also did not exist, was unlikely to break cover and leak the story. The same basically applied to Bond. He could also be expected to remain silent. Where Koldun was now Fitzpatrick had no idea and really did not care. He had contributed to the mess in northern Scotland and was unlikely to stick his head above the parapet.

By now Siberian officials had admitted that a virus had escaped the permafrost when the explosion that created the hole occurred. But they were adamant it was a passive virus and of no danger to humans. The continued closure of the area was, they said, because of safety reasons. The land was, they said, unstable because of the melting permafrost. The whereabouts of the two British scientists continued to be investigated but there was suspicion it linked to an illegal aircraft landing and departure at the airport at Ugolny. It was being assumed that was how they left Siberia but there was no conclusive evidence to link the two incidents.

The blanket closure of the area was an economic disaster for Fitzpatrick. This was a critical stage in the mine's development with preliminary work completed and extraction about to commence. Unable to demonstrate his business plan and timeline were not compromised and that he was on course to deliver when he said he would, banks and investors were becoming twitchy. Cash flow was being hit as costs continued to grow and with no income by which to offset them. The strain on Imperial Mining was like a pressure cooker with the lid screwed down – but with steam appearing through cracks at the edges! Fitzpatrick appealed by letter, followed up by numerous telephone calls, to the governor of the Chukotka Autonomous Okrug, the Russian equivalent of a federal area, based in Anadyr and which covered the area in which both the mine and hole are situated. His plea was for work on the gold mine to continue. It was, he said, in the interests not only of his company and its shareholders but of the economy of the area too.

Meantime, knowing that the wheels of bureaucracy in any part of Russia grind forward with mind-numbing slowness, Fitzpatrick greased a few palms of strategically helpful people in the area which enabled some degree of work to continue, albeit discreetly and on a far smaller scale than otherwise would have been the case. It enabled a small team of expert geologists and miners to continue to work their way towards where seams of gold were thought to be located according to initial survey work including numerous test holes. Simultaneously, work continued on the development and maintenance of the vital infrastructure necessary to support the mine when it became fully productive, including a road to the coast. There it was proposed to build a small harbour in the expectation that climate change and reduced sea icing would eventually enable extracted gold to be shipped.

Imperial Mining's Siberian gold mine is in the rolling tundra wilderness some 120 miles north of the small town of Kanchalan which lies on the Kanchalan River. It is conspicuously more east than other mines in Siberia such as those in Kabul or the Olimpiada mine, or lesser known ones in places such as Karalveem and Valunistoye. Its logistics plan included the road – more like a flattened down track – which is partly on terra firma but has some sections as ice highways across the lakes of the tundra. It was well developed before the compulsory evacuation of the area, having been established to enable exploration equipment to be transported to the mine site. But, as the senior engineer reported to Fitzpatrick, it would also be needed to transport gold out of the area when winter returned and the ice road sections were safe.

"Don't expect it to be on the scale of Olimpiada," he had said somewhat jokingly to Fitzpatrick, referring to the massive 400 metre deep open goldmine some three thousand miles east of their own mine. "Trucks leaving there do so with loads worth around $20,000 a time!"

"I wish!" Fitzpatrick had replied.

"But then each truck costs about $1 million. You can afford them when you're extracting a little over $1 million a day!"

The plan was to enable extracted gold to be trucked to Kanchalan then sent by barge down to Anadyr for shipment or to be flown out depending on the time of the year and the volumes of materials involved.

The call that blew all of Fitzpatrick's plans and schedules came from the mine's site manager. It was an unscheduled call late at night.

"What's up, Flannigan?" Fitzpatrick grumbled down

the phone. It had been another bad day and a long one. He had spent the last three hours battling through a backlog of correspondence and now just wanted to go to bed.

"Well, there you go boss," came the very Irish response. "And here's me with news that'll change your day."

"My day's just about over," Fitzpatrick told him, checking his watch. It was 2315 now. It would only be midmorning in Siberia. "What do you want Flannigan?"

"And here's me thinking a bit of good news would cheer you up," said the Irish engineer.

"For Christ's sake Flannigan, what the fuck do you want at this time of night?" Fitzpatrick was getting annoyed. "Get on with it!"

"We've recovered a chunk of gold," came the reply.

"So what?" barked Fitzpatrick. Admittedly this was earlier than he had expected, especially with the reduced activity in the mine. But to find some gold before hitting the main seams was not necessarily surprising.

"It weighs a little over six pounds!" The voice was triumphant.

"Say that again," Fitzpatrick wanted to make sure he had heard right. At any stage of the mine's development this was exceptional news.

"It's just over six pounds," said Flannigan. "It's 2,750 grams."

"Jesus!" Fitzpatrick's mind was whirling. "That's about, er – about $117,000."

Fitzpatrick reached for his iPhone, clicked through to the calculator and checked, speaking out loud as he did so.

"The gold market was $42.3 a gram last time I looked this afternoon." He did the calculation. "$116,325. Shit!"

"And that's not all," Flannigan continued. "That rock was in an area of loose material. There's as much if not more in smaller pieces. I did the calculation too and got the same results. Only I more than doubled my bottom line because there's at least twice the weight of the main piece in the rest that's been recovered. I reckon we've got around a quarter of a million here right now."

Fitzpatrick was finding it difficult to take in Flannigan's news.

"And," Flannigan went on. "My betting is if we have stumbled across this lot we could stumble across more. And that's way before we reach the seams."

"Am I making your day a little better boss?" the Irishman asked him.

Fitzpatrick was thinking fast.

"Who knows about this?" he asked.

"Only the people on site," Flannigan told him. "And their contracts are standard."

Which Fitzpatrick knew meant mine workers were not allowed to tell people outside the mine about anything to do with volumes of materials being mined and how much gold was being discovered. Such matters are seriously commercially sensitive.

"Keep it that way," Fitzpatrick told him though the instruction was not necessary. Nobody would talk for fear of being instantly dismissed and salaries in Siberian mines are huge.

The implications of the news were enormous. Way after the call with Flannigan ended Fitzpatrick was considering how best to respond. This was fantastically good news, but only if the gold was in his hands – or at least, banked. He had asked Flannigan to consider how to get the gold to him and to phone back when he had some ideas. When the call came the news was not so good.

"We're grounded boss," the Irish site manager told him, his voice far less exuberant than it had been earlier.

"What do you mean by grounded?" Fitzpatrick responded.

"I can't fly anything in or out of here at the moment. There's a ban on all civil flying. Something to do with the pissing about between the Ruskies and the Yanks. Guess you've heard about it boss?"

"Yes," Fitzpatrick told him.

"Well, it means no choppers. They can't keep the ban on for long because so many people around here rely on air movement of goods. But there's sure a ban right now."

"Use the road then," Fitzpatrick told him impatiently.

"Can't do that either boss," responded Flannigan. "We've just had a routine engineer's risk assessment on the road and it's not fit for use at the moment."

"What do you mean – not fit for use?"

"It's a bit optimistic to call it a road," Flannigan told him. "It's more like a track. It's been bulldozed across the land. There's no hard core to it. And it crosses the tundra and a lot of that's wet. It's a mix of small lakes and small islets. It's ok when it's iced but the engineers say the ice is too thin to take the trucks at the moment. So we're fucked boss."

Fitzpatrick thought for a moment. "But what about lighter vehicles. A small 4x4 for instance?"

"I've only got big trucks here boss," Flannigan told him. "And anyway it doesn't matter. If the engineer's risk assessment says the road is a no-go, then it's a no-go for anything on wheels because the company's insurance would be invalidated."

Fitzpatrick thumped his desk with frustration. No sooner had an answer arrived to take the pressure off from the banks than it was gone again. Unless! He had an idea.

"How about if I can get to Anadyr, I could drive a 4x4 to you and pick up the larger bits of gold?"

"Sounds like a plan boss, if you can get to Anadyr and then if you're willing to risk the road. It's up to you. You're the boss. Rather you than me."

"Let me see if I can organise that. I'll come back to you shortly."

"OK boss," said Flannigan. "Just one other thing."

"What's that?" asked Fitzpatrick.

"If you do get to Anadyr and come on by road, bring me a sandwich and a cask of Guinness!"

Chapter 27

Au65°4531.071-169°711.1318GS. Patterson immediately knew what it meant but the implications were mind-blowing. Clearly Au is the chemical symbol for gold. GS was almost certainly George Symons who Lieutenant General Vladimir Antonov recently revealed was a British spy who had visited Ratmanov Island which Patterson now knew from the map he'd seen to be also known as Big Diomede. And here before him, etched into the woodwork of a hut on a remote island in the middle of the Bering Strait, was a message from that man. It was, he guessed incredulously, about 100 or so years old. But it gave him the co-ordinates for where some gold was, or maybe had been – gold that could only be that linked to the Romanov family because that was what Symons referred to in his message the copy of which Patterson had seen at Anadyr-1. And if all this thinking was right, was the gold still where Symons indicated it was? After all, it was a very long time ago. On the other hand, Patterson could not recall reading or hearing any news of a major find of Romanov gold. Surely if a discovery had been made in an extraordinarily remote place like this, such an amazing and historic find would have made headlines across the world.

The tedious days of doing more or less nothing slipped by with still no news about their fate. One way or another they saw Vladimir Antonov, normally only fleetingly as he moved around on his daily duties. He occasionally visited to seemingly check on their wellbeing and to sit in on the few discussions held with Nika and her family. Apart from the fact they were being forcibly incarcerated on this desolate, rocky island by the Russians, they were being very well looked after. New clothes had been brought in for them which, Patterson thought, transformed the Flintstone family, especially Nika. In jeans and jumpers instead of her home sewn animal skin clothes, the transformation was amazing, aided by her hair also having been trimmed.

Nika's metamorphosis produced something akin to an excited young teenager, proudly showing off her new clothes. She had little or no understanding that in doing so she also exhibited just what an attractive woman she was. Patterson noted the excited attention she drew from many of the Russian soldiers – the glances towards her, the nudges, the mutterings. There were only two other women on the island, both Russian soldiers. Their male counterparts, youthful, with high levels of testosterone and a long distance and time away from wives and girlfriends, showed natural interest in this young, shapely woman in their midst. She was conspicuously youthful and feminine but equally they knew she was strictly 'tabu'.

By now, from a continuing, gentle interrogation, more was becoming known about the Flintstone family including their proper family name. Popov, Patterson also discovered via Antonov, was an indicator the family might once have been linked to the Russian Orthodox Church.

Mother and father Popov spent most of their days resting indoors. The unexpected move from Anadyr-1 to this remote island had taken its toll on the physical and mental wellbeing of the elderly couple. Their main concern was to recover. Their son Stepan had worryingly withdrawn into himself, becoming surly and sulky, not concealing his anger at the Russians, hardly conversing with the rest of the family and disappearing for hours on end as he just roamed aimlessly around the island. Patterson hoped he did not become too belligerent which could potentially lead to trouble between him and their captors.

Nika attached herself as much as she could to Patterson. She was keen and eager to learn English. They spent much time in concentrated language sessions or talking as they walked around Big Diomede. She was particularly keen they understood and shared three particular words. Because of her limited vocabulary, though that was expanding rapidly, it took a while to identify the third of the three words she wanted to use. The first, "droog", Patterson eventually identified as being "friend" in English. Likewise, they eventually understood "uchitel" was "teacher". But that third word she had no word for. It was beyond her experience to date. It took quite some time, effort and exploration for Patterson to identify she wanted to use the word "lover" or "lyubovnik" in Russian.

And once they both understood all this she frequently whispered the three words to him, made even more sensual by her heavy Russian accent – "droog; uchitel; lyubovnik."

She was a fast learner but the more she was able to converse with the Scottish scientist the more she conveyed her overwhelming concern about the fate of her family and how her relationship with Patterson might continue. Patterson, increasingly frustrated about their incarceration, had no answers but tried to reassure her as best he could.

"The Russians. What do they do with us?" she asked.

"I don't know," he told her. "They shouldn't be holding us like this. It's against international laws. But there's not much else I can do but moan at Antonov."

She thought about that for a while before asking, "What will happen to you and me?"

"I don't know."

"But I love you. I don't want to leave you."

"I know," he responded but beyond that he struggled to know what to say. He had no idea how they were going to get away from the island or from the Russians or even what would happen after that. Patterson was a man without ties back home. He had had many relationships but the pressures from his profession always dictated that none lasted any length of time or became too serious. Even as he agreed with Nika that he would do all he could to ensure they remained together, another side of him questioned whether he really wanted to settle down with anyone even though he found Nika exceptionally alluring, loving, sexy, fascinating and, mainly because of her naivety and lack of previous connection to anyone outside her family, like nobody he had become attached to before.

Big Diomede is a rugged lump, roughly eleven square miles of rock and bog that rises from the sea to a highest point of some 1500 feet with sheer cliffs alive with sea birds around its frequently battered coast. The sea and the weather dominate everything. The sea is always close by, virtually always in view. Never tranquil, it often looks angry with huge waves that add to the drama of the scenery as they crash into the island's steep cliffs. Rain is frequent and in winter often falls as snow. Some days it rained incessantly, sometimes pounding on the building in which they stayed. It was often accompanied by high winds that stirred the sea into an awe-inspiring cauldron. But other days were relatively tranquil with rich blue skies and such clear air visibility was exceptional. On these days, as they scrambled across the rocky barren island, Patterson looked across at the nearby American owned island which was so tantalisingly close. Was this not their route to freedom? But if so, how?

Patterson noted that a slipway had been built leading to the pathway that linked the rugged shore to the collection of buildings huddled together at the one end of the island by the old observation post and the new missile launcher. The slipway was obviously fairly new and, he assumed, coincided with the recent increase in military activity on the island. Now and then boats would arrive and depart, connecting the tiny island to the small fleet of military and auxiliary vessels anchored in the Bering Strait. Two large fighting ships, grey, enormous but sleek and purposeful, sat majestically a mile away surrounded by a mix of smaller vessels, some military, some supply ships.

With the weather being mostly kind to them, he and Nika explored the island, walking through muddy bogs, sometimes thick with spindly grass, over rugged rocks, and through areas where small wildflowers bobbed in the wind and struggled to survive the raw conditions. Nothing grew to any height on this weather battered island and there was a conspicuous absence of any trees.

And while they wandered around, seemingly aimlessly but constantly developing their ability to communicate, Patterson tested just how much freedom Antonov was giving them. At any time when it looked as if they were heading towards the steps leading to the observation tower, or in the direction of the missile site, soldiers would block their way or there would be shouts from afar clearly telling them they were out of bounds. That apart, they were given a considerable amount of freedom, Antonov realising that to try and lock up his enforced guests was to encourage their antagonism which would make managing them even more difficult. As it was, the senior Russian on the island continued to wait for instructions as to what to do with his five captives. Clearly though his superiors had more pressing things on their mind.

One stroke of luck for Patterson was the old map he had found. It showed lines of longitude and latitude. 65°4531.071 -169°711.1318, it transpired, was a corner of Big Diomede about as far away as it could be from where the huts and the Russians were. Patterson used their walkabouts to head closer and closer to that location without raising the interest of their captors. The precise position seemed to be at the bottom of cliffs, an area he could not see without a concerted effort and one he certainly did not want to undertake with Nika with him. It would have been too conspicuous and he was not inclined to expose Nika to the dangers.

This day had dawned with a thick sea mist. That had happened before but on previous occasions it had cleared quickly, stirred away by the wind and burned out by the sun. Not this day. A sea mist was mixing with low cloud, knocking visibility back to only a few yards. The world became almost silent, colourless and a lot colder.

Patterson had hoped for such a day. Now one arrived he needed to make the best of it – and on his own. What he planned he would exclude Nika from. It was going to be risky and he did not want to endanger her. Nika, however, had other ideas and was far from content at the idea of Patterson being on his own. She tried to cajole him into telling her what he planned to do. With Stepan off on his daily wanderings, they had met in the room he shared with Nika's brother.

With her arms around his neck, she nibbled his ear and pulled him tightly towards her whispering "drook; uchitel; lyubovnik." His hand around her back sneaked up the inside of her jumper to feel her nakedness, unfettered by bra straps. The enticement was enormous. Nika had become a real temptress. He could feel her body against his – as close as could be. Her hand moved below his waist belt.

"Oh no!" he said emphatically. "Not now."

She moaned gently in his ear- "Droog; uchitel; lyubovnik."

"No! I've got to make the most of this weather," he told her, reluctantly removing his hand and gently pushing her away. "I won't be long."

And before she could respond and continue to arouse him he left the room and headed out into the fog.

He knew where he was going. He had rehearsed this enough on their ramblings. He had a clear vision of the route in his mind though following it with the visibility this low was testing. The ground was wet and slippy and the air thick with moisture. It was a dank, cold, bleak and eerily silent morning.

Eventually the sound of the sea did come to him through the fog. It told him he was nearing the end of any knowledge he had picked up on their walks and that he was very close to the edge of the cliffs, even if he could not see it. Cautiously he moved forward, wary of the nearby drop of many hundreds of feet to the sea below. Then it was there! Right before him! The grass and rock mix continued right to the edge and to a blank wall of thick white fog. The sound of the sea was now quite evident but he could not see it. He could not see anything! Where he now stood the cliff disappeared from view in a sheer vertical drop. How far it went he had no idea. There could be a ledge 10 feet away. There could be a 1,000 feet drop. He had no way of telling.

Even as he stood and contemplated what to do next the fog and mist started to swirl and to vary in its thickness. Tantalising glimpses of the cliff before him came into view but were quickly denied as the curtain closed again. Encouraged by the prospect of the visibility improving soon, Patterson made his way cautiously along the cliff edge, now and then peering down and straining to see the sea below each time the mist lifted which it was increasingly doing. Just for the briefest of seconds he saw waves a frighteningly long distance below. Then the mist was thinning rapidly, more of the coastline ahead coming into view as was the rocky shore. It was, he thought, a prodigious drop.

For perhaps 10 minutes he slowly progressed towards a spot high above the place the co-ordinates identified on the map. The actual position appeared to be at sea level and he could not help but speculate if Symons was referring to where some sort of vessel that was carrying Romanov gold had crashed into the cliffs of Big Diomede. The thought was ludicrous, he kept telling himself, yet the wafer-thin evidence he had made it remotely possible. He could not leave the island without knowing the truth.

A good breeze had set in now, accelerating the departure of the mist and swirling the cloud on its way. Into view was the breathtaking vista of the huge seas of the Bering Strait, the stunning but rugged island on which he stood, Little Diomede, seemingly a distance of no more than a short rowing boat trip away and, in the hazy distance, the mainland of Siberia to his right. The whole scene was wonderfully spectacular.

All the time Patterson was straining to see anything out of the ordinary on the coastline way below him. But mostly it was rocky outlets and short, pebble and rock-strewn beaches. His attention was drawn to one particularly long promontory reaching out from the island at a narrow angle to the cliff face leaving a small finger of water between the two. Frustratingly he could not see where it met the cliff below. But there seemed to be the slightest glimmer of a track heading down from the lip of the cliff. Was it a path or just something animal movement had created? Patterson could not tell but it was worth venturing a yard or two along it to see if it opened up a view to the end of the strip of water.

Hanging onto anything he could grab – a rock edge, the slightest bit of vegetation, just the hint of a muddy ledge, Patterson gingerly edged his way from the top of the cliff. He was taking in big breaths, exhaling slowly to try and control his nerves. The drop below was virtually sheer and, he guessed, 300 feet or more. He knew what he was doing was crazy but his geologically related career had taken him on numerous climbing ventures, some quite perilous but, he had to admit, none as perilous as this. The so-called pathway reached a slight curve, barely 30 feet from the top of the cliff. As he reached it so more of the coastline came into view and, looking down, he could now see where the finger of water reached the bottom of the cliff. And there, tucked in right at the end of the stretch of water, as if rammed into the cliff face and hidden from view from the sea by the high profile of the finger of rock, was an only just discernable shape. Patterson had to turn away, adjust his eyes and try again to confirm what he was seeing. Was there something there or was it his imagination? No, he eventually concluded, there was a distinct shape that was not the work of nature. A shape?

The more he squinted at it the more he concluded it could conceivably be the remnants of the bows of some sort of boat. It was so obscure that if you were not looking for any sort of vessel you would not have given it a second glance. But how to get to it? The track ahead petered out. It was so frustrating!

Chapter 28

"Now don't you worry about a thing," Noack had told him, reassuring him that 'Old Betty', his trusty Piper Cessna 172 Skyhawk, had never let him down. But as they flew the 120 miles or so north towards Wales, Bond had a developing sense of pending disaster. Their flight hugged the coast. It was, thought Bond, an extraordinary part of the world. His relationship with Georgi certainly led him into some disastrous situations but it had its compensations. Flying at well below 2,000 feet up the west coast of Alaska was definitely one of them. It was spectacular!

He became mesmerised by the view as he stared out of the window and it was only when they flew over a particularly different land formation he turned to ask Peter what he was looking at. From their low height he could see a narrow finger of land initially curving its way from the mainland but ending in a thin straight section upon which there seemed to be quite a lot of activity.

"It's Port Clarence," Peter told him. "We're about 70 miles up from Nome. It forms a bay between that strip of land and the mainland."

"What's all the activity down there?" asked Bond.

"The Government's concerned to build a new port somewhere around here. They're exploring a number of options and this is one. Another was to do a joint venture with the Russians at Provideniya on the other side of the Bering Strait in Siberia but Russia's recent actions seem to have blown that out of the water."

Bond nodded in understanding. "Why a new port?" he asked.

"There's been a huge increase in the amount of shipping around here in recent times and we know it's going to grow," Peter told him. "Tourism and minerals extraction will mean more ships. They need places to refuel. Places to stop. Places to shelter. Also there's nowhere at the moment from which to mount a major rescue. The Coast Guard is concerned about that. They see more and more massive tourist ships on the Arctic seas and nothing nearby to help them if anything goes wrong. But there's a few problems."

"Like what?" said Bond.

"Like Canada's broke and trying to cut its budget deficit at the moment. Finding money for projects like this is difficult."

"How much broke?" asked Bond.

"I read it's about 1.2 trillion dollars. It's a hell of a lot of dollars. So they are strapped for money to build a port but a port would bring revenue into an area that needs it. It's a problem. A real Catch 22."

The bay fell behind them as the coast turned north heading towards Wales. The weather closed in and Bond lost his view of the coast. It gave him more time to talk to Peter.

"It sounds like life for the Inuits is becoming untenable," he said to his newly acquired friend.

"It's becoming increasingly difficult for people to live in the harsh conditions of the Arctic," Peter agreed. "But this is our tradition. Our inheritance. Our world. And now it's changing. I read the other day that climate change is being blamed for food and water shortages in Bearskin First Nation. That's a community of about 500 in Northern Ontario. Normally supplies get there by road. But warmer weather means the roads haven't frozen. The trucks can't get in. Goods could be flown in but it's too expensive. They can't afford it. Right across the Arctic a way of life seems to be coming to an end. It's a tragedy!"

They fell silent as the aircraft droned northward. Bond's sense of foreboding increased as the aircraft started to react to an increasingly gusting crosswind. The small, aged aircraft seemed to be fluttering as an unexpected storm hit them. Noack tried to reassure them.

"Sorry folks. We didn't see this coming. Old Betty's being battered a bit but we've been through worse. Just hang on in. We'll be down soon."

Peering out of the window Bond could see nothing. Thick cloud seemed to engulf them. But then, suddenly, there was the airfield right below them – very close below but at a startling angle.

Legendary are the stories of aircraft arriving in bad conditions to land at Wales's near 2,000 feet long, gravel surfaced and exposed runway. But Betty's arrival was up there with the best of them. Sliding in towards the airfield at a severely sideways angle, battered by a gusting crosswind that was virtually gone one moment then a severe force the next, Noack as near as damn it got it right. But not quite! Just as one wheel seemed to have well established itself on terra firma but with the other some five feet off the ground, yet another blast of wind caught the underneath of the plane's tail and swung Betty on the one grounded wheel 45 degrees to the runway. Noack was beyond the point of no return in dropping the aircraft down. He became a mere passenger as his beloved Betty lurched violently to port, slid sideways 200 yards across the gravel hard surface, hit grass where she toppled over and stopped.

Bond was first to move, unlocking his seat belt and climbing off his seat, hanging onto it as he felt his feet secure a firm position on the side of the aircraft which was now immediately below him. From there he was soon at the door, wrenching it open and dropping to the ground below just as the airfield's crash tender arrived. He turned to help the other three, none of whom had sustained any injuries. The only victim was Betty, bent, battered and with one wing cracked into two. Noack was mortified and sobbed openly as he assessed the extent of the damage.

By now another vehicle had arrived. A 4x4 from which jumped a young-looking British naval officer.

"Chief Petty Officer Jo Herbert here to meet you, sir," said the uniformed youngster. "But I didn't expect such a dramatic arrival!"

"Neither did we," agreed Bond with a restrained laugh. Together he and Peter climbed aboard the car, leaving the unhappy sight of Noack and his young lady navigator standing in the gusting rain looking forlornly at the sad and broken Betty.

It was a grey day in Wales and the 4x4 was buffeted by the energetic wind that had been the downfall of Betty. They drove the short distance from the airfield to the so-called town of Wales, a motley collection of varying buildings scattered together on land set back from the shore of the Bering Strait. Bond could see the wind was now whipping up quite a sea and in the distance an island and, faintly behind it in the varying visibility, another.

"The Diomedes," Jo Herbert told him. "Little Diomede closest and Big Diomede behind it."

Bond was fascinated by this place. It was hard to conceive a community could survive here. This had to be the epitome of remoteness. There was no planning to this place. Buildings had been erected in a higgledy piggledy sort of way. He noted that many homes seemed to have a small shed-like structure attached. He mentioned it to Herbert.

"It's a sort of an air-lock," he told him. "Helps keep the cold out. About 200 people live here," Herbert continued. "Must be one hell of a tough life."

"The town was nearly wiped out some years ago," Peter told them. "A strange virus travelled aboard dogsleds right across Alaska's hinterlands. It left thousands dead. When it got here it killed almost 200 people, more than half the people who lived here then. It orphaned several dozen children."

Bond immediately thought of the virus that had apparently escaped the holes that had appeared in Siberia.

"It was influenza," Peter continued. "In 1918 it killed an estimated 50 million people worldwide. It killed at a higher rate in western Alaska than anywhere else in the United States."

"Now there's another virus problem," added Jo Herbert and again Bond thought he was going to mention the Siberian virus. But the Navy man had another story.

"There's an outbreak of anthrax in Western Siberia," Herbert told them. "Loads of people have been taken to hospital and 1,500 reindeer have died. It's blamed on climate change. It's an exceptionally warm climate across Siberia at the moment. In some provinces it's been 10 degrees Fahrenheit above the norm. It's thought that the carcass of a reindeer that died in the plague 75 years ago has thawed and bacteria in it has been reactivated. Herds of reindeer have been quarantined."

It was sobering news on such a grey day and the group fell silent until they arrived at the community centre which, it transpired, the Navy had commandeered with the co-operation of the community's elders. The locals were happy to help in any way they could. Feelings were running high against the Russians since the forced movement of the community on Little Diomede. The team from the navy had quickly established close relationships with the Inuit community which rather made Peter's role redundant. Herbert introduced Peter and Bond to the man who was in charge of the rescue of Patterson from the Russians.

Captain Peter Turner was a bearded man whose age Bond found difficult to guess, mid 30s perhaps? He was seated at what would have made a good canteen table – plastic topped with four narrow metal legs. The table top was totally obliterated by a map upon which were various small piles of documents – mostly reports of one sort or another. Five other men surrounded the table. Unlike Turner they were standing and Bond immediately noticed they all wore more or less the same dark blue sweaters and jeans with not a badge or marking on any of them. The group's arrival had obviously interrupted some sort of briefing. Turner, eyes deep in sockets blackened by fatigue, looked up with some annoyance as the perpetrators of the interruption headed into the room.

Chief Petty Officer Herbert reported on the chaotic arrival into Wales of Peter and Bond and the demise, temporary or otherwise, of Betty.

"This motley lot," Turner told the newcomers waving an arm darkened by thick, wiry hair to indicate the men of his group, "are members of the Special Boat Service. If you've not heard of us, the easiest explanation is to say we're the marine element of the SAS which everyone's heard of. A bit like the SAS in boats! We're operationally self-contained and run much to our own rules and standards."

Gene Bond was puzzled. "This seems like a massive and expensive operation to rescue one Scottish scientist."

"Not for us to reason why," Turner responded. "We just do. But as I understand it the powers that be think Patterson may have information about these strange holes in Siberia that maybe now is strategically important. This whole area has become exceptionally politically sensitive in a short period of time. So they want to know what Patterson knows. And I guess they don't want the Russians to find out what he knows."

"But you, Mr Bond," Turner continued, "create something of a problem for me. Since the aircraft you came in is now in bits I think you'll have to come with us on our little jaunt. Otherwise we'll leave you stranded here and I don't think my governors would sanction that. And I'm sorry to say Peter you'll have to fend for yourself. The air ban in this area can't last too long. Apart from anything else the town of Wales relies on air supplies. So sometime soon someone's got to get an aircraft into here."

"Meantime, my lot are going to cause a bit of excitement on the Bering Strait. It only involves canoeing across one of the most dangerous seas on the planet, escaping detection by the Russian fleet that's anchored out there, creating some diverting chaos, grabbing a British scientist away from the Russians on Big Diomede and escaping. That's the plan. Now I ask you, what on earth could possibly go wrong?"

Chapter 29

In Seoul Sum Taeyoung was amazed. In Washington, Tokyo, Paris, London and other major cities around the world, politicians wondered what on earth had hit them.

As if someone was pouring petrol onto a blazing heathland fire, the social media campaign launched by a group of students in France spread across the globe at breakneck speed. Modelled on the way the Arab Spring of 2011 maximised online social media that transcended political borders and governmental media control, the cry from the Paris students for the youth of the world to rally round The Spirit of Hwanung and its nine demands quickly gathered momentum.

The initial target for the French students was their counterparts in other countries – disillusioned youngsters trapped in poverty and with little hope of finding meaningful work and progressive careers. They were already well connected to many individuals around the world ensnared in similar circumstances to their own and it took little effort to generate an upward spiral of young people keen to lock onto something that seemed to represent their frustrations so well.

It generated a wave of varying responses. In London people marched. In Paris they threw bottles and stones and ducked the incoming tear gas from the police. In

Hong Kong they threw Molotov cocktails and received rubber bullets back. The same happened in some American cities.

Much to Taeyoung's bewilderment, a cult dimension rapidly emerged because his declaration contained nine demands. Nine, it transpired, was a number with potent powers. Astonishingly to Taeyoung this was seen to be symbolically significant giving added credence and substance to what he had written as a straightforward set of demands. As the flame that was sparked in Paris grew into a raging, global inferno student researchers identified the hidden meaning of 9 within The Spirit of Hwanung. Indian astrology, they proclaimed, attests there to be nine influencers. Hindu philosophy, they said, has nine universal substances – earth; water; air; fire; ether; time; space; soul and mind. In China, nine (pinyin jiǔ) is considered a good number because the word also stands for long-lasting.

This nine-based structure of The Spirit of Hwanung was deemed highly sophisticated and meaningful and gave further authority to the gathering revolution.

Taeyoung observed this with a degree of incredulity and concern. If that is what people thought about his Declaration, that was up to them. He worried that the intensity of the response was getting way beyond his control and he was mindful that sometime in the near future he would be calling on some of these groups to be his local delivery merchants of packages of death. After all, that was why he invented the Hwanung Declaration! What he did take delight in was the chaos being generated in major cities around the planet.

In America, already reeling from increasing protests and riots as the Black Lives Matter campaign continued to spread and develop in power, so, all of a sudden, The Spirit of Hwanung caught hold in the country's college campuses then brought people onto the streets demanding a different approach to the way their lives are managed. In some American cities this merged with anti-war protest marches as the American administration pondered what to do in response to Russia's activity in the Arctic.

"Where the hell has this come from?" the President wanted to know. It was a question being increasingly asked by both supporters and worried onlookers alike. Without a visible figurehead for a leader, conventional wisdom said the matter would soon die out – would run out of steam. But The Spirit of Hwanung was gaining a momentum of its own and like a domino effect sparked anti-government protest marches in many European cities, then in more far-flung places – America; Hong Kong; Mexico; Brazil. Though the Declaration gave no suggestion as to how the demands should be answered, it was a list so identifiable by others it flamed like a beacon of hope for people who had little.

In Washington the President of the United Nations viewed the developments with some dismay. A major theme of Hwanung protests was the inability of the UN to influence actions across the globe in places such as the Crimea; Syria; the Ukraine and to respond to the plight of those striving to escape into Europe. UN response to the desperate circumstances of millions on the threshold of starvation in Africa was widely considered to be too little and too late. Even within areas of the UN itself, it was perceived by many, the organisation was largely impotent. To the hierarchy within the monolith that is the UN the importance and significance of the global organisation remained largely unquestioned. Despite that, its President felt there needed to be some expression of interested concern and response to the protests of such massively large numbers of people taking to the streets in major cities everywhere. But, he kept asking, who was behind this global revolt? Who was orchestrating it? His was just one voice amongst growing thousands of voices questioning who lay behind the Hwanung demands.

To those parading or rioting on the streets such matters were of lesser consequence. Indeed, vast numbers of people being sucked into what was rapidly becoming the Hwanung Crusade seemed little bothered about such detail or even how they expected the demands they were supporting to be answered. To vast numbers of people it was enough to have something that seemed to represent their concerns. It was enough for them to rally behind.

The tentacles of government machinery in every quarter of the globe were asking similar questions. Where did this all start, how and by whom? Who was masterminding its global spread? As more and more intelligence agencies became involved so Georgi Patarava's unit based in Wapping became overwhelmed with demands for information. Georgi and Bond knew full well Sum Taeyoung had previously masqueraded behind the pseudonym Hwanung. They had no doubt the global chaos now reigning in many areas was attributable to the South Korean.

Patarava had no choice but to feed this idea into the system. As soon as he did, Wapping became the heart of a multi-national, multi-agency debate on how best to respond. Now an individual had been identified as being the driving force behind the Hwanung campaign a variety of notions were tabled as to how best to respond. These varied enormously. At the 'soft' end of the spectrum it was proposed that Sum Taeyoung be arrested and put on trial. That generated a barrage of questions – what would he be arrested for? Who would be the arresting authority? Where would he be arrested? Where would he be sent for trial? The debate rapidly became bogged down in enormous complexities. Sum Taeyoung was Korean. Was this something for the South Korean government? It showed no real appetite for becoming involved.

So if not on his home territory by his own government, where, by whom and how remained unanswered questions.

At the other end of the spectrum was the suggestion that Sum Taeyoung be assassinated. Georgi recalled the discussion with Graeme Samsom from the UK's CONTEST programme. "What would you do?" Georgi had asked him.

"Get rid of the central perpetrator," Samsom had responded.

"Kill Taeyoung?" Georgi had queried.

"Yes," said Samsom.

And they had gone on to talk about the failed attempt to blow Taeyoung up in Seoul.

"But," Samsom had countered, "that wasn't an attack aimed specifically and individually at one person. You attacked a building you thought he was in. What you need is a more specific plan."

And that had led to the question of assassination. Georgi told a multi-agency on-line strategy meeting that he had doubts such an action could be authorised. Samsom had called it 'state sanctioned homicide' and something that he thought was not impossible to get authorised.

The consensus view of the multi-national teleconference was that Samsom was right.

"What we need to do," Georgi suggested to the virtual meeting and echoing the recommendation of Samson, "is to lure Taeyoung into a position where there can be no doubt who he is and where he can be a clean and uncomplicated target."

The meeting agreed. It was also agreed that because the agencies involved in this debate had been tasked by their various governments to come up with a solution and to deploy it, they had the authority needed to take the action being recommended.

"In which case," said Georgi. "Can I win support for this idea? In the very near future the President of the UN will be in Brussels. He is to attend the annual meeting of the Bilderberg Group being held at the Château du Lac hotel. For a number of reasons I think this presents us with the situation Samsom recommended we lure Taeyoung into."

"What's the Bilderberg Group?" asked one conference participant.

"It first met in 1954," Georgi told him. He had done

his homework. "They met at the Bilderberg Hotel in the Netherlands. That's where the name comes from. There's a lot of cloak and dagger stuff about the group mainly caused I guess because their annual meeting is held to Chatham House Rules so nobody outside the meeting knows really what's been discussed. It's a European/American group and people who attend – between 100 and 120 of them – are exclusively high ranging individuals from business and politics."

"Why use this for what we want?" another asked.

"Because it's neutral territory," Georgi responded. "It's not governmental, not national, not even UN. So if anything were to happen there it could not be attributed to any individual nation or even the UN itself."

After a pause, he added: "And it's a high profile enough event for the President of the UN to be attending."

"What about the location?" came another question.

"I know the Château du Lac hotel well enough," Georgi reassured the virtual meeting. "It's a former castle about 20 minutes out of Brussels city centre. It's located in an area that is relatively easy to secure. It has high security certification from a number of agencies including mine."

"If we agree to this how would you execute such an operation?" asked another. Georgi spelt out his plan in detail.

Chapter 30

They say money can buy anything. Alexander Fitzpatrick was doing his best to prove it! He was liberally scattering the stuff around Siberia as he spent his way through a barrage of challenges. His task was perhaps equal in magnitude to that confronting Captain Peter Turner. All the mining executive had to do was find a way of getting to Anadyr, now in a more or less militarily controlled exclusion zone covering part of Eastern Siberia, hire a suitable vehicle to drive 120 miles or so across the tundra, drive north to the community at Kanchalan then the ice track to the mine – then back. That he had been told the so-called road to the mine was now impassable because the ice sections were melting earlier than usual added a certain spice to the task. But the thought of getting his hands on a quarter of a million dollars' worth of gold was a serious incentive to keep going.

The first stage of his journey moved from being virtually impossible to maybe achievable when the Russians, under pressure from local administrations, opened flying corridors in the militarily controlled no-fly zone to enable aircraft to access those communities across Eastern Siberia which could not otherwise be supplied. To people living in these remote parts it was simple. Be supplied or starve. Anadyr was no exception and the 15,000 or so people who lived there would be in dire difficulties without the help only aircraft could provide on a regular basis.

Fitzpatrick flew into Anadyr in a heavily loaded Russian Ilyushin transport aircraft which he boarded in Novosibirsk, the unofficial capital of Siberia located nearly 5,000 kilometres to the west. It had taken nearly three days to get to Novosibirsk and the flight from there was long, arduous, very uncomfortable and massively expensive. He felt drained and ragged as he booked into a hotel in Anadyr and started to inquire about hiring a suitable vehicle for the next leg of his journey.

News of this Englishman hellbent on a crazy journey into the tundra spread across the town which explains why Fitzpatrick was joined at the hotel bar by a giant of a man, six and a half feet tall or maybe more, broad-shouldered, arms as thick as oak tree branches, heavily tattooed, with a beard that looked pretty well out of control. Fitzpatrick immediately categorised him as someone who drank prodigious amounts of beer and probably had a Harley Davidson at home.

"You the guy intent upon freezing to death? On the tundra?" the big man asked as he arrived alongside Fitzpatrick at the bar before breaking into Russian to order a tankard of beer which disappeared into his huge hand as he grasped it. His question to Fitzpatrick had been in English but with what seemed a mixed American/Russian dialect.

"Who are you?" Fitzpatrick responded. He was not necessarily well-known for his tact or civility and being asked so directly and bluntly about his plans by a total stranger immediately rubbed him up the wrong way.

"Most call me Jock," was the unexpected reply.

"Jock?" Fitzpatrick frowned. There had been no trace of a Scot in the man's voice. "That's usually attributable to someone from Scotland." Fitzpatrick could imagine this man tossing a caber but this was all a bit incongruous in a bar in this ridiculous Siberian town.

"Aye. Guess so. Blame it on my grandfather. From Glasgow. Married a Russian woman. Their son became Canadian. He married a French girl. I was born in Alaska. Have mostly lived in Siberia. So how'd you expect me to sound, behave or look? But people still call me Jock." The man spoke in staccato short sentences. His rich blue eyes stared unblinkingly from a well lined, parchment skinned, moustached and bearded face. His uncouth appearance made him look like a social dropout. Someone quite destitute, thought Fitzpatrick. But the quality of his jacket, jeans and decorated boots suggested otherwise. Thanks to a few hefty gulps, the tankard was returned from the giant hand to the bar half empty.

"Planning to head north. Into the tundra. That's what I hear," the big man said. It wasn't asked as a question but that is what it was.

"I might be," grunted Fitzpatrick.

"Why?"

"That's my business." The English mining executive was feeling increasingly uneasy in this unwanted conversation. He reached for his whisky, intent on taking a last swig and getting away to his room.

"It could become mine," the blue eyes were laser-like as if trying to pierce Fitzpatrick's mind.

"What do you mean?"

"I can help you."

"I don't need help," Fitzpatrick said sharply, turning from the bar to look up and straight at the unwanted company.

"Then you're even crazier than I thought," said Jock.

"Why?" Fitzpatrick cursed himself for asking the question. It was inviting more conversation and he had had enough some time ago.

"Because you're fucking crazy man. Setting off into the tundra now is crazy. Going on your own! Even crazier. To turn down help from a trucker? Someone who earns his living driving ice roads. That's crazy beyond being crazy. Pure fucking madness!" And the big man downed the remaining part of his beer and returned the empty tankard to the bar top with a crash, as if to underline his point.

"OK," responded Fitzpatrick with a deal of reluctance. "Tell me more."

"You have no idea. This you're about to try and do," said the big man. "It's dangerous out there. Lethal, man! Where you going?"

Fitzpatrick told him.

"Shit!" Jock was vigorously rubbing his beard. "North of Kanchalan! I don't even know of any road heading north from Kanchalan."

"My company built it," Fitzpatrick told him.

"How?"

"What do you mean – how?" Fitzpatrick's impatience was showing again.

"How was it built? What's its surface? How much water's it going over?"

"I don't know," Fitzpatrick admitted.

"It would be good to know. Before we start out," said Jock, now on a second tankard of beer.

"Hey," Fitzpatrick said with a half chuckle in his voice though there was no humour in it. "Where does this "we" come from?"

The blue eyes stared back at him. "You're going to need me. If you're going to make this journey."

There was a pause as more beer was consumed.

"I guess your road is a track. It'll have been bulldozed through the land. Flattened across the ice. They tow a heavy sledge on snow and ice roads. A massive and heavy bit of kit that carves a route. Then the regular use of trucks keeps it open. They use tracked vehicles to maintain the routes. Over the ice they do aerial surveying. They bore test holes to check ice thickness."

More beer intake.

"Any of that happened on your road?"

"I don't know," Fitzpatrick confessed. The big man looked at him with disdain.

"Then there's how you drive 'em. There's a skill and technique on the mud. Always need to be thinking ahead. On the ice you have to go steady. Don't want to start a wave under the ice. If you do, the ice can start cracking in front of you. Like a submerged bow wave. On frozen lakes you can hear the ice cracking and banging. When it gets real bad it frightens the shits out of you. You drive with the door open standing on the cab step ready to jump if the rig goes in."

As the man spoke Fitzpatrick considered his situation. Clearly he personally knew nothing about driving on the Siberian tundra. He had wide experience of driving a range of vehicles on varying terrain from his days in the army but he had never driven on ice roads. As the big man spoke, the magnitude of the task ahead became increasingly apparent. And, having thrown so much money at getting as far as Anadyr, it would, he eventually conceded with some reluctance, be irresponsible to prejudice that investment without accepting some experienced help.

Grudgingly Fitzpatrick agreed. It immediately solved another problem in that the man with the Scottish/Russian/Canadian/French mongrel antecedents had his own transport, a large and battered Toyota tundra pickup truck. The vehicle was thrown into the deal "for nothing" according to Jock though Fitzpatrick thought the extortionate amount being asked was enough to buy a new truck – and more.

"What's the state of the road?" the big man asked.

"I've no idea. My man at the mine says the warm weather's making it difficult." That is not quite how Flannigan had told it to him but he thought it was enough information for his new co-driver.

"I guess," was the brief response.

The journey was one of the most extraordinary Fitzpatrick had ever made and he was soon thankful he had done the deal with his knowledgeable and skilled companion. The journey from Anadyr to Kanchalan started from the airfield at Ugolny where Jock kept his Toyota in a lockup. According to Jock there was no road link between Anadyr and Kanchalan. Via satellite phone Flannagan contradicted this. According to the Irishman there had definitely once been some sort of road route. It was, he said, developed in the early days of the mine but he confessed that since supplies had started to be flown in regularly by helicopter or by the river in the summer, nobody could remember the last time anyone had driven towards them from Kanchalan.

They headed almost directly north out of Anadyr into a flat, featureless wilderness with distant mountains. Though the weather was being kind with this part of Siberia looking at its best on a bright and sunny day, even at its best, thought Fitzpatrick, this place was pretty foreboding. He recalled reading somewhere that the Arctic tundra is the coldest of the world's ecological zones. It certainly felt like it – yet this was late Spring and the talk everywhere was about an exceptionally warm winter and early summer temperatures.

A forbiddingly endless rolling countryside patchwork of bare rock lay before them with stretches of green made up of short plants or spindly grass indicating near-frozen bogland, and frozen water varying in size from puddles to small lakes. The challenge was to know what lay immediately ahead of the Toyota, to recognise a problem before hitting it. Several times Jock got out from the cabin and used a telescopic probing rod, checking the thickness of ice over a stretch of water and the depth of water beneath. Twice they got stuck in the mud and once had to use the on-board winch to heave the truck from where it was held. It was hard going and slow.

Kanchalan was a welcoming sight and a surprisingly

neatly laid out community with many single storey, red or grey roofed dwellings. The few people about who spotted them waved and they waved back but kept going. It may have been anti-social not to stop but they were anxious not to run out of daytime, though the nights by now were very short. Jock insisted they kept going. It took some time to find the track leaving the township and heading for the mine.

If there had been a road to the mine it was now barely recognisable as an even decent track. The wind and weather had eaten into man's work and it was quickly reverting back to the natural landscape. The Toyota battled on, crossing several small frozen lakes. None were particularly big but at each one Jock shuffled across on foot, prodding the ice with his measuring stick. The longest stretch was perhaps a few hundred yards. By the time they encountered it they were more than three quarters of the journey to the mine. They were exhausted, physically shattered from the continuous lurching of the vehicle and the stress on their nerves.

"Not sure about this one," Jock said, returning from his recce of the small lake. "Ice is pretty thin in places. Water lying on ice in some parts. Not deep. Deep enough!"

He gingerly edged the vehicle onto the lake.

"You can see the ice reacting," he told Fitzpatrick, nodding towards the area in front of the Toyota. "Watch those streaks heading out from us. So long as they remain like patterns it's OK. If they crack, we get out!"

By half way across the icy stretch Fitzpatrick could

hear the ice reacting to the weight and movement of the Toyota. It was all too easy to hear the crack and groans of the ice, even what sounded like muffled explosions. The tension in the car was palpable.

Jock eventually opened his door. There was a blast of ice cold air but he was obviously expecting the worst. Fitzpatrick did the same. He could see ahead to where the land went upwards slightly. It was the shore of the lake. They were so tantalisingly close. But the ice noise was getting louder.

"Out!" shouted Jock climbing onto the truck's running board, steering the vehicle with his right hand on the left hand side of the steering wheel. The Toyota was chugging on at near stalling speed with the throttle almost completely closed. Fitzpatrick clung onto the swinging open door and watched fascinated as the shore crept ever closer but with cracks in the ice starting to spread before them, water now oozing towards the surface.

Time stood still in the frozen wilderness. The four drive wheels of the Toyota were now frequently spinning freely on wet ice, gripping momentarily to keep them moving – just. There was the occasional crash and lurch as they passed over widening holes in the ice. And then the vehicle staggered forward as the front wheels bit into hard ground. The two men returned to the cabin and shut the doors.

"My God," said Fitzpatrick. "That was bloody ridiculous."

"Business as usual," responded his companion.

It took five hours to get to the mine where Flannigan

was waiting for them. That something was wrong was immediately evident. It was written all over his face.

"We've only just heard boss. Otherwise I'd have phoned you."

"What is it?" barked Fitzpatrick.

The Irishman looked anything but his usual confident and buoyant self. He was obviously agitated and immensely concerned about what he needed to tell his employer. "It's the Russians. They've just issued an announcement. They're saying that because of what they call irresponsible and aggressive acts by the United States, they're compulsorily nationalising all mines in Siberia. I think you may have come all this way for nothing!"

"What!" Fitzpatrick exploded. But before he could say more Flannigan spoke again.

"And there's more," he said cautiously. "It's the Americans. They've launched a battle fleet out of Washington with a view to reclaiming their island in the Bering Strait. It's heading up here right now!"

Chapter 31

Despite it representing so much she despised, she loved the view from the top of the Washington Monument. She had only seen it a few times but it stuck vividly in her mind. Her first visit was courtesy of a young backpacking tourist from Eastern Europe who had taken her there when she pleaded with him to do so. The outstanding vista compensated for her poor head for heights though her nerves were further shredded every time the elevator reached the top of the needle-like building and sent a discernable jolt throughout the whole structure. Most visitors did not notice a thing. They did not feel it. She did – every time. She found it utterly unnerving. She had also been taken aback by the blast of upward air as she stepped out of the elevator onto the observation floor. The powerful updraft was another instant reminder she was at the top of the 550 feet plus obelisk commemorating the former President, George Washington.

But she had to admit the view from the top was amazing, even if the focal points were buildings that epitomised the political establishment she so reviled. In one direction, seen over the wide open spaces of the Ellipse and the South Lawn, the iconic White House, unequivocal symbol of Western power, glittered in the sunshine. Swinging slightly to her right she could see the Anacostia River and beyond that the area in which she lived and where she had only recently encountered the Hwanung Crusade for the first time. In front of her, over the Potomac River, stood the less visually appealing Pentagon – harsh, grey, and menacing. Every now and then she was reminded – as if she needed reminding – of the height of the monument as she found herself looking down on passenger aircraft flying along the river, making their final adjustments before landing at the nearby Reagan National Airport. It was impossible not to recall 9/11.

Now she was waiting at the bottom of the monument. She felt nervous but excited. Twenty three years old, the daughter of a naval dockworker who she hardly knew and a Caribbean mother who had battled daily to keep a family of seven children in some semblance of order, Moya Ryan was just about five feet two high, slight in build and with black hair cut very, very short. She was renowned for having a temper which, it was said, she inherited from her father who her mother frequently declared "died early of too much living." He left a reputation for excessive drinking and a valiant effort on behalf of population growth.

The youngest member of the family, life had never been easy for Moya who always seemed to be the target for the consequences of the frequent misdemeanours of her elder siblings. Education had been a disaster and employment non-existent and through her late teens a sense of helplessness and frustration grew to dominate her life. Washington DC was, she thought, the epitome of a community hugely divided between those that have an overabundance of seemingly everything and those who most certainly do not – sometimes even the ability to feed themselves. Even today as she waited she felt destitute and surrounded by people from all over the world enjoying the very evident fruits of their wellbeing.

Just as Janka Koldun had done in The Park Of The Forged Figures, so Moya Ryan waited to do dirty deeds for Sum Taeyoung though she had never heard of the South Korean and never would. It had been a short walk from her home to Anacostia Drive and Poplar Point on the southern shores of the river near the road bridge that headed towards the White House not that far away. It was here she first encountered the Hwanung Crusade. A magnetic sort of curiosity took her there – as it did for many others. She heard drums banging, some music and voices through amplifiers. When she arrived at the riverside road she found something of a carnival atmosphere and some 200 or more people with flags and banners proclaiming support for the Hwanung Crusade. Two police cars prowled by, their officers keeping a watchful eye on this unauthorised event. The Crusade, she learnt from leaflets being handed out, seemed to be an anti-government/anti-establishment campaign based on nine demands for change all of which immediately resonated with her. It grabbed her interest and she edged her way to the front of the crowd to discover more.

She found the nucleus of the rally centred on two people who had a small portable stage, sound system and some telescopic aluminium poles from which flew banners proclaiming the nine demands of the Hwanung

Solution. Clearly skilled in whipping up a crowd's emotions, the two talked about this global crusade that would oust convention and those who had failed to deliver solutions, who had failed the poor, created international divides and ignored the consequences of climate change. They promised an injection of a new, dynamic generation of "doers" whose priority objectives were the nine demands listed by Hwanung.

It made the utmost sense to the young Moya. This was different in that it was talking to her. No other political initiative ever had. This kindled within her a feeling that she could become involved in something that would change the world order, would dismantle bureaucratic structures that, in her perception, seemed to cost a fortune, provide generous income for a chosen few, yet delivered little if nothing. Every one of the Hwanung demands was utterly meaningful to her and she was fascinated by the quasi-religious links to the number nine spelt out by the two who ran the event.

With the noise of the crowd growing and with more and more people swelling its numbers, the police grew anxious that this unlicensed rally was getting out of control. Reinforcements were called in and the meeting broken up with only a minimum of resistance. But that was not before anyone showing keen interest in the Crusade was invited to meet again a few days later at the Washington Peace Centre where plans for action would be made known in detail.

"There is a deadline to this," one of the speakers told the group that attended the second meeting which attracted 30 or so people from the first event. "And if it's not met there's a threat of action – potentially leading to the deaths to thousands. Yes – death! We cannot go on as we have done. We cannot continue to destroy our own home – this planet. We can no longer be ignored by those in authority. They must be persuaded to respond. Before it's too late!"

Similar groups, they were told, were developing across the world. The scale of the Hwanung Crusade was now enormous. Its supersonic speed of expansion had no parallel in political or campaigning history. Now simultaneous action was happening in at least 22 countries. And the clock was ticking! A demand had been laid before the United Nations and world leaders saying unless the conditions of the Hwanung Demands were met within a certain period of time, a threat of deadly proportions would be unleashed. That deadline was fast nearing.

"We need to prepare for the worst," the speaker said. "We need passionate, devoted followers prepared to sacrifice even themselves for the Crusade – for the Hwanung Solution – for the salvation of people on our planet!"

Moya was captivated. "We need foot soldiers," said the young speaker. "Soldiers of the Crusade. Soldiers willing to sacrifice themselves so those who control our lives will at last take appropriate and proportionate action. We call for a response to our nine demands. We will not be ignored."

The assembly of 30 plus was whittled down to a group of four – an inner sanctum – who, they were told, had to swear a blood oath of allegiance to Hwanung and to hold in "secrecy unto death" all knowledge about the organisation and how it functioned. Only once they had done this were they told more.

Sum Taeyoung's plot was unfolding. Strains of the virus extracted from the holes in Siberia had, so it was reported to him, been released on a controlled test exercise in Eastern Ukraine and the breakaway Donetsk region. The continued fighting there was exasperating the challenge of combating what local officials were describing as an outbreak of swine flu which to date had killed more than 300 people. Via Janka Koldun, Taeyoung was informed the official story was a total fabrication, a cover up. The man from Belarus was proving to be a real asset and essentially now the main deliverer of the project thereby enabling Taeyoung to maintain a discreet distance from operational activity.

Koldun, like Taeyoung, was totally amazed at how the flame of social media swept the Hwanung Crusade across the planet. From Detroit to Beijing, Oslo to Cape Town, tens of thousands rallied to the call for a new global order and for the delivery of the nine demands of Hwanung. Recruiting "foot soldiers", as the South Korean called them, was anything but difficult. Establishing a covert, social media based organisational structure proved virtually impossible. But through an osmosis-like process there arose from the seeming chaos what best could be called an arrangement with small groups establishing representation in their respective countries.

The growth of each group and how it behaved varied country to country, group to group but with one common denominator. Each group elected an inner sanctum and it was members of this who took the blood oath. Under Koldun's guidance the laboratory in Donetsk duplicated strains of the virus that would deliver Taeyoung's threat. Following the path established with the anthrax that had killed civil servants around the world, the virus was transported to Paris where the group of students there became the central distribution operation, creating the disguised packages for onward delivery to inner sanctum teams around the world.

As the premier volunteer of her Washington inner sanctum of the Hwanung Crusade, Moya waited at the bottom of the Washington Monument as she had been instructed to do. The appointed time came – and went. Nobody approached her. Ten minutes ticked slowly by. After a quarter of an hour she was beginning to doubt she was in the right place at the right time but each time she ran the instructions through her mind she concluded she was right. So she waited. Twenty minutes later a young man who she recognised as being one of the speakers from the rally at Poplar Point arrived panting heavily.

"Sorry. Sorry. Thank God you're still here. Train late," he explained. He held a colourful shopping bag which he placed on the floor.

"It's all in there," he told her. "Instructions and the kit. It's very simple. All you need to do now is wait. If things go well in Brussels there'll be no need to use this. But if they don't, we'll send you the one word message 'activate'. If you receive that, you know what to do."

She nodded. She understood. The young man left. Moya picked up the shopping bag and headed back towards Anacostia.

Chapter 32

The black limousine sped due south out of Brussels city centre on the road to Waterloo, the driver paying meticulous attention to the rules of the road whilst his passenger relaxed in the rear seat reading the morning's London Times. He had been met at the appointed time at his city centre hotel and had winced slightly at the sight of the driver's garish yellow jacket. But it was not worthy of comment. He assumed it to be some sort of corporate colour in bad taste. He was wrong. It had been strategically chosen. Nothing was being left to chance.

It was mid-morning. A splendid morning of cloudless sky, bright sunlight and hardly a hint of wind. The traffic had thinned in the aftermath of the rush hour as they turned off the motorway onto the relatively narrow, busy N275 but continued to make good progress on the short journey to La Hulpe. There the driver swung the limo off the major road towards the stunningly beautiful Lake Genval and its surrounding park-like area.

Today the predominantly white walls of the castle-like, five star Château du Lac hotel shone in the brightness of the morning. The passenger put down his newspaper to look at the folly on the opposite side of the lake, a view frustratingly hidden much of the time by the sharply cut privet hedges that line many of the narrow roads and are a feature of the area. This morning the lake was a rich blue and the single column fountain a twinkling of cascading silver. Often almost overwhelmed by parked cars, today the area was relatively clear thanks to a widespread security sweep that had left only authorised vehicles anywhere near the hotel.

Inside the building the guests and members who assembled for the conference of the Bilderberg Group were keen to hear from the assembled political and commercial leaders of the world and to network amongst themselves. Few had any regard to the luxurious building in which they would spend two days. Many did not even give a thought to which country they were in today such is the conveyer belt of meetings to which they were accustomed and to which they were herded via cars, trains and aircraft on schedules organised by their PAs.

For those who could see outside their highly focussed lives, some might have been intrigued by the countless strange mechanical displays on show throughout the Château du Lac hotel. Varying in size, shape and complexity and found in nooks and crannies throughout the building, for those who bothered to enquire the answer was quite unexpected.

This strange but appealing building and its resemblance to a castle was built in 1906 by the mineral water company, the Société des Eaux Minérales, attracted to do so by the quality of the springs in the area. They ran it as a health resort. It was in 1934 that the better known company, Schweppes, acquired the building and turned it into a base for their growing soda water and lemonade business. The strange machines to be found throughout the hotel are industrial artefacts from those days.

Georgi had been quite right. The Secretary General of the United Nations was amongst those assembled for the Bilderberg Group annual event. That had been a genuine part of the invitation to Hwanung who Georgi knew to be the South Korean Sum Taeyoung. What neither Taeyoung nor the Secretary General knew was that the man from the United Nations knew nothing about the invitation that had been extended to the man who wanted to hold the world to ransom.

The limousine was travelling at a gentle pace down the narrow lane that circumnavigates the lake. It slowed even further where the road forks, taking the left turn into the Avenue du Lac. The driver, keeping close watch on his passenger through the rear view mirror, saw him taking particular note of the modern building sitting in the centre of the fork in the road, all its shutters closed. To the left the hedge was again blocking the view of the lake. But, just after the fork in the road, there is a gap in the hedge, a metal gate that was opened, and the view of the lake again with the Château du Lac hotel on the far shore and the fountain before it, all now clearly in view again.

With a lurch the large car swung violently to the left through the open gateway. The large man on the rear seat was taken completely by surprise and thrown across the car. The vehicle hit a bump before skidding to a stop on the grass some 20 yards in front of a line of trees that effectively concealed this small field from the lake. The hedge did the same in the opposite direction. The spot had been chosen with care.

Before the passenger could gain any resemblance of composure, the passenger door was pulled violently open. Two men stood by the car, both in black jeans and jackets and with hoods over their heads. One had been tasked with opening the door. The other was the assassin. He fired two bullets from his silenced pistol at point blank range into the head of the passenger, then leant into the car and with the end of the barrel virtually touching its target, fired again into the heart.

The second man undertook several tasks that had been clearly specified in their brief before throwing a blanket over the dead passenger and climbing onto the seat alongside him. Spinning round on the slippery grass, the limo headed out of the field but this time took the right turn at the fork in the road and headed to a disused quarry some 10 miles drive from the lake where the body was dumped. Back at the scene of the ambush the gunman dialled a number on his phone and waited for his call to be answered.

"Samsom" is all he said before turning off his phone, pocketing it, then leaving the field in the car that had been concealed alongside the hedge.

In London Georgi received the call and heard the single word, the agreed code that signalled the assassination of Sum Taeyoung had been accomplished. He sighed. It felt like the end of a chapter, the end of a challenging adversary.

"More like the end of a real pain up the ass!" he contradicted his own thoughts as he phoned Graeme

Samsom from the UK's CONTEST programme to tell him the news. He wished he could tell Gene Bond but recent attempts to contact his friend had failed. He hoped he was alright.

Chapter 33

Bill Patterson was not sure if he was awake before it happened or whether it was the explosion that boomed and echoed across the waters of the Bering Strait that woke him. One way or another he heard it clearly enough and wondered what on earth it was. It was not a vivid crash of a detonation, more a muffled but very loud boom. Almost a minute passed before a nearby claxon wailed, shattering the silence. This had never happened before during his time on the island. It was followed almost immediately by the clatter of military boots as soldiers scurried around outside. Patterson quickly pulled his coat on and hurried out into the cold night air.

It was not quite pitch black. On good weather nights like this it never was. The moon and stars generated enough light to cast shadows and at this time of the year the nights were so short they barely had time to achieve full darkness on cloudless nights. He looked out onto a colourless, black and grey world with darkly silhouetted shapes and a sea that occasionally introduced some white as a wave creamed over. There was no question that the bang had led to the alarm bell ringing and the soldiers taking up predetermined action stations. There was much rushing around going on and orders being shouted by commanders.

Over the water north of the island where the Russian naval ships were at anchor searchlights played on one particular ship. It made for a dramatic picture. The outlines of the grey, bulky vessels could be seen silhouetted against the dying night sky. Powerful beams of light were stabbing across the black sea to illuminate a 22,000 ton supply ship. Alongside her were an atomic-powered Arktika-class icebreaker and one of the newly commissioned, Admiral-class frigates recently built in St. Petersburg. Patterson was witnessing a drama as it unfolded. Arc lights illuminated the supply ship enough for him to see it was clearly lower in the water at the stern and keeled slightly over on its port side.

"Inside! Inside!" a Russian officer shouted at Patterson, indicating he should return to the building from which he had just emerged. Patterson reluctantly and slowly did as he was commanded. What had happened offshore Big Diomede was puzzling him as much as it was the Russians. There had definitely been some sort of explosion and the supply ship was distinctly damaged. But what had caused it? Had it been some sort of internal malfunction? If not, the clear alternative was the ship had been hit by something. But what? A torpedo? If so, where had it been fired from? And by whom? If not a torpedo, what else? A mine? There were no records of drifting mines in the area so who could have planted one? The Russians were scanning the seas with all the sonar they could muster. One of the naval ships had fired off rounds of parachute flares and submersible sound detectors, the former drifting back down to sea, bright white phosphorous illuminating a large area to the north of the island. The rumble of high powered inflatables could be clearly heard as some sought to find any intruders while others contributed to the evacuation of crew from the supply ship.

Patterson kept the door to his building open to try and keep some sort of eye on what was happening. Visibility from here was restricted by neighbouring buildings and there was only one window that gave a view of nothing but a scrubby bit of land. As he peered out from the doorway an arm went round him. It was Nika, obviously also disturbed from her night's sleep by all that was happening. He pulled her close to him then saw Stepan was also up but heading outside.

"You can't go out," Patterson told him. Stepan looked back and shrugged his shoulders. Patterson was sure he knew what was being said but if he did Stepan cared to ignore it and slipped out of the building into the night. Ten minutes followed. If anyone had been timing events they would have realised it was precisely ten minutes to the second after the tranquillity of the Bering Strait was shattered by the first explosion that a second took place. Fully alert though he was, this second bang was enough to make Patterson jump. Nika gave a stifled scream.

Together they ventured outside and up the hillside to gain a better view. Nobody was bothered about them now – at least for the time being. All attention was on the action out at sea. Patterson could see the target was the same ship. This time the explosion had been towards its bows. If anyone had doubted before that the ship was under some sort of attack, those were now utterly quelled.

A full scale rescue was being mounted to take off the crew from the now obviously sinking supply ship. Amidst the chaos a third explosion went off, this time half way along the ship's length. This third detonation caused an upward blast sending decking, chunks of equipment, and a column of fire and smoke heading towards the dying night sky. Flames reflected and flickered on nearby ships. The Scottish geophysicist and the young Russian girl stood together, her hand tightly clasping his as they watched the distant activity in unbelieving amazement.

The perpetrators of the attack had long since gone. When Captain Peter Turner told Bond he was going to "create a bit of excitement on the Bering Strait" it had been, Gene Bond now realised, something of an understatement. Three hours before the explosions a three man SBS team left the American side of Little Diomede in a stealth canoe heading for the larger island, creeping along its coast, then onwards to the group of ships lying to the north of it. Meanwhile, two others set off for the south end of Big Diomede.

"What could possibly go wrong?" Turner had concluded tongue-in-cheek after spelling out his plan to the team assembled around a table at their temporary base in Wales. Spread before them was a chart of the Bering Strait and its two islands. Included in the small group were Peter and two of the Inuits from the community in Wales. They were providing invaluable local knowledge on tidal and wind directions. The commando leader had already taken Bond to one side.

"I'll tell this to you straight," he said. "If I had my way I'd leave you and Peter here. But I'm told to get you back home. Peter's going to have to fend for himself. Have you ever been in a canoe before?"

Bond confessed he had not. But he tried to reassure the naval man that he was very familiar with rowing, as if that was helpful.

"You haven't a fucking clue what this is about," Turner told him cuttingly. "There's no comparison between anything you've ever experienced and what you're about to embark on. Believe me. So I am telling you now – you do what you're told when you're told and without discussion. Right? And you don't move a fucking muscle on the boat or you might have us over. If you're going to be sick, you puke without moving! Right? Understand?"

Bond assured Turner he understood. To say he was apprehensive about the coming trip was a massive understatement. He was frightened to the core.

"One team will leave ahead of the others and will head for the Russian ships to the north of Big Diomede," Turner told his men. "Target will be the supply ship. It's a softer target than the others." And he spelt out how computer controlled, high powered limpet mines would be attached to the ship with the first set to explode an hour after they had been deployed. The attack team would then join the two other canoes off the southern coast of the island.

"There's an inlet in the cliff face," he told them pointing to it on the chart. "Like a tailor-made harbour for us."

The two Inuits muttered to each other then to Peter. Turner looked at him quizzically.

"They say there's a wreck there," Peter translated. "A historic wreck. Been there for as long as anyone can remember."

"Will it interfere with us?" Turned asked.

"No," came the answer and the commando continued with his briefing. The two teams that had gone straight to Big Diomede would establish a beachhead and cliff route and wait for the arrival of the third boat. They would be well positioned on top of the island by the time the mines went off, hopefully doing what was intended and drawing the attention of the Russians on the island to activity at sea to the north.

"We have to work fast," said Turner. "We have an appointment with a V-22 Osprey that'll take us straight back to Alaska."

There was a murmur of surprise amongst his men. "What's an Osprey?" asked Bond. He felt conspicuously like an amateur onlooker to what was going on but was more than aware that the plan very much included him. On that basis, he felt happy to ask questions – even if they were considered stupid. His life might depend on knowing what was going to happen.

"It's an American built tilt-rotor aircraft," Turner told him. "A cross between a helicopter and a turboprop aircraft. It's the only one we've got at the moment. We've had it on trials for a while. It can fly far longer and a damn sight faster than a Chinook. Just the job for what we want. We're lucky to get it."

There were nods of approval from his men. He continued. "When we get to Big Diomede, you Bond will stay with the boats. No way I'm having you freaking around the island and getting lost. You stay put while we go and get Patterson. The Osprey will take us all off and away before the Ruskies realise what's happened. The safety of America is just minutes away."

"All clear?" he asked, looking round the faces that were staring at the chart. There were nods all round.

"Easy," Turner concluded. "What could possibly go wrong?"

Bond realised this was something of a catch phrase for the commando captain. Whatever it was, Bond hoped he was right.

He was lucky. The weather was kind that night and the sea relatively calm. Kitted out in all-weather camouflage clothing and his face blackened like the commandoes around him, Bond clung to the side of the canoe as if his life depended on it. He did not move a muscle until they had successfully crossed the relatively short distance from one island to the other. There, just as Turner had shown it to be on the chart, a jagged finger of rock pointed out to sea and created a small haven of a harbour into which the two canoes manoeuvred on a relatively gentle sea swell. The first canoe that had left before the others was already tethered to the rocks and its crew busy on shore.

Bond got onto dry land only with some embarrassing clumsiness and the considerable help of one of the men with whom he had shared his boat. By then rocket propelled ropes with grappling hooks had been fired up the cliff face and commandos were already on their way to the top. Bond could only look on in awe and marvel at the speed in which they reached the top and disappeared.

Suddenly he was on his own, standing on a narrow ledge of rock with the sea sloshing in and out of the natural narrow harbour. Only now did he realise how cold it was.

Bond strained to hear any noise of action from the island. It was unnerving being out of contact with everyone and having no idea what was going on. He felt unbelievably isolated and alone here in the middle of nowhere. After a while, mention of the wrecked boat came back to him and, for the sake of something to do and to keep him moving in the cold night air, he turned his attention to finding it. There was only one place such a wreck could be and it meant scrambling along the bottom of the cliff face where the rock was wet and slippy, ground to a fine shining surface by thousands of years of constant pounding by the sea.

It did not take long to get to the point where the section of rock jutting out into the sea at an acute angle joined the bottom of the cliff face. Sure enough, jammed at the end between the outward pointing spit of land and the cliff was evidence of some sort of craft. There was not much to see – just some well fashioned timber that may once have been the bows of a boat of some sort or another, its remains having been preserved for years in the frozen or semi-frozen seas of the Arctic. There seemed to be the remnants of a rope tethering the vessel but to get to it would have meant climbing along an even more precarious part than he was currently on. It was not, he concluded, worth the risk and he retreated back to where the ropes dangled down from the cliff top.

Again his isolation was almost overwhelming. He

felt miniscule in this gigantic setting – this remote island in the middle of a sea in the Arctic. And the thought crossed his mind for the first time. What if Turner's question had been answered? What if something had gone wrong? Where the hell would that leave him?

Chapter 34

Moya had opened her package and the accompanying note which she read with growing excitement and a fair degree of nervousness. The message read:

"In at least 22 countries around the world, very special people like you, elected by your peer groups and bound by the same blood oaths, are on stand-by. Action day depends on us receiving an official response from the United Nations. It has a meeting in Brussels tomorrow. If we are successful the Hwanung Solution will be adopted by the world community. If not, we will fulfil our threat and release a deadly virus in 22 or more countries. Tomorrow you will be told whether or not we have been successful."

After a sleepless night, just after she had washed and dressed for the day and was pondering what to do, her phone buzzed. There was a new text message. It simply said "Activate."

She felt a shiver of uncontrolled excitement, anticipation and apprehension run through her body. For years she had felt insignificant and unwanted – virtually unseen. Now she could make a mark and be part of a global movement, perhaps, she thought, even change the course of history. The bag she was handed at the base of the Washington Monument was nothing out of the ordinary – deliberately. It was an anonymous shopping bag inside which was a face mask, a translucent bag with a zip top, and a note as to where the bag was to be deployed and unzipped.

There were several common denominators to actions taking part that day in more than 20 cities around the world. Young cyclists are part and parcel of modern city life and, with cities being as polluted as they are, it is quite usual for such people to wear a face mask to reduce the volume of toxic substances being inhaled. For such a mask to also conceal the face behind it was a prime consideration for those transporting Taeyoung's deadly materials to their destinations. So, across the planet, mask wearing youngsters carrying anonymous bags cycled to exactly the same sort of destination in more than 22 cities.

It would be a four mile ride for Moya. From her shared apartment in Anacostia on the south east side of the city, she rode up to the river then through the place where she had attended the Hwanung rally, crossing the river over the 11th Street Bridge and onwards to her target. All major cities have one. To Taeyoung, the benefit is they are places where people congregate in vast numbers and in close proximity to each other. These are also people not confined to that one location but who head out in all directions carrying with them whatever coughs, colds – or worse – they may have picked up in their close encounters with others on their journey.

Forty million people a year pass through the splendid edifice that is Washington's Union Station. Opened in 1907, its expansive palatial spaces, sweeping, grandiose arch roofs and extensive use of marble gives it a classical appearance. Moya could not help loving the design of the place with its Romanesque influenced architecture and its glittering use of marble. It was more like a palace than a railway station. Her destination was the less opulent recent addition to the station, the modern steel and glass Bikestation where commuters can leave their own cycles or hire one. She approached it from the opposite side of the building to where it is located, thereby having her bicycle with her as she walked through the central mall. She stopped, as any young cyclists might, to sit on one of the wooden benches and take a small bottle of water from her bag. Having consumed it she continued on, absentmindedly leaving her shopping bag leaning against the bench. But this was not the act of forgetfulness it appeared to be. Returning the water bottle to the shopping bag, in the same movement Moya opened the zip of the translucent bag before standing up, grabbing her bicycle and walking off.

Inside the shopping bag the pressurised container with its zip now opened released its deadly content from which Moya would, she had been told, be protected by her mask. The diminutive youngster pushed her bike through to the Bikestation, left it locked up there and caught a bus back home where she showered in the clothes she was wearing, a precautionary measure of her own volition to rid herself of any traces of the virus she expected to be spreading now across central Washington and beyond.

Across the planet the same procedure was being enacted in major railway stations as Sum Taeyoung hit back at the world's leaders who, he thought, had chosen to ignore him.

Chapter 35

With dawn soon to arrive and visibility increasing as the light improved, so Bill Patterson stood with Nika clinging to his arm. From their vantage point on the hilly rocky scrubland to the rear and above the cluster of buildings they could see the supply ship was now lying low in the water, almost submerged and more or less broken in two by the third explosion. Efforts to rescue its crew were now frenetic while helicopters and high speed naval craft searched the area for the attackers.

On Big Diomede a further drama was enfolding as the body of a Russian soldier was found down at the water's edge near the landing jetty. His throat had been cut. A figure had been seen moving fast away from the scene across the rough ground towards the most northerly point of the island. Soldiers were in pursuit and Patterson and Nika could hear the occasional shout and one or two gun shots. They had assumed the disturbance was to do with whoever had attacked the ship.

It was Lieutenant General Vladimir Antonov, arriving with three soldiers, who told them of the death of the soldier, at the same time demanding they returned to their building.

"We think it's the work of Stepan," Antonov told Patterson in English.

"Stepan!" repeated Nika clearly understanding enough of what was being said in English. Antonov reverted to Russian to tell her what he had told Patterson – her brother was at large and seemed to have taken advantage of what was happening at sea to launch his own attack on the Russian contingent on the island. Nika was distraught, looking pleadingly at Patterson for some sort of support which left him floundering, not knowing what to say. He was already well aware that Stepan appeared to have been destabilised by his capture by the Russians. His belligerent attitude indicated clearly how much he hated them. Patterson had thought for some time it would not take much to tip him over the edge and into uncontrollable anger. With Nika sobbing they returned to their building, escorted by Antonov's soldiers. Before disappearing to deal with his growing list of problems, Antonov said he was leaving one soldier with them in case Stepan returned.

The soldier stood outside. With the door closed, Patterson tried to console Nika. Tears were pouring down her face and her body was shaking with uncontrollable sobbing. He held her tight but could not find any appropriate words that she would understand. Not many minutes passed before the door crashed open. Stunned, Patterson and Nika watched incredulously as a man in black top, black trousers, black hood and blackened face with some sort of weapon slung over his shoulder, heaved the body of the Russian soldier into their room and slammed the door shut. Patterson thought Nika was becoming hysterical. Already tearful about Stepan, this new intrusion was almost too much for her to take. She shrieked as the armed man pulled the Russian – who appeared to be still alive but unconscious – into the room.

"Captain Peter Turner, SBS, Royal Navy. Come to take you home Mr Patterson."

"Home?" Bill Patterson queried, increasingly bewildered by events.

"Home," the commando confirmed. "Back to the UK."

The navy man paused briefly. A moment of doubt crossed his mind. "You are the geophysicist William Patterson?"

"I am," Patterson confirmed.

"Just as well to check," Turner half joked. "But we've got to move fast. Now!"

The geophysicist was still struggling. "What about her?" He nodded at Nika.

"Just you," Turner told him as he strapped the Russian soldier's hands together with a plastic noose and stuck tape over his mouth. The soldier was still alive, Patterson was relieved to see.

"I've no brief for anyone else," Turner continued. "And there's no time to talk about it. We've got to move."

"I go – she goes," Patterson responded. It was an impulsive statement uttered with little or no thought behind it.

"Bloody hell man," Turner snapped. "You've no idea what we're putting at risk to get you out of here. Whether or not she can leave here isn't up to me. It's up to the guy whose going to fly us out of here."

Patterson could hardly comprehend what the navy

man was saying. Fly off the island! How? To seek answers now was obviously ridiculous. So he chose to simply say "OK. I'll argue it out with him."

Turner opened the door just enough to be able to see out.

"Come on. Just follow me as fast as you can. More of my men will join us. Whatever happens, just keep going."

Patterson made for the door but Nika held back.

"Come on," the Scotsman encouraged her. "Our chance to escape."

She looked at him. Her face was streaked with tear marks. Her eyes red from rubbing. She muttered words amidst the sobbing.

"I don't understand," the frustration in Patterson's voice was obvious.

"She's talking about her mother and father," Turner told him. "Are they here as well?" Clearly this was an added complication he could do without.

"You speak Russian?" Patterson asked.

"Enough," was the briefest of answers. "Now let's get the fuck out of here."

Patterson looked at the stooped and sobbing Nika. She was the saddest of sights and obviously utterly distressed by these latest events.

"We've got to go," he implored her. She was clearly being torn in half and pressured to make a decision in the most horrendous of circumstances. Should she leave with this man she had come to love but who came from a world she did not know or understand? And could she abandon her mother and father – and Stepan?

"For Christ's sake! Come on," pleaded Turner.

"OK. OK," she said. "OK." The words were just an audible whisper.

Turner was through the door, bent double and running best he could over the scrubby surface of Big Diomede. Patterson was right with him, almost dragging the young Russian girl after him and now aware that to either side and running with them were other armed men, hardly visible. It was a mad dash to freedom and seemed to be a race they were winning when the semi lightness of the dawning day was shattered by the sound of nearby gunfire. Tracer bullets glowed as a heavy calibre machine gun opened up towards them, fortunately way off target. Patterson became aware of more shouting and more gunfire coming from somewhere to his left. Wrongly he assumed it was directed at them. Though he did not know it, Stepan was unwittingly providing a very effective diversion to their escape.

The coast was now clearly in view. The day was rapidly becoming lighter. Patterson realised they were running in a direction he knew and had previously explored. Sure enough, the ropes of the naval team disappeared over the cliff edge close to where he had ventured down the narrowest of pathways some days before. Two of Turner's team disappeared over the edge.

"You next," Turner ordered Patterson. "Can the girl climb down?"

"I've no idea," Patterson told him. "You ask. She may understand you better than me."

He chose the moment to unload a question that had been going round and round his head ever since Turner had first appeared. Now, as they waited at the edge of the cliff and with Turner's men fanned out in a defensive line, he asked the question.

"How come all of this? For me? The lives and risk. The cost. Why?"

"I just do," Turner answered. "Others plan. But as I understand it there was some doubt as to whether or not you were alive. The powers that be needed unequivocal evidence one way or the other. At best that meant me bringing you back and sticking you in front of them."

"And at worst?" Patterson asked.

"Dead or alive. It didn't seem to matter," the navy man answered.

"Very odd," Patterson replied.

"When you get to the bottom of the cliff you'll meet a guy called Gene Bond. All this is largely down to him as I understand it."

Patterson scrambled down the cliff face and stood and watched in amazement and awe as Nika followed him down with hardly any hesitation. On the rocky shore a man approached him, dressed also in navy combat kit and with face blackened.

"I'm Gene Bond," he said. Behind Patterson, Nika was scrambling across the rocks to join them. The remaining members of the naval squad were heading down the cliff.

"I've been here before," the geophysicist was saying to the man before him, ignoring the introduction. Bond was having difficulty in concentrating on any conversation. The sea was now pounding onto the rocks behind him and the developing wind whistled round the cliffs. Somewhere not far away more gunfire could easily be heard and a new sound had joined the cacophony of noises – an engine of some sort and out at sea. Bond turned to squint into the developing wind. Across a sea in which the waves were growing in size and strength with spray flying from the tops of the bigger ones as they were swept away in streamers by the wind, an aircraft was heading directly towards him. To say it was low was an understatement. It immediately reminded Bond of how seagulls play in the valleys between waves – seemingly just for the sheer exhilaration of doing so. This aircraft seemed to be that low.

Head on to Bond, it was difficult to determine how big it was though even at this distance it looked different to any other fixed-wing aircraft he had ever seen. He became aware Turner was shouting at him and Patterson was still talking. To Bond, Patterson and the girl with him presented a disturbing picture. Both appeared to be greatly the worse for their recent experiences. They were grey from fatigue and mud splattered from head to foot from their recent rush across the island. Patterson was trying to make a point to Bond but with the noise of the sea, the incoming aircraft, gunfire not far away and Turner shouting at him, Bond was finding it hard to fathom what he was trying to say.

"It's the missing gold! From the Royal family. The Romanovs. It's in the boat. George Symons the British spy has been here."

Bond's immediate reaction was to think Patterson had somehow become deranged whilst a captive of the

Russians. Certainly what he was trying to say made no sense. Not that Bond was fully focussed on him. His mind was preoccupied with the need to board the aircraft and get away from the island as fast as possible. Looking back out to sea, the aircraft was now close enough for him to confirm he had not seen anything like it before. It was the propellers that did it. One on each wing, they were huge and seemed disproportionate to the rest of the aircraft. As Bond watched, the aircraft, perhaps no more than 50 feet above the wave tops, slowed and the huge propellers pivoted so they were facing more downwards than horizontal. Being so low, the downward blast of the propellers was fanning huge quantities of water in every direction.

Turner and his squad were more or less together and heading towards where Bond stood with Nika. Patterson had moved off down the spit of rock, holding onto the top of the low ridge as he did so, waves lapping at his feet.

"Where the hell's he off to?" Turner shouted at Bond.

Bond shrugged. He had no idea.

"Come on Patterson," shouted Turner above the noise of the Osprey. "We need to get aboard."

"Two minutes," Patterson shouted back.

"What the fuck's he doing?" Turner asked Bond as he reached him. The aircraft was now no more than 50 yards away and slowly moving towards them.

Bond had to talk straight at Turner's ear to ensure he heard. "No idea," he told the naval man. "He's on about gold. Something to do with the Russian royal family."

"Christ almighty!" swore Turner and again shouted at Patterson who had crept further down the rocky spit.

"Patterson. We've got to go."

But the geophysicist had only one thing on his mind. He was totally shut off to any external interferences. Ten feet in front of him he could see the tattered remnants of a rope that disappeared into the sea which still had chunks of ice swilling about in it. Sticking out of the icy water and still recognisable as part of a boat were lengths of timber that maybe once could have been part of its bows.

"Patterson!" Turner's voice echoed back off the cliffs. It was barely discernable above the noise of the aircraft that had nearly reached them.

There was now less than six feet to the rope. In his mind Patterson could see a vision based on the bits of information from George Symons. Somehow the British spy had been involved with the fleeing Russian royals as they continued their escape from the Bolsheviks and crossed into Siberia. Symons had mentioned gold. Had it been with him? Had he still got it after the Romanovs were executed? Had he brought it with him to Big Diomede? Was it in this boat? Patterson had become obsessed with the thought. If it were here it would be the most astonishing discovery in recent times. And now he was so close – less than six feet. He clung to the slippery rock and edged his way closer.

"I'll have to bloody well get him," groaned Turner. Ropes had been dropped from the Osprey and some of the naval commandos were already wading through the waves towards them. Turner shouted to one of his men to ask the aircraft's pilot if he could take the girl. He set off after Patterson.

Bond, waves now engulfing him virtually to his waist as he edged closer to the dangling ropes, was torn between looking where he was going and keeping his balance as he did so, and watching Turner heading towards Patterson. The noise from the aircraft vibrated through him and seeing anything through the swirling waters was almost impossible. At the bottom of the cliff Nika was looking on in horror, hand to her mouth as if to stifle a scream.

The naval officer nearly got to the Scottish scientist – but not quite. Patterson reached the ancient piece of rope that had been preserved for decades in the cold of the Arctic. He let go of his grip on the rock and put his faith in the rope. It was not a good move. With the pressure being applied by Patterson, the rope broke loose from whatever it had been attached to at the other end submerged beneath the icy water. Patterson wobbled. For a moment it looked as if he would regain his balance. But it was not to be. He stumbled, falling forward, tripping over the tip of the spine of rock on which he was standing. His left leg extended towards the timber of the ancient boat, then downwards. As his weight transferred from the rock, so the ancient timbers gave way and Patterson's leg kept going down, his whole body following.

There was a mighty splash as the geophysicist hit the water and the remains of the boat which instantly disappeared under the weight of the Scotsman. Far too late, Patterson turned his upper body and extended his hand towards Turner. It was a forlorn hope. Turner was still a good 10 feet or more away. There was nothing he could do. Patterson was gone. It had taken seconds. By the time Turner got to where Patterson had fallen in, there was no trace of anything – Patterson, the boat, the tatty length of rope. There was just an angry swirl of icy water. The naval commando lay on the rock and extended his arm into the water as far as it could go. He felt nothing, just the searing cold of the water. He looked back towards the aircraft.

Bond stood like a statue in a cauldron of water being churned up by the aircraft. He stared back towards Turner in disbelief. Not far away Nika was on her knees, hands to her head.

It was a shot from the top of the cliff that jerked them all back into action. On instructions shouted from the aircraft, Bond twisted the rope round his waist and found himself being winched up into the aircraft. As he looked down he saw Turner run close by the still kneeling Nika, his hand stretched out towards her in an obvious attempt to get her to follow him. But with more shots being fired from the island the naval commando kept running, more or less leapt at the one rope still hanging from the aircraft and, as the Osprey turned and moved out to sea, was himself hauled up and into the aircraft.

Bond looked back at Big Diomede. On the cliff top three Russian soldiers were firing at them, their guns twinkling in the still half light of the early morning. At the foot of the cliff, a solitary, lonely diminutive figure still knelt on the wet rocks of Big Diomede's shore staring towards where Patterson had disappeared. The sad sight was the last Bond saw of Nika. It would take the Osprey no more than 10 minutes to cross the coast near Wales and to gain the relative safety of American owned Alaska.

Chapter 36

It was not the best place to try and have a conversation let alone a meaningful debrief. But without hesitation they both chose the Russian Bar to meet in London. There was no discussion about it. They agreed the priorities – to have their brains warped by the pounding beat of deep South American rock and roll hammering out of the club's sound system at an alarming volume, whilst losing their senses to a slow but steady flow of black beer interspersed with Vodka chasers. In the mix of that they would somehow hold a debrief.

Waiting for Georgi to bring another couple of black beers from the bar, Bond absentmindedly ran his right hand index finger slowly round the frozen sugar rim of the silver goblet containing his Vodka whilst his eyes contemplated the tall, slim, long haired girl who gyrated on the dance floor and flaunted her body at anyone who cared to look. Bond cared to look. It was quite some body! Memories of Nagriza flooded back. Such an extraordinary, extroverted, unpredictable, effervescent woman. Such a wonderfully generous lover. Bond missed her love, her nakedness and sex, her companionship, her conversation and her wit. He wondered if he would ever get over the way she was snatched out of his life. On the other hand, he often speculated as to how their relationship would have worn over time. Would it have endured? Or would she have eventually become bored with him? He would never know.

"Why was so much effort made to get Patterson off Big Diomede?" Bond asked Georgi on his return. "It must have been a hugely risky project – and expensive."

"Sum Taeyoung – using the pseudonym of Hwanung – you'll remember he used it before – was threatening the United Nations by saying if they did not respond to his nine demands he would release the deadly virus that escaped from one of the holes in Siberia when the permafrost melted. Taeyoung maintained the virus he was going to use had killed the two British geophysicists. What happened to one of those, Jack Bailey, we will probably never know. He disappeared from The Mansion in Scotland. We'd already suspected Taeyoung hadn't got an ancient lethal Siberian virus when what he used to kill top civil servants around the world wasn't from Siberia. It was a form of anthrax made in the rogue laboratory in Donetsk."

"Bill Patterson ended up on Big Diomede and was obviously very much alive, assuming it was indeed him. We picked that up from Russian radio chatter. So to be able to discount with total certainty that the virus from Siberia was not deadly, the powers that be needed unequivocal evidence that Patterson was still alive. So that's why the rescue from Big Diomede. Mind you, they were also interested in anything Patterson could tell them about Siberia, the Bering Strait and what Russia is up to in that area. It's become strategically highly important."

"So Taeyoung never launched a virus attack?" asked Bond.

"Oh but he did," said Georgi. "And because he knew the virus from Siberia was not lethal as he proclaimed it was – because he knew Bailey and Patterson had not died from it – he used the anthrax from Donetsk."

Gene Bond was puzzled. "So did anyone die?"

"No," Georgi told him. "After the disastrous attack on the civil servants that killed so many of them the authorities produced an antidote to combat it."

"It was ironic Patterson died the way he did," Bond reflected. "Was that the curiosity of a scientist or greed spurred on by gold?"

"Who knows?" Georgi replied. "And greed over gold may have cost the life of someone else we've met."

"Who?" asked Bond.

"Fitzpatrick," said Georgi. "You remember. We met him in The Mansion. The man from the mining company."

"Oh yes," Bond said with some surprise in his voice. He had forgotten all about the arrogant man that owned The Mansion, the mining company and a mine in Siberia. "What's happened to him?"

"We're not sure," Georgi told him. "He's gone missing. He apparently drove out to his mine, found its ownership had been taken over by the Russian government, and headed off back to where he had come from. But he never got there. What's happened to him nobody knows. Maybe we'll find out one day when someone stumbles over his frozen body."

"Gold, greed and death. Interesting mix," reflected

Bond. On that sombre note they momentarily turned to the task of drinking.

"Taeyoung's threat," Bond eventually said, "and subsequent attack may have failed but from what I've read the Hwanung Crusade has had an extraordinary impact on the United Nations."

"That's the great irony of this," Georgi told him. "Taeyoung fired up a global campaign that inspired youngsters into concerted action. And you're right. It's extraordinary. The Hwanung Crusade and its nine demands has no leader – no people heading it – but it has now a staggering eight million followers across the planet. Groups are now operating in 25 countries. That's the last count I have. It may be more now. It's all held together through social media. Nothing like this has ever appeared before. Not on this scale."

Georgi paused to half empty his jug of beer and take a few sips of vodka before going on. "This Hwanung thing's got a bit fragmented. Taeyoung was demanding a huge amount of money as well as a response to nine demands. On various recommendations it was decided to eliminate Taeyoung on the basis if you killed off the leadership to this campaign it would die. But it hasn't. A worldwide petition urging a response to the nine demands of the Hwanung Crusade has been signed by nearly eight million people. Eight million! It's caused turmoil inside the UN. So this headless initiative has a self-generating momentum that will lead it to goodness knows where. In various countries politicians have been trying to climb aboard the bandwagon to satisfy their own ambitions. There's a clamour to know who's leading it. But it seems nobody is. That's crazy! But it's new."

Another pause for more beer.

"Maybe this is what the world is going to look like with political structures abandoned because the people think they're ineffective, corrupt, redundant, irrelevant to their needs – maybe all of those things. Maybe they're going to be replaced by some sort of global, pluralistic methodology. You remember the Declaration of Intent I showed you in Scotland?"

Bond nodded though it seemed like a lifetime ago.

"That declaration talked of creating a totalitarian system. Some sort of post-democracy, post-capitalism structure. It quoted the Han dynasty, Confucius, Bahá'u'lláh, and, of course, Hwanung. Who knows? Maybe eight million people have somehow signed into this and leaderless though it might be, it's got one hell of a momentum."

"Maybe it doesn't need a leader," Bond suggested. "It sounds a bit like Autonomism or even Marxism."

Georgi shrugged his shoulders. "Who knows? When you have a moment in time when people are rebelling against conventionalism – and technology is providing a totally new way of conversing and linking between people and which ignores geographical or political barriers – who knows what might happen?"

They sank into their own silence.

"And what's the latest you've got on the American response to the Russian takeover of the Bering Strait?" Bond asked his friend.

"The American fleet continues to head towards it

intent, apparently, on repatriating Little Diomede."

"Christ!" swore Bond. "What then? Hell breaks loose?"

"We all pray," said Georgi. "Meantime we hope to God it'll not get that far. Let's hope it'll be a repeat of the Cuban missile drama."

More silence between them. The music, the alcohol, and now three dancing, semi-naked girls were doing nothing to stop their spirits sinking.

"There is one blessing though," said Bond.

"What's that?" asked Georgi.

"Taeyoung has gone. No need to worry about him again."

Georgi Patarava looked up at his friend.

"He's not dead," he said quietly.

Gene Bond thought for a moment he had misheard. But he knew from the look Georgi was giving him that was not so.

"You must be joking! You told me about the ambush in Belgium. The assassination."

"It wasn't Taeyoung," Georgi replied. "I haven't a fucking clue who it was sitting on the back seat of the limo. But it sure wasn't our South Korean friend. The corpse was photographed and blood samples taken. Nothing matched Taeyoung. The bastard dropped a decoy on us."

"Fucking hell," exclaimed Bond.

"Indeed," his friend replied.

Appendix

Fact or fiction?

Fact

- Anadyr-1 – the former base for a Soviet Union cluster of RSD-10 Pioneer nuclear missiles and a population that at one stage reached 5,000.
- Roman Abramovich once was Governor of the town of Anadyr.
- The mysterious large holes in Siberia. The first was found by reindeer herders in the Yamal Peninsula, sometimes known as 'The End Of The World', less than 20 miles from Russia's biggest and strategically important gas field at Bovanenkovo.
- The Kupol Gold Mine employs some 1200 workers who live in a subterranean world. Sounds allegedly from a Siberia hole sounded like the roar of a furnace but with human screams and howling in the background. Played on American radio it created panic. It was said the sounds came from Hades! It was a hoax.
- Pingos and all about them.
- Nika and her family are based on the extraordinary story of the Lykov family.

- Everything to do with north Scotland except the location of Bond's cottage.
- The threat of a 21st Century water war spreading across the Ferghana Valley.
- The disastrous story of the Aral Sea and Munak.
- Wales, the Diomede islands and the Bering Strait
- Flying Bird Tea Shop in the Insadong district of Seoul.
- Russia hoarding gold.
- Siberian gold rush including communities being moved to make way for mines.
- The activity of the US destroyers Curtis Wilbur and Lassen in the Southern Seas.
- Spratly Islands and China's artificial islands (and runways) being constructed on top of reefs.
- Drifters night club – based on the now defunct Opposite Lock Club in Birmingham, UK.
- The Russian Bar – based on a similar establishment in Liverpool.
- Examples of people being moved compulsorily to make way for developments.
- The Devil's Ear.
- Everything to do with the Olimpiada mine.
- Professor Anders Levermann of the Potsdam Institute for Climate Impact Research. Research and all related references.
- All climate change and ice melting references.
- Lake Poopo.
- Ice imported for the Alaskan dog sled race.
- China sending ships on northern route via Bering Strait to Europe and N America.

- An etched stone tablet kept in the Louvre in Paris depicting a treaty brokered by Turkey to end the world's first water war.
- Very ancient viruses, some more than 30,000 years old, have been released as the permafrost has melted.
- The car park at Fresgoe and the sign warning that atomic particles have been found in the area and people should not pick material off the beach.
- The (Russian) National Control Defence Centre – is located on the banks of the Moskva River.
- The history of the sale of Alaska to America.
- The history of the Bering Strait and the two islands.
- The unpretentious environs of Wesley's Café.
- The beautiful Halladale Estuary.
- George Symons of the British Secret Service Bureau.
- Yekaterinburg and the Russian royal family.
- The Old Believers.
- Belarus was a major manufacturer of biological warfare materials when it was in the USSR but has subsequently closed factories down.
- Everything about Donetsk as a breakaway state and its biological manufacturing facilities.
- The secret chemical research establishment in Shelkostantsiya.
- Man arrested in Los Angeles having made threats against the White House. He told officials he had built a "microbe bomb" containing a virus that had been produced in the Ukraine.
- Deaths in Ukraine from a virus.
- The facts in the "Declaration of Intent".
- All about the North Pole in Fairbanks.

- Article by Professor Peter Wadhams of Cambridge University.
- International Arctic Research Center.
- University of Alaska and its Permafrost Laboratory.
- 197 steps on Big Diomede to the lookout point.
- Everything about Nome.
- Inuits as correct term.
- The article by Shiela Watt-Cloutier.
- 60% of its youngsters out of work in Greece.
- The CONTEST programme.
- Bilderberg Group and its history.
- The Château du Lac Hotel, 30 kilometres south of Brussels city centre and its history.
- Piper Cessna 172 Skyhawk.
- New harbour at Port Clarence.
- Canadian debt.
- Problems at Bearskin First Nation.
- Anthrax outbreak in Western Siberia blamed on climate change causing an ancient reindeer carcass to thaw.
- The SBS and its equipment.
- The building of and driving on ice roads.
- The view from the top of the Washington Monument.
- Atomic-powered Arktika-class icebreaker and one of the newly commissioned, Admiral-class frigates recently built in St. Petersburg.
- Everything about Washington's Union Station.

Fiction

- Everything to do with Imperial Mining Inc.
- Everything to do with Georgi Patarava including the European Secret Service and its hidden London base.
- The Mansion – based geographically on the Big House.
- SDBI and everything related to it.
- The supposed legal basis for the Russian take-over of the Bering Strait – as far as I know it's my pure fiction that Russia has any territorial water rights to the Bering Strait.
- Everything to do with Nika and her family at Anadyr-1.
- Russia expelling people from Little Diomede.
- Paris Guerriers Urbains.
- America sending a fleet of warships into the Arctic to confront Russian claims of ownership to the Bering Strait and reclaim occupancy of the island of Little Diomede.
- As far as I know there is no natural inlet or wreck at 65°4531.071 -169°711.1318.

Some Useful Connections

David Middleton Author	*My novel writing activities*	www.davidmid-dleton-author.com	@david-mid2014
2degrees Community	*UK based 2degrees Community is online membership group of 43,300 professionals*	www.2de-greesnetwork.com	@2de-greesnet-work
Acclimatise	*Globally operating UK consultancy advising on climate change*	www.acclima-tise.uk.com	
CALEXIT	*California independence campaign (see my book 1 "The Final Shah Mat")*	www.yescalifor-nia.org	
Climate Change Solutions Ltd	*UK events organising campaigner*	www.climate-change-solu-tions.co.uk	@Cli-mateC-Solution
David Middleton Communications	*The platform for my project activity*	www.davidmid-dletoncommu-nications.uk	@david-mid2014
Edie	*UK based provider of daily information on sustainability*	www.edie.net	@edie

Environmental Leader	*US daily publication*	www.environmentalleader.com	@ELDaily
ForumfortheFuture	*UK based non-profit organisation working to solve complex sustainability challenges*	www.forumforthefuture.org	@Forum4theFuture
Green Biz	*US group advancing opportunities at the intersection of business, technology and sustainability.*	www.greenbiz.com	@greenbiztweets
Green HuffPost	*The green section of the Huffington Post*	www.huffingtonpost.com/section/green	@HuffingtonPost
Greenpeace UK	*The action orientated campaigning group*	www.greenpeace.org.uk	@GreenpeaceUK
Guardian Sustainable Business	*Guardian newspaper's sustainability initiative*	www.theguardian.com/sustainable-business/about-guardian-sustainable-business	@GuardianSustBiz)
International Arctic Research Center	*Alaska based research centre*	www.iarc.uaf.edu	
MEBC	*Midlands (UK) business network focussed on environmental issues*	www.mebc.org.uk	

Mother Nature Network	*The world's most visited online network for news and information related to the environment and responsible living.*	www.mnn.com	@mothernaturenet
Permafrost Laboratory	*Part of the University of Alaska*	www.permafrost.gi.alaska.edu	
Potsdam Institute for Climate Impact Research	*German scientific institute – global change, climate impacts and sustainable development.*	www.pik-potsdam.de	
Sustain	*UK alliance for better food and farming*	www.sustainweb.org	@uksustain
Sustainability West Midlands	*The sustainability champion for the West Midlands (UK) as designated by government*	www.sustainabilitywestmidlands.org.uk	
Sustainable Cities Collective	*US based initiative focused on urban life*	www.sustainablecitiescollective.com	@sustaincities
TreeHugger	*(US) is the leading media outlet dedicated to driving sustainability mainstream.*	www.treehugger.com	@treehugger

UKBCSD	*UK branch of the WBCSD*	www.ukbcsd.org.uk	
WBCSD	*A global, CEO-led organization of over 200 leading businesses and partners working together to accelerate the transition to a sustainable world.*	www.wbcsd.org	
World Resource Institute	*A global research organization that spans more than 50 countries*	www.wri.org	@worldresources